Last of the O'Rourkes

Kate Douglas

Hard Shell Word Factory

With much appreciation to my critique partners; Kathryn Awe
and B.J. McCall, to my editor Libby McKinmer and to
Kat Malone, who, from the time I finished Honeysuckle Rose,
refused to quit whispering in my ear: My story.
Tell MY story!

© 2003 Katherine A. Moore
Trade Paperback
ISBN: 0-7599-3806-7
Published April 2003

eBook ISBN: 0-7599-3805-9
Published March 2003

Hard Shell Word Factory
PO Box 161
Amherst Jct. WI 54407
Books@hardshell.com
http://www.hardshell.com
Cover art copyright Kate Moore Photo
Printed in the United States of America

Prologue

SATISFACTION, A SENSE OF completion...satiation tempered with desire, so much like the aftermath of orgasm. It should not have been so easy...he fought the urge to laugh aloud, recalling his gut-clenching fear, his trembling fingers as he'd grasped the steering wheel, yanked hard and veered the car tightly to cut the other motorist off at precisely the right moment.

Precision counted. Precision and planning. He'd relish that moment forever—the shocked expression in his victim's eyes, the brief flash of recognition, the terror of impending, unalterable death.

If only he'd known...he'd never once imagined the gratification, the power, the unbelievable sense of control.

His first kill.

Now this pleasure...watching from the shadows, relishing the aftereffects of his deed, visualizing the next steps in this most thrilling game of cat and mouse.

Kat and mouse? No...he was the cat...feral, a killer. A killer who had tasted first blood.

He'd toyed with his prey long enough.

Smiling in anticipation, gliding silently through the grove of ancient olive trees, he disappeared into the shadows .

Chapter One

A BREEZE. FINALLY A faint breath of air, barely enough to lift away the cloying scent of incense and flowers, but sufficient to stave off the persistent nausea for another moment.

Kat Malone leaned against the rough trunk of a twisted olive tree, doing her best to remain at least partially hidden in the shadows of the small grove. She watched silently as, inch by inch, the simple oak casket disappeared into the freshly dug grave, all the while wondering if there wasn't some way to speed up the process short of goosing the pallbearers. She'd managed to get through the interminably long High Mass and the equally lengthy graveside service, but she knew she couldn't last much longer.

Her skin felt clammy and her stomach churned. The old tree offered welcome support, but if she didn't find a place to sit down soon, she'd probably pass out right here in the cemetery.

Of course, at this point, it probably wouldn't make any difference.

She closed her eyes, swayed slightly, and swallowed past the foul lump in her throat.

Fingers clamped about her arm, vice-like, startling her, but steadying her as well. She looked up, up into the icy green eyes of Riley O'Rourke.

The man who'd just been buried.

No. Riley's eyes are blue...they've always been blue....

She fainted.

HER WORLD GRADUALLY EXPANDED from dark to light, opening like the aperture of an old camera. Her initial fear subsided, giving way to confusion. Riley held her firmly in his arms, his brisk steps carrying her back into the olive grove, out of sight of the other mourners.

No! This wasn't Riley. It couldn't be. Riley was dead, buried moments ago. Riley of the sparkling blue eyes.

I saw them bury you, damn it! She thought of breaking free of the man's steady grip, but lethargy held her arms and legs immobile. Instead, she absorbed what information she could about him.

Know your enemy. One of the first rules she'd learned. An

important lesson, it had saved her life more than once.

A stray thought intruded. *Why do I immediately think of him as the enemy?*

Bemused and disoriented, Kat studied her captor. This stranger, this image of the gentle man she'd loved, was subtly different from the easy-going FBI agent. It was more than the eyes...much more. If possible, his hair was even darker, a little bit longer, his demeanor more intense, his scent...she took a deep breath, inhaling an intoxicating blend of expensive after-shave and man that made her want to shut her eyes and inhale all over again.

Geesh, Malone. Get a grip! She jerked fully awake and struggled enough that he loosed the arm under her knees until her feet touched the ground. He steadied her with one hand while his other arm lightly supported her at the waist.

She inched away, out of his reach. Confusion sharpened by a brief stab of pain followed her.

Riley's dead. He's dead. He's....

"You're not going to keel over again, are you, ma'am?"

Kat shook her head in quick denial. She keyed on his voice. It was different, definitely not Riley's. Deeper...softer. Almost threatening.

Kat Malone never backed away from a threat. Suddenly feeling as if she were back in familiar territory, she raised her chin and brushed a wisp of hair out of her eyes. "I wouldn't have keeled over the first time if you hadn't scared the crap out of me. I thought you were Riley."

"My brother's dead."

"I'm well aware of that fact." Kat stared at him a moment, quickly assimilating the almost imperceptible differences between this man and the man she'd loved. So, Riley had a brother.

One more thing he'd neglected to tell her.

She sighed, closed her eyes and swallowed. "I've spent the morning watching his grieving widow and loving family and friends bury him."

"From the tone of your voice, I assume you're not a close friend of the family." He cocked his head and looked down at her as if she were some sort of bug on the ground.

She studied him a moment before answering, noting the impeccable fit of his black suit, the crisp white collar and cuffs, the perfectly knotted tie. Definitely not Riley. The resemblance was uncanny, but Riley couldn't have acted this arrogant if his life depended on it.

"Until I read his obituary," she said, watching for his reaction, "I didn't even know there was a family. At least, to be specific, a wife."

"Ah. This is beginning to make sense."

"Are there children, too?" she asked, swallowing the bile that wouldn't stay down. She'd really make this guy's day if she puked all over his shiny black shoes.

"Riley and Clarisse were unable to have children."

"I see." Kat swallowed again. "Well, it certainly wasn't Riley's fault."

"What do you mean?"

Even the way he tilted his head as he waited for her answer reminded Kat of Riley, reminded her of the sweetness of the man, the humor...the duplicity. Kat blinked herself back to the present.

"I mean, Mr. O'Rourke, that I loved your brother. I've loved him since the day I met him during an investigation we both worked on well over a year ago. I thought he loved me, too. I changed jobs and transferred out here from Pennsylvania because he asked me to. We talked about marriage, about settling down and raising a family, all the things couples in love generally discuss. Only he neglected to tell me he was already married. In fact, he never said a word about the wife. Who, by the way, must be the one with the fertility problems, because it certainly wasn't Riley."

He stared at her as if she'd suddenly grown a third eye, then lowered his gaze to her flat stomach. "Why would you say something like that?"

"I say that, Mr. O'Rourke, because I'm pregnant with Riley's child."

His reaction stunned her.

"You lying little... How dare you..." He clenched his fists as if he might take a swing.

Kat stood her ground. She'd stared down larger, angrier men than this, though she didn't have a clue why he was so upset. It wasn't like she was accusing *him* of fatherhood. "Put a sock in it, O'Rourke. I have no reason to lie. Your brother and I had an affair and I got pregnant. It happens all the time."

I just didn't expect it to happen to me.

"Not to my brother, it doesn't. Just what kind of scam are you trying to pull?"

Scam? Kathleen stared intently at the man glaring back at her. What in the hell was this jerk's problem? She swallowed and took a deep breath to give herself time to think of a fitting answer. She blinked and swallowed again.

Then the need for a snappy comeback disappeared entirely. Kat leaned over and puked all over Mr. O'Rourke's fancy black shoes.

KAT WASN'T CERTAIN IF it was humiliation or shock that kept her quiet when Riley's brother pulled his Jaguar up in front of her little bungalow just as the fire truck was leaving. She didn't say a word when Mr. O'Rourke opened the car door for her and helped her out of the low-slung Jag. She even managed to accept, with what she considered remarkable aplomb, the presence of three squad cars and a phalanx of uniformed police officers hovering around her front door.

Then her landlord barred her way at the bottom step and refused to let her pass. Kat saw red.

"Bug off, Morton. You'd better get out of..." She lunged at the little weasel.

O'Rourke grabbed her elbow and stopped Kat dead in her tracks. "What's going on here?" he demanded, looking down on Mr. Morton even though the landlord stood a step above. Kat tried to jerk her arm free.

O'Rourke's grip tightened, firm but not bruising.

She glared at him.

He ignored her.

"I told you the last time this happened I wanted you out of here, lady. This time you pack your bags and get." Morton pointedly avoided eye contact with O'Rourke. He scowled at Kathleen. She noticed a tiny fleck of saliva at the corner of his mouth and wished her stomach hadn't chosen this moment to finally settle down.

She'd really love to puke on *his* shoes.

"The last time?" O'Rourke's gesture encompassed the squad cars as well as the smoke still drifting out of the side window of the little house. His grip on Kat's elbow tightened. He tilted his chin and looked down his rather patrician nose at her. "This isn't the first time for *what?*"

The patronizing look on his face fired Kat's adrenaline into overdrive. Damn, the man was infuriating! Just who did he think he was, talking to her like that? He might be Riley's brother, but the two obviously had nothing in common. His disparaging attitude gave her the strength to yank her elbow out of his grasp. She flashed him one of her famous if-looks-could-kill stares.

He didn't flinch.

In a brief flash of insight, she realized she really did owe him an explanation. He had, after all, come to her rescue this morning, whether she'd needed it or not. Kat took a deep breath, turned her back on her sputtering landlord and gestured toward the police captain coming their way.

"Follow me." She brushed past O'Rourke and reached out to shake hands with the officer. "Hey, Sandy." She grabbed his outstretched hand. "I take it my stalker's back?"

"I'm sorry, Kat. We had the place staked out and everything. He must've gotten in during the shift change. Torched the place this time. Really trashed things."

The landlord shoved himself in front of Kathleen again. "I repeat, Ms. Malone, I want you out of here. Today. Don't plan on getting your deposit back."

"Stuff it, Morton. You owe me twice that deposit for all the times I've caught you peeking through the blinds. I don't give freebies. Now out of my way." Kathleen was aware of O'Rourke standing off to one side quietly taking in all the commotion. She turned her back on the landlord and tried to push the image of the tall, raven-haired Irishman out of her mind as well.

Damn, he looked so much like Riley it gave her the creeps. But there was none of Riley's easy going style, none of the loose-limbed awkwardness or easy manner she'd found so endearing.

A wave of nausea swept through her. *Look where endearing got you this time, sweetheart.* Well, she'd never been known for her intelligent decisions regarding men.

"You probably ought to come in and take a look...let us know if he took anything," Sandy was saying. "Be prepared, though. It's bad. Really bad." Still muttering about the damage, he turned and led the way to the front door.

Kat followed Sandy down the walk to her tiny cottage behind the landlord's house and ducked under the yellow CAUTION tape stretched across the front porch. She was aware of O'Rourke following silently behind her and had to stifle a grin when one of the officers allowed him through but restrained the fuming landlord.

She wasn't prepared for the mess that greeted her. "Oh, my God." Once again a strong hand at her elbow steadied her. She heard the sharp hiss of in-drawn breath.

"You're not going to be sick again, are you?" His voice was so close she almost jumped.

She shook her head. "No," she whispered. "I'm okay."

"That's a relief. Though I wouldn't blame you if you did throw up. This kind of wanton vandalism would make anyone ill."

"Gee, thanks." She tugged her arm free of his grasp and stepped away. *Damn!* She'd loved this little place in spite of her slimy landlord. A quiet, furnished little house that actually had some character to it. Now it was splashed throughout with painted vulgarities and threats, not done with a spray can but brushed on thickly, red paint over wallpaper and cabinets, across the appliances in the kitchenette.

Red paint. Dripping blood-red paint.

A fire had melted the small plastic trashcan near the sink and black soot streaked the walls. Long cobwebs hung from the ceiling, invisible until the soot had given them substance. Greasy black smears covered every unpainted surface where investigators had dusted for prints.

Sandy tapped her on the shoulder. "We'll need to get Mr. O'Rourke's prints so we can figure out which ones don't belong here."

"Different O'Rourke." Kat's hand went to her belly, consciously cradling the life she carried. "Sandy, meet Riley's brother, the other Mr. O'Rourke. Riley was killed in a car accident four days ago."

"Ah, gee, Kat, I'm sorry to hear that." He held his hand out to the man beside her. "Sandy Wilson, SFPD," he said. "Kat and I have worked on a number of cases together since she transferred to the San Francisco office. I assumed you were Riley. You look just like him...we only met once before. I didn't know he'd been killed. I am truly sorry for your loss. He seemed like a helluva nice guy."

"Seamus O'Rourke." O'Rourke shook hands with the officer. "Riley and I are...were...fraternal twins, but other than our eye color we were almost identical. Your confusion is perfectly understandable." He gestured toward the vandalized kitchen. "What's going on here?"

Kat glanced at him out of the corner of her eye, surprised by the lack of emotion in his voice. He'd dismissed Sandy's sympathetic remark about his brother's death as if they discussed a stranger.

This guy was definitely nothing like Riley.

"Kat's got a stalker." The police captain frowned, his frustration evident. "We figure it's someone she helped arrest somewhere along the line. There've been references to a few things in his...um...writing."

Seamus glanced once again at the stained walls and the room littered with filth. Anything to take his mind off thoughts of Riley. His brother had obviously spent time here in this room. Had most likely made love to the beautiful blonde. Maybe there on the couch? Seamus blinked away the image just as Wilson patted Kathleen on the back. The friendly act made him bristle.

"You got someplace to go tonight, kid?" Wilson's hand still

rested, much too comfortably, on Kathleen's shoulder. "You can't stay here until it's cleaned up and the fire damage repaired."

She shook her head. The thick blond hair swung softly with the slight motion. "I'll get a hotel room. Thanks anyway, Sandy."

"You know you're welcome to stay with us. Jane loves having someone to fuss over."

Kat smiled sadly at the captain and shook her head once again. Sighing audibly, she turned away to inspect the damage.

"How about you, O'Rourke? Got an extra room at your place?" Sandy watched Kat as she poked aimlessly through the mess. "I worry about her. This guy's scary and I don't think she appreciates the danger she's in. Kat's too damned stubborn for her own good."

"What? You want me to take her home? I hardly know the woman." Seamus stared at her a moment, trying once more to fathom the relationship between his irascible twin and the tall blonde.

The tall blonde who might possibly be carrying his brother's child. The odds were against it, but what if....

"That's your loss, then, isn't it, Mr. O'Rourke?"

Hell, now even the police captain was pissed at him. Seamus clenched, then unclenched his fists, finally accepting the inevitable. "You're right. She can't stay by herself." He glanced down at his spotless black shoes and shook his head. "She's had a pretty harrowing day."

Why did he feel as if he were making the gravest error in his life? Before he could stop himself, Seamus glanced back at the captain. "She'll stay with me until she finds someplace suitable."

"Excuse me?" Kat swung around from her inspection of a pile of burned books. Ice formed on her clipped words.

"I said, Ms. Malone will come with me." Seamus stepped over the rubble and offered a helpful hand to her arm. She jerked out of his grasp and glared at him. He backed away.

"Over my dead—"

"It very well could be." Wilson spoke to Kat, but it was obvious his words were meant for Seamus. "The attacks are growing more violent, Kat. More personal. You can't deny that. It's risky, you being here alone and all. It was different with Riley in and out of the place like he was. This pervert could never know for certain you were alone. That's changed. If I were you, I'd take Mr. O'Rourke up on his offer."

"Well you're not me, damn it." She glared at both men.

Seamus thought he'd never seen bluer eyes in his life. Riley'd always been a sucker for blue eyes.

Hell, Riley'd been a sucker for anything in a skirt. The legs sticking out from under her short little black number were as long and sleek as any Seamus had ever seen. Riley hadn't stood a chance.

Thank goodness Riley and Clarisse had reached a mutual agreement in their marriage long ago. Clarisse had her affairs, Riley had his, and no one got hurt.

Yeah. Right. Seamus hadn't given Riley's women much thought. Now that he'd actually seen one, touched her, looked into her angry blue eyes, he was suddenly aware of the human toll.

This woman had most likely gone into the relationship with her heart wide open. Riley'd always been a silver-tongued devil, the kind of man women loved to love. Usually, though, the women he chose were worldly enough to understand that, for all his flowery words and lofty promises, he'd be gone the moment the winds changed.

But not this one—this tall, cool blonde with crystal blue eyes and the face of an angel. She'd believed his brother, believed in the dream.

Not only had she believed, if what she said was true, she'd accomplished the impossible.

She carried Riley's child. The child neither brother had ever imagined would exist.

It changed everything. This angry woman, obviously a cop of some kind, had accomplished something Seamus and his brother had never, not in their wildest fantasies, dreamed could happen.

If she's telling the truth, she's pregnant with Riley's child.

Hope blossomed where only loss had survived. *If she's telling the truth...* Stunned by the potential of his changing reality, Seamus finally accepted unimagined possibilities.

He was no longer the last of the O'Rourkes.

AT LEAST HER STALKER hadn't found the new toothbrush she kept in the medicine cabinet. It was about the only thing he hadn't ripped, burned, painted, pissed or defecated on in her home. Kat squeezed her eyes shut.

My stalker. She had to quit thinking of him like that...proprietary, almost as if he belonged to her. Hell, nothing belonged to her anymore. The bastard had methodically destroyed what few personal belongings she'd brought to San Francisco during the past three break-ins at her last two residences. She couldn't let herself think about the past, the small treasures she'd lost, the mementos she'd never be able to replace.

It was almost as if he was systematically removing every trace of Kathleen Margaret Malone from the planet. When all her things were gone, she'd be next.

Without warning, Kat leaned over and threw up in the sink.

Shuddering, she raised her head and stared at herself in the mirror. The fingers of her left hand traced the firm contours of her belly. *Get a grip, Malone. He hasn't killed you yet.*

Kat rinsed her mouth and brushed her teeth. Carefully she washed her face and hands. She knew she'd never feel clean as long as she stayed in this house, but still she lingered.

She was very aware of Seamus O'Rourke waiting, probably impatient as hell, in the main room. Why did he bug her so much? Her rational mind appreciated the fact he'd offered her a place to stay until she could get something more permanent, but the rest of her brain found him overbearing and arrogant as all get out. As irritating as Riley'd been easy-going.

However, unless she wanted to spend the next few nights in some motel room, Kat figured she might as well take him up on his offer of a place to sleep. At least until she could find an apartment.

Hopefully, one with a decent security system and a landlord who didn't get his kicks staring through window blinds.

Riley'd never mentioned a brother. Now that she thought of it, Riley hadn't mentioned a lot of things. Her mind kept straying back to the wife—a tall, gorgeous blonde wearing the designer suit, standing less than grief-stricken at her husband's graveside. She'd been leaning heavily on the arm of an equally gorgeous man. From the vibes Kathleen had picked up, she didn't think Riley would be mourned too long from that quarter.

Well, damn it, she'd mourn him. He'd given her the best months of her life. She'd even been excited when she found out she was pregnant, though she'd been almost four months along before the changes in her body, the slight thickening of her waist, the persistent nausea, had made her suspect anything.

Kat grimaced at her pale reflection in the bathroom mirror. "You always were a bit slow on the uptake, Malone." She glanced down at her flat belly, amazed there could be a new life growing there. She still couldn't think of it as a real baby, a child she would someday hold in her arms. In her mind it was just a "whatsit." An anonymous little thing that made her feet and waist swell in what felt like equal proportions. An intruder that activated her barf reflex on a regular basis.

She'd waited almost a month to tell Riley.

Be honest, Malone. You didn't believe it yourself. She'd planned to tell him, though, that last evening when Riley had called and said he was on his way over. She'd planned to tell him, not certain if he'd be upset or thrilled.

Still not certain if she was upset or thrilled.

She'd been hurt when he didn't show up, but not worried. Riley'd broken dates before, but he always had an acceptable excuse, a reason, she realized now, that usually made her feel guilty for mistrusting him. After their missed dinner engagement, she'd spent the next three days in court giving a deposition on that damned hijacking case...then she'd picked up the morning paper.

Picked up the paper and read that Riley James O'Rourke, beloved husband of Clarisse, brother of Seamus, son of the late Mary and Alfred, was dead.

Another head-on collision on the freeway. It was just one more messy accident to tie up the rush hour traffic and inconvenience hundreds of tired commuters trying to find their way home.

With his death, everything in Kathleen Margaret Malone's world suddenly shifted perspective. The tiny being growing inside her no longer had a father. The future Kat had nearly fantasized into reality had suddenly, like so many of her dreams, disappeared into thin air.

Once again, she faced the world alone.

She picked up the foamy toothbrush and realized her fingers were steady. In fact, she felt almost preternaturally calm, as if this were just another day in a humdrum world, or as the old cliché went, the first day of the rest of her life.

Which it is.

She took a deep breath, rinsed off the toothbrush, stepped out of the tiny bathroom and walked into the living room beyond. Seamus O'Rourke turned and nailed her with a piercing gaze. Kat hesitated, then took another deep breath.

She'd faced down killers, disarmed smugglers, even caught a murderer or two. Riley's brother actually seemed to think he could order her around. Kat almost smiled with her recovered sense of self. She was not a victim. Never had been, didn't intend to be. Seamus O'Rourke appeared to be under the impression he was calling the shots. It was going to be interesting when he finally figured out she'd been letting him get away with it all morning.

Kat met his glare with one of her own, then tucked her toothbrush into the breast pocket of her suit and picked up her handbag.

It was time for Mr. O'Rourke to learn that life, as he expected it, was about to change.

HE TURNED HIS HEAD as the dark green Jag sped past, though he doubted the bitch would recognize him, especially in this nondescript Buick. Of course, it wouldn't do to be spotted right now, right here...not with red paint staining his slacks. Too bad they were ruined, but it was worth the loss.

Turning the key in the ignition, he took a deep breath and grinned in anticipation. This was too good to be true. Another O'Rourke, identical to the first. A sobering thought, though. He hadn't known there was another one. Success depended on knowledge. Knowledge required study.

He pulled in behind the Jag and followed at a discreet distance. There was no rush. None at all. After all the months of planning, of dreaming about this moment, he'd never once considered how much he would enjoy himself.

Smiling broadly, he followed the dark green sedan through the rolling streets of San Francisco.

"MAKE A LIST. I'LL send the housekeeper out for whatever you need for the next couple of days, at least until you're in condition to shop for yourself."

Seamus turned off the ignition and stepped out of the car before Kat had a chance to respond. She'd been fuming throughout the entire ride from her house to his. By the time he opened her door and reached down to give her a hand, she was ready to explode.

She ignored him, stubbornly folding her arms across her middle. *Damn him.* She'd wanted to drive her own car, but do you think he'd take her by the cemetery to pick it up?

"I'll do my own shopping as soon as you take me to my car. I'm not getting out until you do."

"Your car will be delivered within the hour. I've already sent for it."

"How?" She glared out of the corner of her eye. He glared back. "You don't have the keys."

"I took them out of your purse."

"You what?" She unzipped her bag and scrambled through the garbage that seemed to collect in there of its own volition. *No keys.* "You had no right to go through my bag."

"It was done under the watchful eye of the police captain. In fact it was his idea. He didn't want you driving after the emotional strain you've been through. Now please get out of the car."

She figured she could sit here a while longer to make her point, but it wouldn't prove a thing. Besides, if she didn't find a bathroom soon she'd probably wet her pants. It was truly amazing what pregnancy did to a perfectly healthy body. She didn't see Mr. O'Rourke taking lightly to piddle stains on his expensive leather upholstery.

She swung her legs around and stepped out of the car before Seamus could once again offer his hand. For some reason it felt like a victory. A very small victory, but one nonetheless.

A strident voice in the back of her mind reminded Kat she was the one supposedly calling the shots. She pushed the voice aside, grabbed a tight hold on her tiny victory and followed Seamus into the house.

"THIS WILL BE YOUR room." Seamus opened the door and stepped back, waiting for her comment of appreciation, her acknowledgment of the tasteful decor.

Instead she brushed by him and headed directly for the bathroom as if she'd been here a thousand times before.

"You're not going to be sick again, are you?" *Please*, he thought. *Not here.* He glanced at the toe of his shoe, wiped clean after this morning and wondered if he'd ever wear this pair again.

He heard the toilet flush, the sound of running water, then she was standing in the doorway wiping her hands on one of his grandmother's delicate hand-embroidered towels. "Thought I was gonna pop." She tossed the towel on the counter behind her. "Nice room." Kat looked around as if she'd just stepped into a Motel 6.

She dumped her bag on the bed and slipped her fitted black jacket off her shoulders, then casually removed a lethal looking pistol from a previously unseen shoulder holster.

Seamus thought for a minute he might be the one to throw up.

"What in God's name is that?"

"It's a pistol, nine millimeter Ruger, to be exact." She carefully unfastened the holster, slipped the harness down her arm and folded the whole contraption into a neat bundle. "Riley carried a gun. You knew that. We have very similar jobs with the same kinds of risks. So what's the big deal?"

"Riley wasn't pregnant," was all he could think to say.

"Well, of course not." She rolled her eyes. "Look, if it's a problem, I'll leave. I can find a room in town, but the gun stays with me. I've had three attempts on my life in the last year alone. You saw what my apartment looked like."

"Just what is it you do, Ms. Malone?" He knew, as with Riley's work with the FBI, she was some kind of investigator...at least that's what the police captain had alluded to. Somehow, though, the reality of a loaded gun tucked neatly under the arm of this tall, slim blonde with the look of a fashion model and the mouth of a street walker wasn't all that easy to digest. Neither was the stark image of the weapon lying on his grandmother's crocheted bedspread,

"I'm a field agent for the Department of Transportation. Or was, that is, until I barfed in my partner's car on stakeout. I've since been assigned desk duty for the duration of my pregnancy." She flashed him a dry, but tired, smile. Seamus had the odd sensation of having been punched in the gut while tumbling down Alice's rabbit hole.

Not a particularly pleasant feeling.

Good Lord, the woman was magnificent when she smiled.

"That doesn't tell me what you do, though, does it?" He struggled for a sense of balance. "Do you have to carry a gun?"

"You are an uptight fish, aren't you?" She smiled again, and once more he felt dizzy with the glory of it. "I guess, to be perfectly explicit, my job requires me to track down crooks within our transportation system. Truck drivers embezzling goods, smugglers bringing things in or taking them out of the country, mob activity—whatever illegal actions someone can think of that affects how goods are moved." She smiled again, holding her hands out as if for understanding. "When you deal with crooks, it's a good idea to at least match their firepower."

"I see. I guess you surprised me. To be quite honest, you don't look the part."

"No, actually, I look like a hooker. A high-class hooker is how my supervisor describes me, but still a hooker. I think that's what got me the job in the first place. I do a lot of undercover work."

She said it with a twinkle in her eye, but her play on words still made his palms sweat. Leave it to Riley to fall for a street walker, or someone who made her living looking like one. "Is that how you met my brother? Working undercover?"

"No. I met Riley on a job in Utah. My partner was the one working undercover. I was his back-up. We were out from the office in Pittsburgh. Riley was brought in from the San Francisco bureau. We hit it off." She glanced down at her perfectly flat middle. "Yeah, you might say we hit it off real well."

"You don't act like a woman in love." Her choice of words grated over raw nerves. Seamus stepped closer. "How do I know you're telling the truth? How do I know you're carrying Riley's child, not some other man's bastard? Hell, how do I know you're even pregnant?"

Seamus knew how to use his size and presence, but instead of backing away from him as he expected, she stood her ground. Her stubborn poise infuriated him. Seamus felt his muscles tense, knew his control was ready to snap.

"Good Lord, O'Rourke. You think I go around puking on people for fun?" Her tired reply undid him.

He practically shouted at her. "My brother was the one with the fertility problems, Ms. Malone. Didn't Riley tell you? It wasn't Clarisse's fault they couldn't have children. It was his. Now you come along outta the blue and tell me you're pregnant and Riley's the father, and you expect me to just swallow your story?" He reached out for some inexplicable reason and raised her chin with his fingers. "Hell, you don't even look pregnant."

He wasn't sure what he expected to see, but it certainly wasn't the flash of vulnerability followed by a rush of blazing anger. "I don't give a rat's ass whether you believe me or not, O'Rourke." She slapped his hand aside. "I may look like a whore, but I don't act like one. As for mourning your brother, well, it's difficult to mourn a man who didn't exist. I fell in love with Riley O'Rourke, a fun-loving, sweet-talking Irish devil who promised me the stars, who swore undying love and said we'd always be together. I don't have affairs with married men, Mr. O'Rourke. I didn't fall in love with a liar and a cheat. That man can go to hell for all I care and I'll not mourn him."

He felt like a deflated balloon, all the fight gone out of him. "Sadly, Ms. Malone, neither will I." Seamus bowed his head and turned to leave the room. Guilt twisted his gut and clamped a cold, hard fist over his heart.

He'd spent his life covering up for his twin, pulling him out of one scrape after another, making excuses for him, compromising his own values to save Riley's tail, wishing him dead more often than not.

One thing he'd learned, Seamus realized. He'd never wish anyone dead again because the guilt was almost unbearable.

He would, however, do one more thing for Riley. He took another long look at Kathleen Malone. She stood in the middle of the room he would always think of as "Gran's room," one hand protectively covering her flat stomach. Silently Seamus vowed he would watch over her.

He'd watch over the sassy blonde with the face of a saint and he'd be there for the child she carried.

Riley's child. As close to his own as any child would ever be. That brief flash of vulnerability in her eyes had told him more than any lie detector, any blood test, ever could. There was no reason to doubt her word.

She did indeed carry Riley's child.

He took a deep breath, let it out slowly. "You must be tired." He paused, one hand on the doorknob. "Why don't you rest. Come down when you feel like it and have some dinner. If you like, I can take you into town later to shop for a few things to replace what was...damaged. Or take your own car. It's entirely up to you."

"You're damned right it's up to me." She held his gaze a moment, clear-eyed and steady, then abruptly turned away and stared out the window.

Women. Seamus glared at her rigid back, searching unsuccessfully for the trace of vulnerability he was certain he'd seen earlier. *Shit. You try to be nice....*

He turned and stalked out of the room.

The door clicked behind him and Kathleen burst into tears. Damn, it had been one hell of a day. And damn it again, but she didn't want to cry.

But her hormones were totally screwed, she was tired and pregnant and sick to her stomach, and Riley was dead.

She hadn't been telling the truth when she said she wouldn't mourn him. She would. She'd miss his laughter and kindness and the plans they'd made.

Plans he'd obviously never intended to keep, damn him. And damn his insufferable brother Seamus as well. For being kind, for worrying about her, for giving her refuge when she needed it most. She didn't want to owe him a thing. Nor did she want to be intrigued by a man who epitomized all the uptight personality traits she despised. A man who looked exactly like the one she thought she'd loved.

That man obviously never existed at all.

Damn. Damn. Damn it all to hell.

Kat stripped her clothes off and crawled between the sheets, too tired to shower, too emotionally exhausted to care. One hand rested protectively over her belly, protecting her child. Riley's child. The child Seamus told her was impossible.

Later, she thought. She'd worry about it later.

OH, THIS WAS ACTUALLY fun...and so easy. There was no need even to stop the car. He merely noted the location and glided quietly past the mansion.

Chapter Two

SHE VAGUELY RECALLED SOMEONE opening her door during the night, but Kat didn't fully awaken until the morning sun filtered through the heavy damask curtains and birdsong filled her mind.

She showered in the perfect little bathroom, combed her wet hair back off her face, then realized she had absolutely nothing to wear.

She checked the closet and practically giggled out loud. The entire thing, from one end to the other, was filled with perfectly pressed, clean white shirts. Identical clean white shirts, exactly like the one Seamus O'Rourke had worn to the funeral the day before.

Kat thought of Riley's rumpled suits and wrinkled shirts and wondered once again how twin brothers could possibly be so different. Then without a second thought, she grabbed one of Seamus's perfect shirts and put it on.

The tail fell half way down her thighs and the cuffs dangled over her hands, covering her fingers. She folded the crisp cotton back to her wrists and checked herself in the mirror to make sure she was covered. Her stomach growled and a familiar wave of nausea reminded her she hadn't eaten since breakfast the day before. She needed something soon or she'd spend the rest of the day feeling like crap.

The doctor had promised the morning sickness would end by her fourth month.

"One more lying male," Kat muttered. Here it was well into her fifth month and she still spent way too much time with her head over the toilet.

With a last glance at her reflection, Kat headed downstairs in search of a meal.

SEAMUS FOUND HER there half an hour later, munching on a piece of toast with jam and reading the want ads in the morning paper. His morning paper. The one he liked to read in precisely the same order each day. He always began with the business section and stock quotes, which appeared to be the same section Kathleen Malone had already folded in half and covered with coffee rings from her dripping cup.

The nervy woman was even wearing one of his shirts. He started to say something, to announce his presence, but just then she shifted in her chair and tucked one bare foot up under her thigh. The shirt slipped a fraction higher, exposing a bit more of her leg.

It was a spectacular leg. Long, lean, well muscled, an athlete's leg. He studied it a moment, allowing his imagination a brief foray into the realm of fantasy, suddenly aware of what he'd missed by never bringing a woman here before.

It was actually kind of embarrassing to admit, if only to himself. In all his thirty-six years, he'd never stepped into his kitchen in the early morning hours to find any woman other than his grandmother seated at the kitchen table.

It had never felt right, somehow, to bring a woman into his home. In his mind, Seamus realized, that was tantamount to making a commitment, something he had no intention of doing. No, you took a woman out to an extravagant dinner, and if the evening progressed in a satisfactory fashion, you booked a room in a very nice hotel.

Then you left a rose or chocolates on the pillow and slipped away before dawn. He'd tried to explain it to Riley one time, how much simpler it was to avoid the complications of relationships that were doomed to failure. Riley had merely laughed.

Seamus had reminded Riley that most women wanted a husband and children. The O'Rourke twins would never be fathers. A shared childhood illness had seen to that. Riley's smug grin had told Seamus the truth...his irresponsible twin had been relieved that children weren't a risk he'd be taking. He'd gloried in his vast conquests among the female population. Even marriage hadn't slowed him down.

No. Nothing had slowed Riley O'Rourke. Not until a hit and run driver on the James Lick Freeway in San Francisco took the Irishman's life.

Seamus had never before considered what he'd been missing. An image flashed into his mind, of waking up in his own bed with Kathleen sleeping next to him, of sharing a quiet morning cup of coffee after a night of lovemaking.

He rubbed his thumbs over his fingertips. His palms were damp with sweat.

Kathleen looked up, as if suddenly aware of his presence. "Oh." She smiled that devastating smile of hers. "Good morning. I didn't hear you come in. I hope you don't mind..." She gestured toward the coffee maker, the grounds scattered amid toast crumbs and a smear of jam on the otherwise spotless counter. "I kind of made myself at home. If I don't have toast or crackers right off the bat, I get squeamish." She gave him a crooked smile, remembering, he was certain, how he'd responded to her version of *squeamish*.

"Oh, and...uh...I borrowed your shirt."

"I noticed." How could any man *not* notice? He tried to ignore how she looked.

It wasn't easy ignoring a woman as naturally beautiful as this one. Yesterday she'd been so emotionally overwrought, he'd been so upset, he really hadn't allowed the force of her beauty to register. This morning it was impossible to ignore the natural shine of her shoulder length hair, the high, wide cheekbones, the generous mouth.

Not to mention the lean length of her, the athletic grace so evident in every movement. He didn't even attempt to contain the involuntary sigh that escaped him. For the hundredth time in the past twenty-four hours, Seamus envied his brother. Envied Riley the casual way in which he'd lived his life, the manner in which he'd so easily dumped all his problems on his "older" brother.

Why hadn't he seen it before? Why did it take Riley's death to make him finally understand the truth? Riley embraced life. Seamus endured. Riley had laughed and conquered. Seamus followed the rules. Hell, he'd not only followed them, he'd welcomed them. Rules had protected him, had allowed him to back away from every personal challenge he'd ever faced.

Seamus, the perfect son, was doing his best to make the ghosts of his parents proud. He'd even studied for the priesthood because he thought it would have made them happy.

Thank God his grandmother had convinced him he had neither the calling nor the aptitude. But he'd still walked away suffused with guilt, wondering why he hadn't been able to figure that out for himself.

The alpha male had definitely been the one they'd buried yesterday, he thought ruefully. Which left him, Seamus O'Rourke, holding the bag as usual, waiting for the hammer to fall, the bell to ring, the timing to be off.

He'd always felt this way, so uncomfortable within his own skin. He was perfectly aware he made up for it by projecting an image of strength...one he didn't necessarily feel.

Especially now, with Riley's woman sitting at his kitchen table, her sleek form barely covered in one of Seamus's typically conservative white cotton shirts.

"Is that all you're going to eat?" Immediately he regretted his demanding tone. "I mean, with the baby coming..."

"It's all I can stomach in the morning." She grimaced, then smiled. "I'm taking my prenatal vitamins and eating better later in the day, when my stomach's settled a bit more."

"We definitely want your stomach settled." He turned his back on her and poured his coffee.

SHE SMILED AT HIS dry quip as she watched him, struck once again with the resemblance that wasn't perfect, the subtle differences she found so fascinating.

This morning, wearing a dark maroon robe, his hair still tousled from sleep, Seamus looked more like Riley than he had the day before, but everything else about him was different, unique to himself.

Where Riley had moved in a loose-jointed, almost clumsy manner, this man's grace was as much a part of himself as a cat's. No movement wasted, everything precise.

He made her nervous, made her skin feel tight and her heart pound just a bit faster. It was almost as if she were waiting for something to happen—the way she felt on a job where danger lurked.

Here in this spotless kitchen with the morning sun shining brightly and the scent of fresh ground coffee in the air, danger definitely lurked.

Kat watched Seamus take down a box of cereal from one cupboard, a bowl from another, unable to stop the constant need to compare him to his brother. Riley'd been Don Johnson to this man's Nicholas Cage, easy going and affable to dark and dangerous. Seamus projected raw power, leashed and restrained, but prowling just beneath the surface.

She'd loved Riley as much for the ease she felt in his presence as for his striking physique, coal black hair and twinkling blue eyes. Seamus had the look, but the presence was all wrong. It sucked the air from the room, filled the space and demanded it be acknowledged.

He challenged her personally. And Kathleen Margaret Malone never, ever backed down from a challenge. Maybe his comment hadn't been meant as humor. Had it been an insult?

"I didn't mean to ruin your shoes." She hoped he was perfectly aware from the tone of her voice there was no apology intended. "I didn't puke on them on purpose."

"My shoes will survive," Seamus replied, looking over Kathleen with a judgmental air. "My shirt, however, will never be the same."

She glanced down at the line of grape jam dribbled down the front. "I'm sorry. All right?" She covered her embarrassment with another attack. "It's not like you don't have a whole closet full of them."

"You're right. I do." He glared at her. "And if I want any of them to remain intact, we'd better take you shopping as soon as possible."

"*We* aren't taking me anywhere. I'm going alone. Don't you have a job or something to go to?"

"I work at home." Suddenly the wall beyond her shoulder appeared to catch his interest.

"Doing what?" Kat consciously toned her voice down as her anger drained away. She'd always been volatile, knew she could be abrasive, but she really didn't have a right to be so rude to the man in his own house. He had, truly, shown her nothing but kindness. He'd even given her, a total stranger, a place to sleep.

"I'm a writer."

Now his spoon full of cereal seemed to demand his attention.

"Wow, really? Like mysteries or thrillers? What do you write?"

He mumbled something unintelligible.

"What?" she asked. *Something about food?*

"I write food and wine columns for magazines, if you really must know." His expression said, *I dare you.*

She giggled, then bit her bottom lip for control. *Food and wine?* This big, sexy man with the broad shoulders, booming voice and air of danger surrounding him, wrote about food? Kat sucked both lips between her teeth. It wasn't enough. She couldn't stop it. Her laughter exploded, full and unrestrained while he carefully wiped his mouth with a white cloth napkin and glared at her again.

He'd done that a lot this morning, she thought. She hiccupped, wiped her eyes, and giggled again. "I'm sorry," she said, not really sorry at all. "It's just that you look so much like Riley, and he and I both think beer and hamburgers cover all the food groups. It's not easy to picture Riley as a food critic, you know, other than 'hey Sid, ya burned the bun'."

He was still glaring. "I'll remind you once again, Ms. Malone. I am not my brother. Another thing...you need to learn to put him in the past. My brother is dead."

He might as well have slapped her. Maybe she deserved it, but he didn't have to deliberately say things to hurt her. She was hurting enough already. "I'm very aware Riley is dead." She rose stiffly to her feet. "You don't have to remind me, but I'll remind you, Mr. O'Rourke, that when I lost Riley, I lost more than a lover. I lost my memories of him as well. The Riley O'Rourke I loved never existed at all." She brushed the crumbs off the front of her shirt and onto the tile floor, smearing the grape jam into a long purple slash across the white cotton.

"I'll take myself shopping, thank you. Don't expect me back for a couple of hours. There are some rentals I need to check on."

"Ms. Malone...Kathleen."

She paused in the doorway, but she didn't turn around.

"I'm sorry. This has been a trying time for both of us and I apologize." His mind was spinning, almost out of control. What should he do? He didn't want her to leave. He couldn't tolerate her here. But he'd never rest knowing there was someone out there, stalking, waiting, unless he knew he could protect her.

No, not her. The baby. Riley's baby.

She'd drive him nuts, living here under the same roof. He wouldn't be able to abide her unconventional ways, her attitude, her sloppiness, the gun in the bedroom, her coffee stains on his morning paper.

Damn it all! Riley had called him an anal retentive ass and Seamus had adopted the description as a badge of honor.

He'd never denied Riley was right on target.

He still couldn't allow her to leave.

"Kathleen," he repeated, sighing regretfully the moment he reached his decision. "Please don't go. I'd like you to consider this as your home, at least until the baby's born. It's only right, as Riley's sole surviving relative, that I offer you a place to stay during your pregnancy."

Slowly, Kathleen turned around and faced him.

At least he'd gotten his offer out without stuttering...but why was she staring at him like that?

She shook her head, a look of disbelief on her face. "You're kidding, right?" She grabbed the back of her chair and leaned forward. His eyes were drawn to the deep shadowed V between her breasts and the sudden realization she wore nothing at all beneath his shirt.

"You don't honestly think I'd stay here with *you?* Not only are we complete strangers, we obviously don't even like each other!" She laughed, sarcasm dripping from every word. "I don't think so, Mr. O'Rourke. I don't need a keeper. Thanks anyway."

"I'm only offering you a room." *What could this woman possibly be thinking?* He looked away, away from the shadows beneath her eyes, the shadow between her breasts. He concentrated instead on the bowl of cereal turning to mush in front of him.

"I'm not offering my room and certainly not my bed. We don't have to like each other for me to want to help you. My brother got you pregnant. He's dead now. That makes you my responsibility and the offer stands."

He waited a moment for her answer, then when none came, added his final argument in soft, placating tones. "Ms. Malone...Kathleen, there's no need for you to live alone, especially with some nut following you around making threats on your life. That would be foolish, especially when I've got more than enough room here for both of us. This is a very large house."

Seamus silently congratulated himself on his convincing argument when suddenly the image of the filthy threats splashed in blood-red paint across Kat's walls flashed into his mind, filled him with a sense of dangerous urgency. Kathleen needed him. She'd understand that.

Wouldn't she?

"You self-righteous, egotistical fool! There is no place big enough for the two of us to co-exist. The earth is not big enough. Now get this straight...no man is responsible for me, especially you, you sanctimonious ass. How can you sit there looking at me out of Riley's face, talking to me as if I haven't got a mind and a will of my own and tell me I need you to take care of me? I don't need any man, especially Riley O'Rourke's evil twin!"

She thought *he* was sanctimonious? Egotistical? Hell, she'd just described herself! Seamus leapt to his feet, boiling with righteous fury. His chair skittered back and clattered to the floor as he leaned over the table, his lips just inches from her angry face.

A mere fraction from her mouth.

"You *do* need a keeper, lady," he yelled, all semblance of control gone. "And for some stupid reason I'm offering to take on the job!"

Then a horrible thought struck him. What if she'd decided not to keep the baby...Riley was gone, what if...? He backed up, almost tripped over the chair lying on the floor behind him. "That's it! You're planning to end the pregnancy, aren't you? You're planning to get—"

"What I do with this pregnancy is nobody's business but mine." She returned his glare with one of her own. "Just as where I choose to live is no one else's business, especially yours. Kat Malone goes it alone." She carefully enunciated each word. "I've lived that philosophy since I was a little girl. It will always be true. I am responsible for myself."

"But..."

"Goodbye, Mr. O'Rourke, and thank you for your kind hospitality." She brushed her hands together as if to wipe away crumbs. He felt as if she brushed him away as well.

"I'll be leaving shortly. I won't be coming back."

It took a conscious effort for him to shut his mouth as she turned and stormed out of the room.

HE HATED BROODING. RILEY'D made fun of it. His grandmother had lamented over it. But hell, he was good at it. Seamus toyed with his cereal, staring aimlessly at the soggy flakes of bran something-or-other that were supposed to start his day off right.

Well, damn it, it was a little late for that.

He wished, for the hundredth time, his grandmother were still alive. She'd understood him, his deep love/hate relationship with his brother. She'd felt much the same about Riley herself.

She'd know what to say now, to help him find control. But Gran was gone and Kathleen Malone was upstairs dressing in that little black suit she'd worn to his brother's funeral, strapping that deadly looking gun into the harness under her arm, preparing to walk out of his life forever.

Taking Riley's baby with her. He closed his eyes, dreading the thought of her choice. How far along was her pregnancy? It was impossible to tell, but she looked so slim, so decidedly non-pregnant, she couldn't be too far along. *What if she took the easy way out?* Riley was dead. She had a job that certainly didn't sound as if it catered to motherhood. How could he convince her to continue her pregnancy and carry the child to term?

Carry to term, give birth...then turn the baby over to him?

Impossible.

He watched as another cereal flake disappeared beneath the milk.

Maybe not. The idea had merit. She couldn't possibly want a child, not a woman like her. It shouldn't be all that difficult. Money wasn't a problem. He had a good lawyer who could handle the legalities. Seamus and Ms. Malone wouldn't need to ever see each other again, not if it were handled properly.

He looked up from the bowl of soggy cereal and stared at the empty doorway. She'd stormed from the room almost ten minutes ago. He still felt her presence.

"O'Rourke!"

Kat's scream galvanized him. Swearing under his breath, Seamus raced out of the kitchen and up the stairs. He paused long enough to grab the only weapon he could think of, his grandmother's brass-tipped cane.

The stalker, somehow, had found Kathleen.

Her door was closed, but he forced it open without even trying the handle. He raced into the room with the cane raised.

She huddled on the carpet next to the bathroom door, her face as pale as the white shirt she still wore, holding a towel tightly between her legs.

A towel covered in blood.

"Seamus," she cried. "Help me. I don't want to lose the baby."

The baby!

He picked her up off the floor and, holding her close to his chest like a child, sat in the big rocker next to the bed. She trembled. Was she in pain? Was it fear?

Fear of losing the baby.

She'd already chosen to keep it.

A deep sense of relief sharpened by unrelenting terror energized him. Seamus grabbed the phone and dialed 911, gave the dispatcher the necessary information and waited.

Kathleen clung to him, pale, vulnerable, so unlike the harridan who'd stormed out of his kitchen moments before.

Had their argument caused this? "You'll be fine." He stroked one finger along the line of her jaw, silently saying the prayers of his childhood, projecting the calm demeanor he'd practiced over the years. There was no need for her to know he trembled as much as she; no reason to frighten her with his own fears.

"Seamus." Her voice was nothing more than a whisper. "I'm so sorry. I don't want you to think I ever considered...would ever..." Her body stiffened. She grimaced, a low moan of pain ending in a sob.

"Shhh...it's okay." He brushed the damp hair back from her eyes, prayed for an end to her pain. He'd never felt so helpless. "You'll be fine. The baby will be fine. We'll work everything out when you're better. I'm sorry. I didn't mean to lose my temper. I want to take care of you, Kathleen. You and the baby."

She thought about that, about turning all her worries and fears over to this stranger who wasn't really a stranger at all. His face was already familiar, his voice was deep, soft, and so reassuring. As much as he angered her, she somehow knew she could trust him, and could count on Seamus O'Rourke to keep her safe.

He would watch over her...over their baby. Thinking that, believing him, she allowed herself to fade into oblivion.

SEAMUS FOLLOWED KATHLEEN'S AMBULANCE through the foggy morning streets of San Francisco, staying as close behind as traffic lights and traffic would allow.

Then he followed her into the hospital.

Seamus hated hospitals, the smell, the impersonal bustle of too many people intent on their business, the sounds of others hurting, the tears of those whose loved ones were beyond pain.

Usually, he loved efficiency. Now, it merely proved a barrier between him and Kathleen. He handled the paperwork without thinking, paced until his legs were numb, sat and willed Kathleen and the baby well.

Coffee cups stacked up on the small table beside him. Janitors came and cleared them away. A candy striper offered him a bagel and a smile. He could only summon a blank stare in reply.

Time passed. He knew it must be passing, but the minutes blended into hours and the hours meshed, one into the other, so when the doctor finally tapped him on the shoulder he could only gape at the woman and resent the interruption to his brooding.

"Mr. O'Rourke?"

He nodded, afraid to ask.

"I'm Dr. Jeffries...your wife's physician. I want you to know she'll be fine."

Wife? He didn't correct her because he didn't see the need. Kathleen was all right. "The baby?" He looked into the doctor's sad brown eyes that had seen much more pain than a young woman should bear.

"She hasn't lost the baby, at least not yet. There's still a risk. She's just over five months along. Survivability for the fetus at this point...well, we want to keep her overnight, keep her on an IV until the pregnancy is stabilized. If she doesn't abort within the next twenty-four hours, I think she'll be fine. She'll have to limit her activities over the next few months. No lifting, no bending—" She paused, as if measuring Seamus's temperament. "—no sexual activity."

He nodded, sighed, smiled at the doctor. "That won't be a problem." It was difficult to ignore the irony of the situation. "May I see her?"

"Of course. Follow me."

Kathleen's normally fair complexion was the shade of alabaster, the dark blue shadows under her eyes the only hint of color. Seamus paused in the doorway, alternately hating and loving his brother that he, Seamus, should be standing here now, worrying himself sick over a woman he hardly knew; worrying about a child that wasn't his, a child he wanted more than he'd ever wanted anything, ever.

A child with a very fragile hold on life.

Kathleen sensed him close by, slowly turned her head and looked his way. For a moment, Riley stood there watching her, a look of infinite sadness in his eyes. Then he smiled and walked into the room and it was Seamus standing by the side of the bed, awkwardly patting her hand, telling her how glad he was that she was going to be all right.

"I could still lose the baby." She wondered why her lips felt so stiff, why the words were so difficult to say. It would solve so many problems, she thought, if the unthinkable happened. She could walk away, go on with her life, and pretend none of this had ever taken place.

Pretend little "whatsit" hadn't existed in any form, ever.

She felt a deep sense of sadness, a feeling of incomparable loss at what might never be. Hot tears scalded the corners of her eyes. She wanted to brush them away, but lacked the energy.

"You won't." The strength behind his words made it true. He lightly touched her face, wiped the errant tears away with his thumb, then once again covered her hand with his.

"I..." God it was hard to apologize, to retract all those things she'd said in anger.

He didn't give her the chance. No, he was moving right ahead, a veritable bulldozer where her intentions were involved. "This time there's no discussion. You'll stay with me. The doctor said you can't be alone. You'll need bed rest until you're completely stabilized, then you're to take it easy over the next few weeks if you want to prevent a miscarriage. Since I work at home, I can be there for you. I have the extra room and my housekeeper will be thrilled to have someone to coddle."

He glared at her and for a moment she thought she saw a flash of humor in those green eyes of his, but it was quickly shielded. "So don't even try to argue, Ms. Malone. Not this time, because it just won't work."

"At least I know I'll eat well." She unobtrusively pulled her hand out from under his. She'd learned a long time ago it was important to pick your battles. She didn't have the energy to fight this one right now. "I would assume a food critic only allows the best?"

"Exactly." He smiled briefly, looked down at his suddenly empty hand and shoved it in his pocket. He cleared his throat and stepped back from the bed. Kathleen almost smiled at his uncharacteristically awkward movements, as if he didn't know where to look, what to say.

"They keep calling me Mrs. O'Rourke." She studied his face, watching for his reaction.

He flushed, cleared his throat again and looked just over her shoulder. She wondered what was so interesting about a blank green wall.

"It made it easier to get in to see you to find out about your condition. If you're not related, hospital policy is...they don't..." He was obviously avoiding eye contact. "I'll correct it right away."

"It's not important," she said, wondering why that was so. Usually her identity was her mainstay, the thing that gave her control. Now, the only important factor was this fragile life inside her. Or maybe not so fragile, the way it was hanging on, fighting to survive.

"Is there anything you need?" he asked, still not meeting her eyes. "A clean gown, toothbrush, comb...?" His voice trailed off.

"I don't own a nightgown." She wasn't sure why she even said such a thing, even if it was true. "At home I sleep in the nude. Here I get this dandy little thing with a slit up the back." She smiled when he blushed. *Why had he seemed so threatening earlier this morning?* One thing for certain, he was definitely nothing like Riley, something she suddenly found terribly appealing.

She glanced at the little plastic bowl of personal items the nurse had left. "Maybe a comb or hairbrush? Everything else seems to be provided."

"I'll take care of it." The look of relief on his face said a lot more than he probably realized. Kathleen was still grinning when he turned and quickly walked out of the room.

HE CALLED MRS. ANDREWS and explained they'd have a guest for the next couple of weeks, hopefully longer. When he told the housekeeper it was a female guest who would need extra care because of a difficult pregnancy, he could almost hear the old gal's wheels turning.

He'd let Kathleen answer any questions. Knowing Hazel Andrews, there'd be plenty.

Seamus wasn't certain, at this point, what to tell people.

His agent was going to have a field day. Frank made no secret of the fact he thought Seamus was gay. Seamus had never seen any great need to correct him. It certainly kept his philandering agent from constantly trying to set him up with one woman or another of questionable reputation.

The lack of women in his life, his interest in food and the arts, his impeccable style of dress and non-existent social life had been proof enough for Frank to make all kinds of assumptions about his client.

Having a beautiful woman...a beautiful, *pregnant* woman...living in his home was going to really throw the little guy for a loop!

Seamus chuckled aloud. He almost looked forward to his next conversation with Frank.

He knew he was an oddity in this day and age, but that didn't usually bother him. Today, though, as he walked down the long green hallway to the hospital gift shop, he wondered what his friends...and his agent...would think of his basically celibate life.

He'd never been in love, other than the occasional young man's crush. As an adult, his affairs had been few and far between, always discreet, and never—not ever—emotional. He'd never felt the rush of passion he read about. Had never known a desire so deep as to bring him back for a second night with any of his infrequent partners.

He'd never understood the power of love between man and woman.

He wasn't certain why it hadn't happened, though he honestly suspected his own behavior was a backlash to Riley's. Even his youthful decision to become a priest had followed one of Riley's more outrageous escapades.

Thank goodness Gran had convinced him you didn't become a priest because you're embarrassed by your brother's behavior, no matter how awful the transgression.

No, his fairly celibate lifestyle hadn't been the result of his religious beliefs. He guessed he'd just never met anyone interesting enough, or challenging enough.

Then there'd been the issue of children...or lack of them. He'd never gotten to know any woman well enough to explain, never cared enough for it to be a concern.

Besides, he'd had so many other things to worry about over the years.

There'd been Gran and her long illness after years of raising her twin grandsons. Of course, there'd always been Riley and the worrying and wondering over exactly what kind of scrape his irresponsible twin was going to get into next. They'd all been shocked when he ended up in law enforcement, but it was probably the only thing, other than Seamus, that had kept him out of jail.

Well, Riley'd definitely gotten himself into a scrape of monumental proportions this time. Once again Seamus was putting his life on hold to bail him out. Taking a woman under his wing who not only didn't appreciate his help one iota, but who seemed bound and determined to fight him and insult him every step of the way.

This was definitely going to be a difficult pregnancy...for both of them.

Muttering to himself, Seamus stared at the array of hairbrushes and combs in the tiny gift shop and wondered what sort of bristles worked best on hair the texture of silk.

Chapter Three

RIGHT ON SCHEDULE. HE glanced down at the gold Rolex encircling his wrist. It hadn't been easy getting that twit of a housekeeper to start talking, but once he'd gained her confidence, she'd been impossible to shut up. Irritating old biddy. Nothing he hated more than interfering women, but she'd been full of surprises and more than willing to talk to the nice young man surveying the neighborhood for a magazine article on San Francisco's Victorian mansions.

Once he'd steered the conversation to more personal matters, the bitch had really dropped a whammy. Mr. O'Rourke was bringing home a houseguest...and she was pregnant! The gods were definitely smiling on him today.

He smiled in return. This added an entirely new dimension to his plans. He could afford to wait.

Wait and anticipate the pleasure.

"GOODNESS. THIS PLACE IS huge." Kathleen stared through the windshield at an ornately carved stone entry leading to a massive but beautifully restored Victorian mansion. "I can't believe I didn't notice this before...or the neighborhood. Not just the Sunset district, but the outer Sunset... Wow! I'm impressed."

She kept her words light and teasing, but the memory of her first trip to Seamus's house filtered into Kat's thoughts. Of course she hadn't noticed the house. She'd been consumed with anger, frightened and fed up with her stalker's latest attack, and completely frustrated by Seamus O'Rourke and his overbearing attitude.

Frustrated and confused, and trying so hard not to mourn a man she'd loved. A man who had lied to her, who'd had the audacity to die in a stupid car accident. How could she ever forget Riley and get on with her life, if she was faced with his brother on a daily basis?

She couldn't possibly stay here for the rest of her pregnancy. The three-and-a-half months remaining stretched out ahead like an entire lifetime.

"I drove directly into the garage last time." Seamus glanced at her, as if weighing her mood. "After what had just happened to your home, I figured it wasn't a good time to show off mine."

Kat returned his clear-eyed gaze and decided, if he'd really been trying to protect her feelings, he wasn't so bad after all. "Thank you, I guess." She shouldn't think about her ruined little house. Somehow she'd forget about Riley.

Save what you can and move on. That she could do. She'd been doing it most of her life. Shaking off the memories, Kat teased him. "Well, it's really beautiful. Guess food critics make better money than I realized."

"We eat pretty well, too."

His eyes were twinkling and she suddenly realized it was the closest thing to a joke she'd heard from him. She grinned in reply. It was a start, after all.

Of what, she wasn't certain.

He got out of the car, came around to her side and was suddenly leaning into her open door to pluck her from the seat.

"I can walk," she insisted, batting his hands away, but he just cocked one very dark eyebrow, unfastened her seatbelt and lifted her out as if she weighed nothing at all.

His arms felt rock-hard under the soft fabric of his suit, his grip secure and warm. It was easier than it should have been to just give up and wrap her arms around his neck. Just as it was absolutely impossible to ignore the way his scent tickled her senses. What was it about this man? He wasn't anything like Riley, but then her reaction to Riley hadn't been the same, either. Never this heart thudding, breath-stopping shot of awareness whenever they touched.

She didn't like it. No, she didn't like it a bit.

Riley'd been fun and easy and completely non-threatening. Safe. Kat was suddenly thankful for the long robe Seamus had brought to her at the hospital. Thankful for the protection it seemed to offer. Not that she actually *feared* Seamus....

The front door swung open and a little gray haired woman fluttered out of the way. "Oh, the poor dear." She clucked her dismay so much like a character in a bad movie that Kat almost laughed aloud.

And wondered, for the hundredth time this morning, just what, exactly, she'd gotten herself into.

"This is the lady I told you about—Kathleen Malone. She'll be our guest for a while." Seamus brushed past the chattering woman as if she weren't even there. "There's no need for you to follow. I'll get her settled." The last was said looking over his shoulder as he quickly climbed the long staircase.

Kathleen peeked over his shoulder and suppressed a tired giggle at the look of shock on the tiny woman's face. She decided to keep her mouth shut and just go along for the ride.

He sat her carefully in the rocker, the same chair where he'd held her in his arms the day she'd nearly miscarried. He'd been trembling that morning, almost as much as she.

Kathleen still wondered about his reaction. Had he been angry still, or afraid for her?

No. It came to her suddenly, the truth of it all. He had merely worried about the baby, the unborn child who appeared to intrigue him so completely.

Riley's child. Seamus's last link to his brother? She'd have to think about that one. Seamus and Riley obviously hadn't had what anyone would call a conventional relationship, especially for twins.

She still wasn't certain if they'd hated, tolerated, or even *liked* one another.

Seamus pulled back the covers of the bed and fluffed the pillows. Kat waited patiently, biting her tongue when she would have teased Riley about his domestic skills. She had to keep reminding herself Riley was gone. This man didn't know her or her often warped sense of humor, any more than she knew him.

But he'd brought her into his home, offered her sanctuary and care even knowing there was someone out there threatening her, knowing he might be putting himself at risk for a woman carrying another man's child.

She was definitely going to have to think about that one. She knew instinctively Riley wouldn't have done as much, and wondered if he would even have accepted responsibility for his child.

Riley's brother had. Without question or complaint, he had taken her in as if there were no other alternatives. Maybe, she thought, for a man like Seamus O'Rourke, there was no alternative.

His sense of honor was something Kat couldn't deny. She'd seen evidence of it time and again throughout her week-long stay at the hospital. It was a part of him—the integral sense of decency and integrity lacking in so many men.

Not merely lacking, but nonexistent in Riley.

Riley's dead.

She had to quit making comparisons.

"Let me help you." His quiet offer halted her thoughts, and his arms wrapped around her and gently settled her into the wide bed.

She didn't even attempt to struggle. What was the point?

"This room is so feminine." She noticed for the first time the intricately patterned damask curtains, the matching rose carpet, and the crocheted bedspread covering the big four-poster bed. "Not my usual style, but it's really beautiful."

"It was Gran's room." There was softness in his voice that hadn't been there before. "She raised my brother and me after our parents were killed. She was a truly good soul, loving, full of mischief but always there for us. Not a day goes by that I don't miss her."

He shook his head, as if he suddenly realized how much of himself he was giving away. "Anyway," he said, briskly rubbing his hands together, "If you'll make that list we talked about the other day, I'll have Mrs. Andrews pick up what you need."

"Mrs. Andrews?"

"Hazel Andrews, my housekeeper. She comes in for a couple of hours every day."

"Ah." She grinned. "The little sparrow at the front door. Does she always chatter like that?"

"Always." He smiled directly at her for the first time. It hit Kat with the equivalent of a physical blow. She placed a protective hand over her middle. Suddenly, Riley's ready smiles and easy banter faded under the power of this man's strength, his solid character.

His honor. There it was again. She shook her head, an imperceptible shudder. Honor wasn't a word she used all that often in her world, where the line between good and evil, truth and lies, was so often...and easily, crossed. Now, every time she looked at Seamus the word came to mind.

Along with other words, like intractable, arrogant, chauvinistic, stubborn... She was running through an endless list of possibilities when he suddenly leaned over and tucked the blankets up under her chin.

"Mrs. Andrews runs the place with an iron fist. Don't let that silly chatter fool you. She can be a real harridan."

"I'll remember." Kat yawned, surprised to feel so exhausted and yet so energized at the same time.

"Rest." He dropped his hand briefly to her shoulder and squeezed for emphasis.

She wanted to reach up and cover his fingers with her own, to thank him for his kindness, but he slipped away and was gone before she turned thought to action.

HE STOOD JUST OUTSIDE her door, his hands shaking, his heart pounding an erratic tattoo. His mind pulsated with her scent, his skin shivered under the memory of her softness, the essence of her life and the life she carried when he held her oh-so-briefly in his arms. He closed his eyes, savoring the recollection, the image of her lying in the old four-poster bed, her silken hair pooling across the pillow.

Thirty-six years old and he'd never before carried a woman in his arms, never tucked one into bed, never felt this deep, visceral yearning that threatened his sanity.

So this is what it's like.

Oh, the need had been there—the pure, physical need for sexual release. He'd never played the games his brother had played—the flirtations and affairs that had always been so meaningless to Riley— he'd been so determined to be everything Riley wasn't.

So he'd lived like a damned monk most of his life, working and channeling his energy in productive directions, avoiding relationships and passion as if love itself were a sin. The few women he'd slept with had been too much like him—passionless, preoccupied, uninterested in more than a one-night fling, a simple physical release free of complications or emotion.

He'd allowed nothing to interfere with the important things in his life—his work, his writing, his professional success.

Seamus stiffened against the wall as that same life slipped into painful focus. It was a life devoid of living. No one cared about his sacrifices, his accomplishments. Until now, even he hadn't realized what was lacking. Somehow, for all his philandering, could Riley have been right?

No. Absolutely not. Riley's choices had been selfish and self-serving. But in his own way, Seamus realized, so had his. He'd enjoyed playing the martyr to Riley's excesses; had relished his position of self-righteous power.

A position that had suddenly, unequivocally, lost its appeal.

"Just my luck," Seamus muttered, closing his eyes against the agonizing truth. It didn't seem either right or fair that his sexual awakening would occur in the hallway outside his beloved grandmother's old room.

However, considering the way his life usually worked, it was entirely apropos that the first woman he'd ever really wanted, the first woman who'd given him a glimpse of the passion he might be capable of feeling, carried Riley's child.

To top it off, he didn't even know if he liked her.

Some day, he thought, pushing himself away from the wall and heading down the stairs, he might find humor in the irony of the situation.

Not now, though. Definitely not now.

He shoved his needs into that overwhelmed compartment of his brain where such things were stored and went into his office to work on his column.

KAT WATCHED MRS. ANDREWS flutter about her room, dusting, arranging, cleaning things that were already clean while generally driving Kathleen nuts. She thought about just getting out of bed, grabbing the pair of soft blue sweats Seamus had gotten for her, climbing into her car and driving away.

It had been over three weeks. The doctor had said just today she could get up for an hour at a time, as long as she took it easy. Kathleen figured she could go one hell of a long way in an hour.

It was either that or go quietly insane. Which, the way things were progressing, was probably the shorter trip.

She missed her new friends, mostly people she'd met since transferring to San Francisco. With the stalker still on the loose, she'd hesitated to call anyone for fear of putting their safety at risk.

She really missed her old body, the slim, athletic one with hormones neatly arranged and functioning as they should. This body felt fat and bloated and awkward. A body ruled by a tiny, anonymous "whatsit" that had suddenly developed feet and knees and elbows...and a penchant for soccer at two a.m.

She hadn't realized how much she would miss her job. Even a desk job was preferable to this half-existence, flat on her back like a beached whale. She hoped the doctor would release her soon to return to work. Thank goodness she had plenty of sick leave, but the boredom was driving her nuts.

Not that there wasn't plenty to do. Kat glanced at the pile of books stacked next to the TV controls, at the brand new VCR and a dozen tapes of her favorite movies, at the magazines scattered across the bed, and almost laughed.

Especially when she thought about the magazines. Just this morning Mrs. Andrews had pointed out a column Kat hadn't seen before, one about the psychology of food written by a Dr. Frederick James. Then Mrs. Andrews had whispered, as if it were a state secret, that Frederick James was one of Seamus's pseudonyms.

So, of course, Kat read the column. Then reread it in disbelief, learning all kinds of amazing things about the sensual aspects of food, in this case, potatoes.

She'd never really thought of potatoes as sexy, but after reading what Dr. James had to say about those odd shaped little tubers, Kat knew she'd never face a baked potato with the same aplomb again.

Not only was his writing shrewd, cutting and subtly erotic, it was intelligent and humorous as well. A real eye-opener, Kat decided to learn what thoughts were hidden behind the uptight attitude of her oh-so-formal host.

Poor Seamus. The man obviously didn't have a clue what to say to a woman unless he was giving orders, but he sure could turn a phrase or two on paper. She'd love to get him to relax, to let his hair down a bit and maybe smile again.

He'd definitely become a challenge. As bored as she'd been, Kat figured she needed all the challenges she could find.

Daily, he came to her room precisely at ten a.m. to check on her, always with Mrs. Andrews in tow. He stayed exactly ten minutes. They discussed world news, happenings around and about San Francisco, and the weather. Of course, Kat's only view of the weather had been through the bedroom window. She'd tried asking him about his work, but he'd neatly changed the subject. He didn't want to talk about hers. She wasn't sure if he was afraid of her or just didn't like her, but as far as Kat could tell, he was definitely avoiding her.

That rankled. Men usually fell all over themselves to get her attention, at least in the beginning. Then her sassy mouth and bad attitude generally ran them off, but she'd been as pleasant as she could be with Seamus.

Maybe that's the problem.

She checked her watch. Nine fifty-eight. At least she knew when to expect him. She fluffed her hair around her face, bit at her lips for more color. Pinched her cheeks and glanced at the small mirror next to the bed.

Suddenly she realized what she'd been doing...and stopped.

At exactly ten, Seamus walked through the door.

"I THOUGHT YOU MIGHT like some color in here." Seamus had to crane his neck to see around the huge bouquet of roses and irises he carried. "I just cut them this morning."

"Oh, Seamus, they're beautiful."

Not as beautiful as you, he wanted to say. Of course he'd never be able to say anything like that without looking and sounding like a complete jackass. Riley could have carried it off, not Seamus.

"The yard's full of color," he said instead, setting the vase on the bedside table. "We've had such unusually warm weather for March, everything's early. Anyway, I just talked to your doctor. She suggested, if you're feeling up to it, that you spend some time outdoors."

Kat ripped back the covers and swung her legs over the edge of the bed before he even finished speaking. The long cotton gown he'd gotten for her hitched halfway up her thighs and he turned his head to give her a chance to tug it down.

When he looked back, it was still there. Kathleen Malone was a woman obviously unconcerned with the amount of leg she showed.

"Do I get to walk? Will you let me go down the stairs all by myself?" She mimicked a child's voice, tilted her head as she spoke. Her blue eyes twinkled through a fall of thick, blond hair.

She couldn't possibly be flirting with him, could she? "No...um...that...ah...probably wouldn't be a good idea. Too many steps." Seamus swallowed deeply, aware of a near manic response to her light banter. Frantically he glanced about, searching for Mrs. Andrews.

The diminutive housekeeper had suddenly disappeared. He didn't even know why he'd looked for her. *She* certainly couldn't lift Kat.

He could and he did, swinging her lightly into his arms, settling her weight against his chest and silently thrilling with the soft glide of her arms around his neck. He had to get past this wanting her, thinking about her throughout the day when he had his articles to write, deadlines to meet. It wasn't easy. Already Frank was bugging him about the next chapter of his book.

He carried her down the long flight of stairs and settled her into one of the garden chairs set out on the small patio in back. She had a view of the ocean, the sweet scent of citrus, and the hum of bees and hummingbirds.

"Thank you, Seamus."

He could leave her here, with the intercom to call him in case she tired, leave her and get back to his work where the air was easier to breathe and his heart knew its proper cadence.

"Will you sit with me a while?"

No! I can't! He closed his eyes in defeat. "Sure...for a minute or two." He pulled up a second chair, not too close, but still close enough he smelled the soft floral scent he recognized as the soap in Gran's bathroom, close enough to reach out and touch Kathleen if he chose.

She turned her face to the sun's rays and closed her eyes. "You have no idea how good this feels. I've missed being outdoors and my usual activity. I'm not someone to lie around in bed all day."

"Not the soap opera, bonbon type, is that it?" *Not with that slim, athletic body.* The image of Kat Malone in sports gear and running shoes flashed into his mind. He shoved the image away.

"Not me. I've never watched as much TV in my life as I have the last few weeks. I hope I never do again. What a waste of time!" She smiled, then stared toward the edge of the garden wall. "It's strange, you know." She toyed with a rose bud growing close by. "I feel so isolated here, as if the world is miles away, yet you've got neighbors all around."

"That's what drew me to this place. Gran's house, where Riley and I grew up, was beautiful, but the area was too noisy. I brought her here to live with me. We were both a lot happier. It's better for work. I like the quiet, the sense, but not the reality, of isolation. Does it bother you?"

"Not a bit, which surprises me. It's probably because I'm feeling so weird...hormones and all. Pregnancy's a whole new thing for me...for you, too, I guess."

"You could say that." He chuckled. "This whole situation is strange, if you want to know the truth. The only woman who's ever lived here is Gran, and she's been gone for years now."

"You've never married?"

"No." Even he was aware of the sadness in his voice. Aware and surprised by it. He'd never really thought of marriage.

"Why?"

Such a simple question. He watched her slim fingers caress the perfect white rosebud, while memories filled his mind. "There was always something else." He knew the answer wasn't enough, but it was as honest as he could give. "School, Riley, my grandmother, my work."

"You must be the older twin."

"You're right. How did you guess?"

"Because I was the oldest child and I always felt responsible for everyone else, especially my sister, even when she was old enough to make her own choices."

"What did she choose to do?" he asked, curious now.

"She chose to die."

"How?" And how could she calmly sit there and say that?

"Drugs, men, poor choices. Her body was found next to a freeway just outside of Riverside a couple of years ago. They never caught her killer."

"I'm sorry, Kat."

"Yeah. Me, too. I miss her, even though we used to fight over everything. Me being a cop and all."

"I argued with Riley the night he was killed." Seamus stared in the direction of the Pacific, seeing only his brother's face, a face that might have been his own. "We fought about you, I guess, though I didn't know who you were. Only that there was someone he was seeing and someone Clarisse was seeing, and I had to step in and try to shove my morality down his throat. Again."

"I fought with Susan, too." Kathleen covered his hand with hers. "But I did it out of love, Seamus, just as you argued with Riley out of love. If we didn't care, we wouldn't have been angry with the choices they made with their lives. I was doing all I knew how to do. I can live with that."

"I don't know if I can." He sighed, remembering all the pointless arguments that had driven him and Riley apart over the years. The resentment. Even now, the knowledge that this glorious, irritating woman had belonged to his brother left him feeling cold and angry.

"Yes." She reached out and turned his face to hers with the tips of her fingers. Smiled impishly. "You can. Any man who can make a potato sound sexy can do absolutely anything he wants."

"I see you've been reading Mrs. Andrews's magazines." He didn't want to discuss his writing, but he covered her hand with his, pressing it against the side of his face.

The gesture seemed to surprise her, but she didn't pull away.

"I found your column to be...um...educational?" She grinned. "But then I'm not much of a cook." She paused. Her expression sobered. "Seamus..." Her fingers spread under his, stroking his cleanly shaved chin. "Think about what I said. You aren't responsible for Riley's sins and you certainly have no reason for guilt. He was your brother and you loved him, or you wouldn't have cared enough to be angry with him."

"Easier said than done, but I'll think about it." His hand covered hers a moment longer, then he lifted her fingers away and set her hand gently in her lap. "I have to get back to work."

"Is that a potato I hear calling?" Kat cupped her hand over her ear and grinned. "Flirty little thing."

She was definitely going to drive him nuts. Flirtatious and teasing like this... It was all he could do to control himself. His face still tingled where she'd touched him. His hand itched to grab hers again. He wanted to touch her, to hold her, to make the child growing within that glorious body his.

He wanted to make Kathleen Malone his.

Thank goodness she didn't have a clue. He grinned sheepishly to cover feelings he was still unsure of, then stood up and headed back to his office.

Her laughter followed him through the door.

KAT DOZED IN THE lounge chair, although full sleep eluded her. The past few weeks' inactivity was so unlike her usual frenetic pace, but for the life of her, she couldn't muster the energy to fight. Even her brief verbal exchanges with Seamus left her exhausted.

Everything about Seamus exhausted her. No, she thought. That isn't fair. It wasn't exhaustion she felt. It was excitement. *Fighting* her reaction to the damned man was exhausting!

She pondered the implications a moment, half asleep, half dreaming. It wouldn't do. Not at all. If Riley O'Rourke had taught her anything at all, it was that she'd been right all along. Men could be friends or they could be lovers. They couldn't be both. Once they became lovers, they took control, took your love, took your heart, took your trust, took everything that made you *you*.

What did they give back?

Of its own volition, Kat's hand traced the subtle roundness of her abdomen. *Oh, damn, what they give back!*

She liked Seamus O'Rourke. She couldn't help herself. He drove her nuts and made her want to scream, but she liked him and admired him, and she wasn't about to screw up a good thing. Friendship was a rare commodity. She didn't have that many friends, and the ones she had kept falling in love with other people and getting married.

The shrill ring of the telephone startled her fully awake. She heard Seamus answer it, his deep voice an incomprehensible rumble drifting through the open window of his office.

She suddenly realized she'd never seen his office, and in fact, hadn't explored the house at all beyond the guest room and the kitchen. She'd drifted through the past few weeks, existing but not participating in life. Where had her insatiable curiosity gone? She'd always been a snoop. That was why she made such a terrific investigator.

A hummingbird hovered near a sweet-smelling branch covered with lemon blossoms. Kat stared at the tiny creature, enthralled by the rainbow of colors reflecting off the perfect little feathers, hypnotized by the whirring wings.

Hypnotized. That was the only explanation that worked. Seamus had worked his hypnotic magic on her, taking control of her life, her thoughts. The days since Riley's death had an almost dreamlike quality to them. For the first time in her life she hadn't had to worry about a thing. She'd left everything to Seamus. She'd given him control.

Kat Malone goes it alone.

Only Kat Malone hadn't done a damned thing alone. *Rephrase that...Kat Malone hasn't done a damned thing, period.*

She stood up. Her legs felt shaky, but she stood. Other than trips from her bed to the bathroom, she'd barely taken a step in three weeks. Of course she'd feel shaky. Lack of exercise tended to do that to a person.

"I want my life back." There, she'd said it. Of course, she'd barely whispered the statement that was more of a plea...the only one to hear was the hummingbird. Kat stretched and felt the strength pour into her arms. She leaned over and almost touched her toes.

"Won't be doing that much longer," she muttered. Already her body had ripened. The flat stomach she'd always had was rounded and firm in her sixth month of pregnancy. She no longer felt comfortable with the woman she'd always been and wondered constantly if she'd ever know that woman again.

Ever feel that woman's inner strength again.

Seamus had been there when she needed him, offered help before she even knew to ask. He'd made it too easy, too comfortable. It was time she found her own place, made herself strong again. She'd need her strength when the baby came. It wasn't going to be easy. Single mothers never had it easy.

Kat Malone goes it alone. She'd repeated that mantra almost all her adult life. Repeated it when she'd faced a dozen armed men during a raid, holding them off until her partner finally arrived, and again when she'd been locked in the trunk of her car, her head bloodied and her hands tied during a botched stakeout.

She'd whispered the phrase over and over the morning she'd read Riley's obituary.

It had held extra meaning then. "So what's the big deal?" she muttered, then looked around, almost expecting an answer. That was foolish. She'd always been alone.

Seamus's voice carried through the open window as he continued his phone conversation and the rich sound of it made her frown.

Now was as good a time as any. At least she could go up to her room, make some calls, set the wheels in motion for her move. Kat slipped quietly through the French doors leading to the staircase, then carefully climbed the steps to her room. She paused halfway up and held her palm to her stomach. The tiny flutter of motion reassured her all was well.

She'd never gone on that shopping trip and nothing from her vandalized rental had been salvageable. She eyed the blue sweats, thought of the slim-fitting black suit hanging in the closet, ran her fingers over her swollen belly and grabbed the sweatpants.

She was holding the sweatshirt in her hands debating the need for a bra to support her growing breasts when Seamus burst into the room.

"Excuse me." Kat didn't even attempt to cover herself. Modesty had never been her strong point. "Did you want something?"

"I...I..." He glanced away, then shrugged and leaned back against the door, closing it behind him. "Don't you think you should put that on?" he asked.

"I was just going to." Kat slid her hands into the sleeves and raised her arms. The soft blue top slipped easily over her head, covering her completely. She tugged it into position and folded her arms across her middle. "Is that better?"

"Not really." His smile looked tense. "But it does make it easier to carry on a conversation."

Kat shrugged her shoulders and waited.

"I looked outside and didn't see you. I didn't know where you'd gone."

"Here. To my room. What's the big deal?"

His chest expanded, he closed his eyes as if in prayer, then exhaled. "The big deal, Kat, is that you've got some crazy out to kill you." He pushed himself away from the door to tower over her as he tapped each point off on the palm of his hand. "You're six months pregnant and recently almost lost your baby. You've hardly been out of bed for three weeks and here you've just climbed the stairs without assistance."

His voice rose steadily with each transgression. "I looked out my window and you weren't there," he shouted. "I was worried. That's the big deal."

"Seamus, we need to talk...quietly." Kathleen turned away from him and sat down on the edge of the bed. "This is ridiculous. I'm a grown woman, used to doing things for myself. I think it's time I moved out and got my own place."

He opened his mouth to respond but she held up her hand to stop him. "It's not that I don't appreciate all you've done, but I can't let myself become so dependent on you. I'm feeling a hundred percent better. My morning sickness is finally gone and there's no reason I can't find myself a nice little apartment with good security, go back to a desk job until the baby's born, and get back to my life."

"There's an excellent reason you can't do that."

If Kathleen hadn't known him better, she would have thought he smirked. "Why not?"

"You don't have a job to go back to. At least not until after you have the baby."

"Says who?" She jumped up from the bed and confronted him. "If I'm feeling okay, they have to let me work."

"You've been placed on extended disability leave. Your doctor recommended it and your supervisor agreed."

"They can't do this to me. Not without my approval." Pacing back and forth, Kat worked her way through various forms of murder. She wasn't certain who the target was...her stalker, her supervisor, her doctor or Seamus. *Maybe all four.*

"Yes they can, and they have. Kat, listen to me..." He grabbed her by the shoulders and gently slowed her pacing. "It's not just for you. The police are trying to catch this guy, but so far they haven't had any luck. They don't even know for sure who they're looking for. In the meantime, anyone who works near you is at risk. They know this psycho's after you, but they don't know who he is. We don't think he's figured out where you're staying right now, but someone's tried to hack into the department's computer as well as the hospital records on the OB/GYN floor. I guess hackers leave a kind of signature—something that tells the investigator it's probably the same guy who's been following you.

"You're safe here, for now. Once you're out on your own, writing checks on your own account, using the phone, credit cards, whatever, he's going to find you. While you're pregnant, you can't risk that. You can't risk an innocent life because you're too damned hard-headed to accept help when you need it. You can't risk the lives of the people who work near you."

"I... Damn!" She glared at him, hating him and his sensible argument. Kat slumped under his gentle grasp, aware of the heat emanating from his strong hands, the beat of her heart, the sense of defeat simmering in her soul. "How do you know this? Why haven't you told me?"

"Believe me. I didn't know. Not until your supervisor called. That was him earlier. He thinks your stalker might be one of the men you helped arrest on that case in Utah where you met Riley. Two of the men slipped bail. The FBI's got APBs out on both of them, but no word on where they might be. Your ex-partner and his wife have been notified since they were in on the bust, but so far it looks as if this guy just has it in for you. Kat, be reasonable. I saw what he did to your house. He's crazy and he's after you."

"If I stay here, I put you at risk, too," she muttered. His large hands were rubbing her shoulders, doing crazy things to her chest, making it harder to breath. His thumbs caressed her collarbones; his fingers massaged the tight muscles along her neck.

"I'll keep you safe. Just let me take care of you for the next few months," he whispered. "Let someone else worry about things for a change."

It sounded so tempting, felt so tantalizing. Kat gazed up at Seamus out of heavy-lidded eyes and inexplicably wondered what it would feel like to kiss Riley's brother. The two men's lips were shaped exactly the same, but Kat knew instinctively the comparison would end there. Her eyes closed in anticipation. This had to be Seamus's call. She didn't want the attraction gnawing at her heart, coiling inside and building with each touch of his hands. Did not want it at all.

Couldn't live without it.

She felt boneless under his gentle touch, even as his large hands held her, slipping over her shoulders, embracing her. She sensed him drawing closer, felt the heat from his body, inhaled his unique scent. His words soothed and comforted, the mesmerizing rumble of his voice enthralled, hypnotized...suddenly Kat's eyes popped open and she twisted out of his grasp.

He's doing it again!

She'd almost kissed him...almost let him kiss her. She didn't want...could not want...that.

Hell. She didn't know what she wanted.

"What do you want from me?" she demanded.

"To help you." The look he gave her was as confused as she felt. "That's all. I guess I feel responsible for you, okay?"

"I told you, you're not responsible. Your brother got me pregnant, my job got me the stalker and... What's in this for you?" Suddenly she stopped her tirade. Stared at him. At his lips.

HE COULDN'T DENY IT. He'd wanted to kiss her. Almost had kissed her. Was still kicking himself for not kissing her.

She blinked, narrowed her eyes. "Why can't you be honest with me? What do you really want?" She turned away and paced like a cat, all fire and fury, eyes flashing, words tumbling out, spitting anger, her hands curled like claws.

She was absolutely magnificent.

"I may look like a whore—"

"Don't say that." He took a step toward her, his hand out. "Please. Don't."

She backed away.

He dropped his hand to his side.

Her chin came up. She glared at him. Her words, soft and controlled, had all the more power to hurt. "I told you I don't act like a whore. Nor am I looking for a relationship. I don't want to get involved with anyone. Especially you, Seamus. My God, you're Riley's brother!"

She might as well have slapped him. He stepped back, putting as much distance between the two of them as possible in the space between the bed and the door. Kat's face paled. This time her hand reached out. He wondered if she somehow wished she could call the words back, apologize for insulting him.

Did she even realize how much she'd hurt him? Seamus took a deep breath, struggled for control, felt the bands tighten across his chest. He clenched and unclenched his fists, hating Riley now more than he'd ever hated his brother in all his life.

"All right." The words felt as if they'd ripped from his very soul. He spat them at her, words filled with venom, filled with the black hatred for all that Riley had taken from him. "You want honesty. You'll get honesty. You asked what I want from you? It's simple, Ms. Malone. I don't want you. I don't want anything to do with you. You're the means to an end. I want the baby. That's it. I want my brother's child."

IF ONLY HE HADN'T been disturbed, he might have heard what they argued about. He'd been close enough until that twit of a housekeeper practically tripped over him. Well, she wouldn't do it again.

He rubbed his leather-gloved hands over his thighs, flexed his fingers and replayed the feel of the old woman's life ebbing beneath his grasp. He'd only come today to observe, to study the dynamics between Seamus O'Rourke and Kathleen Malone.

Killing hadn't been on the schedule, but she'd left him no choice.

Once it happened, he'd wanted her to see him, to recognize him in that last moment as she hovered between life and death, suspended in his powerful, crushing hands.

He'd waited too long. That was disappointing. His glance shifted to his left, to the tip of a worn shoe sticking out from under a perfectly trimmed juniper. His body thrummed with power and he took a deep breath before turning his gaze to the window just above him on the second floor.

The power within him increased. His need grew. He'd heard the door slam when the other O'Rourke left.

The bitch was there, alone. Pregnant. Vulnerable.

There was no plan, but neither was this impulse. He never acted on impulse. No, he thought, this is a brilliant opportunity to move forward. A chance to gain more power.

He slipped through the open door into the kitchen.

Chapter Four

"STUPID. HOW COULD YOU possibly be so damned stupid?" Seamus abruptly halted his frustrated, furious pacing across the back deck and stared at the upper window, the one to Kathleen's bedroom. The enraged words he'd shouted at her banged about inside his skull like discordant cymbals.

He bowed his head, closed his eyes in self-disgust.

He'd really screwed it up now.

Any minute she was going to come flying down the stairs. He'd hear that beat-up little car of hers peel out of the driveway and he'd never see her again.

Maybe it was all for the best.

What right did he have wanting his brother's baby? Even more despicable, what right did he have wanting Riley's woman?

The few short weeks since Riley's death had driven home some hard truths. Seamus knew he was avoiding the real issue—that all the years he'd condemned Riley, he'd envied him even more, and had wanted to enjoy the freedoms Riley had without the guilt that was Seamus's constant companion.

Now Riley was dead and Seamus not only wanted his brother's child, he wanted Riley's woman as well. Well, he'd definitely screwed that up. *What an ass...* Here he'd promised to protect her and he'd threatened her with the worst possible thing anyone could say to a mother-to-be. He'd scared her badly. Frightened her enough to run far and fast, to put as much distance between herself and Seamus O'Rourke as was humanly possible.

She didn't want his protection. She didn't want his friendship. She'd point blank told him she wanted nothing to do with Seamus O'Rourke.

Get over it, O'Rourke. He slammed his fist into the palm of his hand. He might as well forget both the baby and the mother. She'd brought him nothing but trouble. Trouble and aggravation.

No! He shook his head in denial. Who was he trying to kid? Maybe he'd only known Kathleen for a few weeks, but if he'd only be honest with himself, Seamus knew he couldn't imagine life without her.

Now there was no chance at all of a life with her. What he'd said, what he'd done, to Kathleen Malone had been the cruelest, most hurtful thing he'd ever done to anyone in his life.

Seamus sat down on the stone retaining wall at the edge of the deck. He stared out over the blue Pacific, but Kathleen's image filled his mind. He couldn't escape the stricken look on her face.

The fear in her eyes. No matter what else Seamus thought of Kat Malone, he admired her pride, her self-assurance, her strength. He hadn't understood her vulnerability, and hadn't considered the pain she must be feeling. He'd been hurt by her words, angry with her. Now he felt only shame.

His attack had been lower than cowardly. He'd frightened Kathleen in the worst possible way, set into motion a mother's worst nightmare—the thought of someone wanting to take her baby away from her. All because she'd rejected him.

Rejected him because he was Riley's brother.

It still hurt, but he should be used to that by now. Kathleen didn't know how he felt. What she'd said hadn't been intentionally cruel.

Not cruel in the manner Seamus had been. He scrubbed at the taut muscles along the side of his neck and sighed. He'd never be able to convince Kathleen he wasn't after the baby. It would be a lie anyway. He did want her baby.

Unfortunately, it was only now apparent he wanted the baby's mother just as badly.

Seamus glanced back at the heavily draped window. The curtain twitched as he looked up. Kathleen must be watching him. She hadn't left yet.

Why hadn't she gone? Could she be as confused about him as he was about her?

Seamus grinned in spite of himself. There was still a chance, if he could only figure out what to say.

Should I tell her she confuses the hell out of me? Tell her she makes me crazy, makes me angry, makes me want her so I can't sleep at night, can't concentrate during the day?

No. He'd better start slower. Groveling and an abject apology came to mind. Somehow, he had to make her listen.

Seamus snapped off a perfect white rose on a sturdy stem. It never hurt to come prepared.

KATHLEEN STARED AT THE door, immobilized by Seamus's angry threats. Oh, he hadn't actually said he'd take her baby away from her, but he'd certainly implied as much. She wouldn't stand a chance going up against a man with the obvious wealth and good name of Seamus O'Rourke.

Protectively she cradled her belly in her hands and fought the urge to crawl into bed and pull the covers up over her head. How could she have possibly been attracted to O'Rourke...to either one of them?

Sparkling green eyes, dark hair and absolutely the world's most kissable mouth came to mind. Kat's eyes stung with frustrated tears. Where were the answers?

The baby delivered a strong kick beneath her fingers.

Mobilized, Kat spun around and headed for the closet. She'd leave now before Seamus could stop her, before he could follow...before she caved in to wants and desires only now beginning to roil to the surface, confusing her even more.

She had friends who would welcome a visit from her, regardless of the circumstances. Kat thought of her old partner, Mike Ramsey and his wife, Rose. They had a bed and breakfast just east of San Francisco in the Sierra Nevada foothills. If she hurried, she could be there before dark.

They'd help her. Best of all, they could be trusted not to tell Seamus where she was.

Kat reached for her shoulder holster and her purse, then realized she was still wearing the blue sweats Seamus had given her. Tight fitting or not, she was leaving in exactly the same little black suit in which she'd arrived.

"Damned if I'll take anything of yours, Seamus O'Rourke." The child she carried suddenly came to mind. O'Rourke acted as if the baby belonged to him.

Kat patted her slightly rounded tummy. "Well, you don't, sweetheart. You're mine, and we're gettin' the hell out of Dodge." She pulled the sweatshirt up over her head. The collar band caught on her chin and she stretched her arms high over her head to tug it free.

It wasn't actually a sound. It was a feeling, a sense of the air in the room suddenly being displaced.

Before Kathleen could turn around and confront Seamus, strong fingers wrapped around her wrists and slammed her face first against the wall. Still trapped in the heavy folds of the sweatshirt, she twisted and bucked against the rigid body pressed along the length of her back.

She didn't scream, couldn't scream, could only pitch and roll in a futile effort to free herself from the iron grip about her wrists. The sweatshirt ensnared her. Caught just under her chin, it covered her face and arms like a heavy cotton shroud.

A knee rammed between her legs, the muscled thigh trapping her solidly against the wall. She felt the textured wallpaper against her naked breasts, the edge of the decorative molding biting into her cheek. She flung her head back, hoping to crack her attacker across the nose or chin.

The cold, sharp edge of steel against her abdomen stopped her, froze her in time and space.

Kat felt his hot breath through the folds of fabric, smelled stale cigarette smoke and chewing gum. Heard each harsh breath he took, his face so close to her ear she knew when his lips moved.

Trembling, silently screaming for Seamus, Kat waited.

The pressure of the knife increased.

The baby! A low, animalistic moan escaped her lips.

Her attacker laughed—the first sound he'd made. Kat wracked her brain, searched her memories.

All she could think of was the baby. The razor-sharp blade was a mere thrust away.

"What do you want?" Her voice was a stranger's with the harsh growl of her terrified breathing almost drowning out her own words.

"You."

Who is he?

"It's always been you. Well, I really wanted the other one, but then I saw you and..." A dry cough rattled against her ear. "Besides, she's married."

The knife bit into her stomach, the pressure of the blade emphasizing each word. "You might have been. Married. Life's funny that way, how things might happen, then *poof!* They don't. That guy, O'Rourke? Weird how much they look alike, isn't it? Well, the other one was going to leave her, you know. He was planning to leave his wife for you, you little slut, but that's neither here nor there. Right now, sweetheart, it's just you and me."

"How do you know that?" If she could only keep him talking, maybe... "How do you know he was going to leave his wife."

"That's the best part...I bought him a drink. That little bar where the two of you used to meet? Remember the night you stood him up?"

She remembered. Only she hadn't stood him up. She'd worked late that night and had forgotten to call. They'd laughed about it the next day, once she and Riley realized they'd gotten their wires crossed once again. "I remember."

"I saw him sitting there all alone and offered to buy him a drink."

His harsh laugh filled her ears. "He didn't recognize me. Didn't have a clue who I was. He sat there and told me all about this special woman he planned to marry, how he'd finally decided he couldn't stay in an unhappy marriage. Hell, I felt like a fuckin' damned Dear Abby! He recognized me later, though. Right before his car hit the wall. He knew who I was then."

"What do you want?" That voice! *So familiar.* She'd heard it before, knew she should be able to place it. "Why are you doing this?"

"You ruined my life, that's why. I coulda plea bargained my way out of this if you hadn't testified against me at the preliminary trial. You and that FBI agent. Like I said though, he knew who it was that got him."

The pressure of the knife against her belly increased. The blade wasn't cold anymore. The heat from her body had warmed it. How could that be, when she felt chilled clear through? This guy was admitting he killed Riley? It wasn't an accident? Kat's mind spun out of control while her heart pounded in her chest.

Fear and anger warred, each emotion battling the other.

"I was planning to kill you. I didn't know about this, not for sure."

Suddenly the blade moved away from her flesh, replaced by fingers tightly encased in leather gloves. Kat trembled as the fingers trailed lower inside her sweatpants, circled the roundness of her growing babe with frightening gentleness, a lover's caress.

She trembled, tried to twist away from the violation of his touch. Anger consumed her, overwhelming, uncontrollable anger. This man had killed Riley. It wasn't an accident!

As if sensing her irresistible need to fight back, Kat's assailant tightened the grip on her wrists. His thigh forced her legs farther apart, his chest held her flat against the wall.

In a parody of intimacy, covering her body as if he were her lover, the intruder whispered in Kat's ear.

"Now...now, I think I'll wait."

Kat shuddered, unable to accept her helplessness, not strong enough to fight him off. Damn, if only she weren't so weak, if only she'd been able to maintain her usual strength, this jerk would never have gotten her in this defenseless position!

He chuckled, obviously enjoying her vulnerability, her helplessness. "There's a great deal of satisfaction that comes from the planning, the execution, Ms. Malone. You're afraid of me. I like that. You weren't afraid before."

I wasn't pregnant before!

Kat drew one harsh breath after the other, struggled to control the spiral of fear coursing through her veins. She would not give her assailant the satisfaction of knowing how vulnerable she felt.

The blade was back, the edge just above her pubis. A tiny whimper escaped Kat's throat. *Oh God, please. Not my baby.*

The cut, when it came, didn't even hurt. Not at first. Kat felt the trickle of hot blood, the jerk of his arm as he drew the blade across her belly.

She heard fabric tearing, realized it was duct tape, and felt the wide strips binding her wrists before she even felt the burning sting from the blade.

Her legs buckled. He shoved her to her knees, over to her side, then wrapped her ankles as firmly as he'd bound her wrists. The intruder worked silently. Kat heard his harsh breathing, and an occasional grunt or curse.

He ran a strip of tape around her face, binding the sweatshirt close against her mouth and eyes. Kat drew a frantic breath in through her nostrils, struggling to suck air through the heavy fabric. She wondered if he planned to suffocate her or just let her bleed to death.

She had no idea how deeply he'd cut her. It hurt like a hot wire burning from pubis to hip.

Dear God, don't let it kill me. Don't let my baby die.

Kat's thoughts spun out of control. He hadn't killed her. Yet. She was bleeding all over Gran's carpet. Seamus was going to be furious. She was naked from the waist up, her breasts uncovered. He hadn't fondled her. Hadn't raped her. Why hadn't her attacker killed her? Who was he?

"There."

Trussed up with duct tape, her eyes covered by the heavy sweatshirt, Kat lay on the floor and forced herself to take even, shallow breaths. Her bare nipples puckered in the chill air, warm blood pooled along her side. She sensed the man going to the window, heard the soft swish of damask drapes as he pulled them aside.

"This is great." He laughed. "That dummy's just sitting down there, staring out to sea. Shit."

She heard him back away.

"Don't think he saw me, but we can't take chances. Now, listen."

Suddenly the cigarette smell was in her face; the sense of someone hovering over her overwhelming.

"This is what I want you to think about, Ms. Malone. Think about that little baby. Think about how cute he's going to be. Then think about how you'll feel when I kill him."

The air stirred. Kat shuddered, willing the nightmare to end.

"Then think about how I'll kill you."

Kat waited a moment, afraid to struggle in case he watched her. She'd almost convinced herself he was gone when she heard the steady tread of someone on the stairs.

She shuddered in reaction. Lightheaded from lack of oxygen, she drew her knees up into a fetal position borne of fear and pain.

"Oh my God! Kat... Oh, God, honey."

Hands feverishly ripping at tape, a steady litany of curses, the sweatshirt torn away from her face, then gently rolled down over her shoulders to cover her nakedness, a deep, restoring lung full of air.

Sobbing with the need to breathe, the need to cry, Kathleen threw herself into Seamus's embrace. He sat on the floor and cuddled Kat in his arms, holding her as he would a small child.

Something warm seeped through the sleeve of his shirt. Seamus glanced at his arm. It was covered in blood.

Kathleen's blood.

He frantically dragged the waistband of her pants down, exposing a long, surgically precise cut running from just above the blond thatch of her pubic hair to the sharp edge of her hipbone.

"Oh, shit. Kathleen, I..." He grabbed the phone to dial 911.

Kat yanked it out of his hand. "No," she cried. "No ambulance, no hospital. Seamus, we've got to get out of here. He killed Riley, Seamus. It wasn't an accident. He's going to kill my baby! We've got to—"

"You're hurt. You're bleeding all over the place. You need to see a doctor." He could handle this. He could sit here on the floor, hold her in his arms and calmly argue the fact that she really needed to go to the hospital, really needed stitches to close the slash across her belly.

No, he couldn't.

This was not something open to discussion.

"No. No doctor." Kat shook her head, took one deep, steadying breath after another. The visible tremor that rocked her frame subsided more with each exhalation.

She brushed the tears away from her eyes with the sleeve of her sweatshirt. All the tension seemed to drain out of her. Seamus sensed her gradual withdrawal with the return of her self-control. The look of fear in her eyes was replaced with stubborn determination.

She struggled to sit up and scooted out of his lap. He wanted to drag her back into his embrace, but the distance between them now was more than physical.

Kat calmly pulled the waistband of her pants out to inspect the injury herself. "It's bloody, but it's not deep. It doesn't even hurt too badly. If you've got some little butterfly bandages and antiseptic ointment we can take care of it here. It's just a scratch, really."

"Kat...I'm so sorry, Kat. I should have been here. How did he...?" *I can't even keep her safe in my own house.* The image of her small cottage, the walls splashed with foul threats in blood-red paint collided with the image in front of him. Kat sitting cross-legged on the carpet, a blood-red stain seeping across the front of the pale blue sweatpants.

Here, in my own damned house. He wanted to kick something, to shout his anger and frustration to the heavens. He thought of the gun laying on the table next to Kat's bed, of the man who had so brazenly invaded the privacy, the safety, the *sanctity* of his home.

The same man who killed Riley? It wasn't an accident?

"He had to have already been in the house." Kat's voice was contemplative, questioning, overly professional. Seamus realized she must be distancing herself from the attack, protecting herself by looking at the incident from a detective's viewpoint, not as a victim. This was Kat Malone, Department of Transportation investigator, consummate professional, her thoughts racing as she discarded, then accepted the various scenarios leading up to the attack.

She studied Seamus a moment, her brows knit into a thoughtful frown. "You and I argued, you left, I got up and went to the closet to change into my suit."

She followed words with action, standing up and walking across the room to the closet. She made a quick detour into the bathroom and grabbed an old towel, pressed it against her belly as if the wound were merely an inconvenience, then stood next to the wall by the closet.

She glanced over at Seamus and frowned again. "I was really pissed at you. Don't ever threaten me again."

If the circumstances hadn't been so dire, Seamus knew he'd be laughing. Kat had slipped back into her "tough broad" persona as if the attack had never occurred. "I'll remember that." He stood up. "How'd he manage to sneak up on you?" He'd ask about Riley later. Now he didn't want to even think about Riley.

"I was changing clothes, and had my shirt over my head, with my arms in the air. I knew someone was in the room, but just figured you were coming up to apologize for being such a jerk." She dared him to argue the point.

"I did eventually. Come up to apologize, that is." Seamus leaned over and picked the battered white rose up off the carpet. He handed it to Kathleen. "Will you? Forgive me?"

"Yeah. I'm still pissed, but I'll forgive you." She gave him a weak smile then sniffed the rose. She stared down at it for a long time. As Seamus watched, first one tear, then another dropped to the creamy petals. Suddenly, her hands started to shake, her shoulders bowed, and her face appeared to crumple.

Seamus caught her as she collapsed against him, sobbing, her hard-won control shattered, her body trembling with the delayed reaction to fear. He held her tight against him, rubbed his hand along her spine, whispered nonsense in her ear.

Kissed her, oh so gently, along the contour of her jaw, the tender skin of her throat. Kissed her and held her while she cried, and for long moments after, while she struggled so valiantly for control.

"It's okay, sweetheart."

He felt her chest expand against his as she drew in great shuddering breaths.

"I don't cry. I never cry." She sniffed against his tear-dampened collar.

"I know. Blame it on the hormones, baby. Blame it on hormones and the fact that someone just tried to kill you. I think you've got good reason to cry." He smiled grimly into her sweet-smelling hair, nuzzled and inhaled with his eyes half closed. There was no describing the sense of relief he felt, the sense of having been given a second chance. He hugged her even closer.

Her arms tightened around his waist. "He said Riley's death wasn't an accident, that Riley was going to leave his wife for me. Riley actually *told* him that one night in a bar. The bastard bought him a drink knowing full well he was going to kill him. Then he said he was going to kill me, but he changed his mind. He said he'll wait until I have the baby, so he can kill the baby while I watch. Then he'll kill me. The cut was just for emphasis."

Seamus went cold. How could she stand there and repeat her assailant's disgusting threats and actions in such a calm, businesslike manner? He took a deep, steadying breath. He had to keep her safe. Somehow, he had to convince Kat to stay with him, to let him protect her.

Like you just did?

"What's weird..." Kat paused, interrupting his self-recriminations. She sighed against his collar. Seamus tensed as he waited for her to continue. "He had my arms trapped over my head so my boobs were bare, his hand in my pants to cut me, and obviously I'm not wearing underwear. Most guys, especially when they've got you vulnerable and trapped like that, most guys would cop a feel. This guy didn't. He touched my stomach, caressed it, actually, but it was just to emphasize the baby to make it more frightening. I'm sure of that. He was more interested in the pain he could cause me, physically, psychologically, emotionally. There was nothing sexual in the attack, unless the control he had over me is what gives him a rush."

She pulled back to look directly at Seamus, but didn't step out of his embrace. "I can only think of one guy like that, one guy who gets his jollies out of the fear he could cause. His name is Tim Anderson and he's a college preppie type, clean-cut and brilliant, but definitely weird. He was part of a hijacking gang my partner and I helped break up last year.

"It was the case where I met Riley. We've worked on other cases since then, but in this particular case, your brother headed the interrogation. Anderson would've known who Riley was. Both Riley and I testified against him at the preliminary trial. I heard he'd skipped bail along with one of his partners, a spoiled rich kid named James Dearborn. Dearborn's a bit out there, but I don't think he's got a cruel streak—not like Anderson.

"In fact, last I heard, his attorney was working on a plea bargain that would get Dearborn into some sort of halfway house. I don't think he's facing the big prison time like Anderson. At least he wasn't until he skipped out." She shook her head, the soft fall of her hair brushing against Seamus's chin, reminding him once more of how quickly he could have lost her.

An aggravated sigh escaped Kat's lips. "It doesn't make sense. If it is Anderson, I don't know why he's singled me out. My partner's wife was essentially the one responsible for the breakup and arrest of the entire gang. I was just there in the background. Riley and his partner did the interrogation. I sat in on it and added what I knew..." Frustration etched deep lines in her brow.

The decision was easy, really. Seamus rested his hands on Kat's shoulders. He glanced at the towel she'd stuffed inside the waistband of her sweats to staunch the flow of blood. It seemed to be working. Then he looked directly into Kat's crystal blue eyes.

"First we need to take care of that cut. If it's more than your so-called *scratch*, we're going to the hospital. Then we're going to report this incident to the police. Hopefully we won't need to go to the station because I want to get us out of here as soon as possible

"I've got a place in the North Bay, near the Russian River. It's up in the redwoods above a little town called Monte Rio. It's isolated, but close enough to Santa Rosa to get you to a hospital when the baby's due. Kat, you have every reason not to like me, not to trust me. I've failed you already, but I can promise I won't fail you again."

She studied him, her eyes wide and unblinking. Seamus didn't have a clue what was going on behind that steady gaze. She shrugged her shoulders, gave him a quirky smile. "You didn't fail me, Seamus. You pissed me off, but you didn't fail me."

She stepped back out of his reach. Turned away from him and pulled the heavy curtains aside. "I keep telling you, you don't owe me anything, including your protection, so there's nothing to fail." She rubbed her hand roughly across her forehead. "I don't know how clearly I'm thinking, if you want the truth." She swung her head around and studied him for a long, thoughtful moment. Seamus felt like a little kid, called to the front of the classroom for talking out of turn.

"I've got friends I can stay with, but I don't want to put them at risk. As far as you, Seamus, I don't care if you're at risk. Does that bother you? You said you want my baby, not me. Well, I want my baby, too, but we'll deal with that when the time comes. The most important thing, in my mind, is that my baby is safe, and he or she won't be safe until the guy who attacked me is behind bars."

Or dead. Seamus's glance stole to the heavy pistol encased in the leather holster. "Why don't you call the police captain—what's his name?—Wilson? Tell him what's going on, what you suspect. Tell him I'm taking you someplace safe, *but don't tell him where.* I don't want anyone but the two of us to know where you are. Not even your supervisor. Do you have a cell phone?"

She nodded her head in agreement.

"Make the call to the police department from the phone here at the house. Dump the cell phone. The stalker might have a way to trace yours. We'll take mine for emergency calls only. There's also a phone at my place in Monte Rio, but the number's unlisted and I'd just as soon keep it that way. Here—" Seamus dug through his pockets, found a gum wrapper and scribbled out a number on the scrap of paper. "Give Wilson this number to my cell phone to use only if he absolutely has to. I'll get some food together and we'll find you some clothes. I've got some old sweats and shirts that'll work for now. We can buy stuff when we get settled."

He glanced around the room. *What else?* His housekeeper. Where was Hazel? He recalled a long grocery list taped to the refrigerator door. "I think Hazel's gone shopping. I'll leave her a note to tell her we'll be gone for a while, but not where. I don't want her working here until we catch this guy. It's too dangerous."

He tried to erase the image of Kat when he'd found her. He couldn't get it out of his mind. Hazel could use a vacation anyway. He took a deep breath.

"First things first. We need to get you patched up."

"I can do it. I've been cut worse." She stretched the waistband of the sweats out and swiped at the trickle of blood with the towel. "It really *isn't* much more than a scratch."

Seamus looked at the long slash across her belly and wanted to disagree, but decided not to. "It sure scared the hell out of me when I saw all the blood."

"How do you think I felt when it happened?"

She actually grinned at him! She was either courageous as hell, or too dumb to know how close she'd come to dying.

"The knife was so sharp, I couldn't tell how deeply he'd cut me." Still holding the waistband away from her injury, Kat walked into the bathroom and settled one hip on the tile counter. "It burned and I could feel blood, but since none of my innards seemed to escape and the baby was still kicking, I figured we'd both survive."

She looked up, a wide grin on her face, but Seamus read the underlying fear. She'd been terrified. Frightened for her baby's safety, for her own life. He couldn't think of a response that didn't sound totally inane.

"Well, doc...you gonna patch me up?"

"Yeah. I'll patch you up." He took another deep, calming breath before grabbing the first aid kit out of the cupboard over the toilet. With her typical lack of modesty, Kat shoved the sweats down to the edge of the incision and lifted the hem of the sweatshirt up, exposing the firm skin of her softly rounded abdomen.

Seamus glanced up from the first aid kit and practically choked. Kat had cleaned the blood away from the cut with the towel, leaving a dark red slash running from her hipbone to the soft thatch of blond pubic hair at the juncture of her thighs.

Even with the pregnancy beginning to show, her body was beautiful, flawless except for the wound that, to Seamus, was an abomination that still couldn't mar perfection.

Her hands were rock steady. It took all the control Seamus possessed to keep his from trembling as he doctored her injury. Kat looked away, like a little kid waiting for an injection. Seamus grinned as he carefully spread a line of antibiotic ointment along the cut. When his knuckles brushed the soft mound of blond hair, Kat's head swung around.

"I'm sorry. I didn't..."

"It's okay. Guess I'm just a little sensitive." Kathleen chuckled. "You know, hormones and all."

The thought of Kathleen, hormones and just how sensitive she might be was all the incentive Seamus needed to finish the job quickly. When he was satisfied she was properly bandaged, he offered Kat a hand.

She ignored it and shoved herself off the counter. "I'm going to call Sandy. I'm really exhausted, Seamus, but I feel like I want to get as far away from here as possible. I've definitely gone over the doctor's suggestion for an hour of activity, but maybe I can sleep along the way."

"Call the doctor, too. I don't want to take any chances."

Kat turned to look at him over her shoulder. "I think it's a bit too late for that, don't you agree?" She smiled at him, but he noticed the lack of luster in her eyes, the strain in her face. "Thank you, Seamus. For everything. Even if you do have an ulterior motive. I just want you to know I'm sorry about Riley. I keep thinking if he was planning to leave his wife for me, then maybe he really did love me. I guess it isn't important anymore. What is important is he was your brother and I'm sorry he died before you two got to work out whatever it is that's between you. Whether it was murder or just an accident on the freeway, he died way too soon."

"You're right. Though I don't know if it would've made a difference in how we felt about each other." Seamus carefully replaced the extra bandages before meeting Kat's steady gaze. "Tell Sandy about the stalker's claim...that he murdered Riley. Though you realize, Kat, he might have made the story up just to make you feel worse."

"I'm aware of that. I guess, well...I've forgiven Riley. It wasn't easy, but I've had a lot of time to think about things. It bothers me that you've still got this thing between you that's not resolved." Kat shrugged her shoulders and grabbed the cell phone.

Seamus cleared his throat. "Don't worry about my hang-ups over my brother. They're not your problem." Kat nodded, then punched in the numbers to Sandy Wilson's office. Seamus closed the door quietly behind himself as he left the room.

How could he possibly tell Kathleen *she* was the biggest thing ever to come between the brothers O'Rourke?

She carried Riley's baby. Now she had reason to believe Riley had truly loved her before he died, and that his death might have been murder, not merely an untimely accident.

Seamus tried to take a deep breath, but the pain in his heart left him momentarily gasping. Riley was dead, but nothing had changed. Nothing at all. He clenched his right hand into a tight fist and stared a moment at the whitening knuckles, fought the sudden urge to slam his fist through the wall.

"Looks like you win again, brother." Seamus briefly recalled the feel of Kathleen's supple body when he'd held her in his arms, the perfect fit of her head just beneath his chin, the soft brush of her silky hair.

The look on her face when she said she'd forgiven Riley. He shook his head in disgust. Everyone always forgave Riley. That was the way of it. Charmed and bedeviled by the handsome Irish rogue.

Shrugging off the pain, denying the dream, Seamus headed to his room to pack. It was one thing to compete with a cheat and a liar. Seamus knew he didn't stand a chance in hell against a martyr.

DAMN, THAT WAS TOO close! He practically giggled aloud as he slipped out the front door to the sound of Seamus's footsteps taking the stairs two at a time. Close, but satisfying. He could never have planned a move that smooth, a scene so terrifying. Threatening her baby.

Damn...where had that come from? It was brilliant! Disguising his voice...now that was fun.. Using the vernacular he'd learned in jail, talking tough.

He'd never called a woman "babe" in his life!

He'd never cut one with a knife, either. His breath caught in his throat, his fingers twitched with remembered pleasure. A warmth spread throughout his body, and settled neatly in his groin.

He adjusted his slacks to better contain his erection and settled himself behind the wheel of the rented Ford. Time to back off, even if the need drove him onward. Time to let the seeds of his threat develop and bear fruit.

He drove away without once looking back.

Chapter Five

KAT DOZED OFF AND on as Seamus negotiated the heavy traffic on Highway 101 heading north, out of the city. It was easier to sleep, or even pretend to sleep, than to attempt to figure out the enigmatic man sitting, silent and brooding, next to her.

His hostility had been apparent from the moment they left San Francisco. This stranger was completely opposite the caring savior who had found her bound and bleeding on the bedroom floor. That man had held her in his arms, reassured her with tender kisses and soft words.

He'd made her feel safe.

As safe as she could feel with anyone who wanted to take her child away. Unlike her stalker, though, Kat knew Seamus meant neither her nor her baby harm. He only wanted what he thought should be his. She'd set him straight eventually.

Now his jaw was clenched and his posture unbending. Tension and animosity flowed from him, an almost palpable entity between them. Kat shivered from a chill the Jag's heater couldn't come close to warming.

Was he angry with her or her stalker? Angry with the entire situation, the complications she'd brought into his life? Could it be the fact his brother had died with so much between them unresolved, or maybe, just maybe, was he upset that Riley might really have loved her?

That didn't make sense. Seamus had made it perfectly clear he had no interest in her at all, only in the child she carried.

Kat shivered again and pulled the afghan she'd brought with her more tightly around her shoulders. She turned her face against the soft leather of the Jaguar's interior and closed her eyes. None of it made sense. Not Seamus, not Riley, not the stranger stalking her and threatening her unborn baby.

Her fingers fluttered lightly across her swollen belly. She still found it hard to believe she carried a new life there, wondered when or even *if* she'd feel that rush of maternal love she'd read about. Even now, little "whatsit" existed in her mind as an abstract, in her body as an alien being determined to take over...in her heart, not at all.

Absentmindedly she scratched at her stomach. The bandage

covering the shallow wound itched. She thought about taking it off.

"Does it hurt much? I still think you should've let the doctor look at it."

Kat flinched, raised her head and stared at Seamus. She scooted around in her seat but kept the afghan pulled protectively about her shoulders, then stretched her long legs out in front of her. "It doesn't hurt. Just itches. The bandage itches."

"That's good. Itching's better than hurting." He glanced quickly in her direction. She blinked at the brief eye contact, then turned away and stared down at her toes.

Seamus gazed a moment longer at the fall of silky blond hair hiding her eyes, then turned his attention back to the road. He rolled his shoulders in an attempt to release muscles knotted with tension, but he knew his discomfort couldn't compare to Kathleen's. She appeared beaten, exhausted. Dark circles marred the flesh beneath her eyes, and creases bracketed her mouth. She looked every one of her thirty-five years and then some.

It was all his fault. Damn! How often was he going to fail this woman? "Are you okay, Kat? After weeks of mostly bed rest to have a day like this..."

She turned stiffly and nodded her head. "I'm fine. Just get us there." She stared at her toes again, obviously lost in thought.

Seamus practically groaned under the weight of her despair. He missed her spark, her confrontational attitude. Hell, as much as he hated to admit it, Seamus missed the Kat Malone who drove him nuts.

"Okay," he said. "I guess, after what's happened...I wish you'd at least let me take you to a doctor to make sure everything is all right. I know your obstetrician said you'd be okay, but she's just going by what you told her. I don't imagine you went into all the details of the morning, did you?"

Kat grunted her reply. Seamus figured it was open to interpretation. "Look...I don't want to take any more risks than we have to, Kat. You almost lost the baby once..."

This time her head whipped around, passion and fury flashed from her blue eyes. Kat practically exploded, her voice raw with hostility. "The baby is fine. I am fine. I'm not going to risk *my* baby's health doing anything stupid, get it? Damn you!"

She punched the seat next to her leg, evidence of her mounting frustration. "The only reason I'm putting up with you right now is you're a means to an end. Understand? I'm six months pregnant, I've got some crazy bastard threatening to kill me and I'm smart enough to realize I can't take care of myself like I normally would. The way I wish I could. Do you have any idea how much I hate depending on you right now? Don't think because I've agreed to come with you that gives you some kind of claim on my baby. It doesn't. This baby is mine. Mine alone, and we are both fine. Does that answer your question?"

Kat pulled the afghan back around her shoulders, slammed herself back against the leather seat and stared straight ahead.

Seamus didn't answer. Biting his lip to keep from laughing out loud made it difficult to talk. If Kat had been a kitten, her fur would be standing on end. The image gave him a satisfying sense of relief.

Kat was back.

"I'm going to take a different route to the cabin," he said after a few minutes of the loudest silence he'd ever heard. Kat didn't even acknowledge his comment. "It's longer, but it's a beautiful drive. Winds through lots of back roads through the redwoods. Not a lot of traffic."

So if anyone is following us, I'll know soon enough.

He didn't want to upset Kat any more. His constant checking in the rearview mirror did little good in the stop and go traffic they'd encountered since crossing the Golden Gate Bridge. Their stalker could be in any one of a hundred cars or more.

Once Seamus turned off onto the quiet country road it would be easier to spot anyone coming up behind. He glanced once more in the rearview mirror, then checked both side mirrors.

Kat still watched him, that hostile, wary look in her eyes as unsettling as the warmth he'd seen in them earlier today. She had every right to be angry with him, every right not to trust him. It was better this way. As long as she believed he wasn't interested in her, that he only wanted the baby... No, he couldn't let his thoughts wander in that direction.

Seamus sighed. One day he'd been a perfectly happy middle-aged bachelor, working on his columns, writing his book, leading a comfortable—if boring—life. Now here he was, spiriting an absolutely gorgeous, pregnant woman into hiding and watching the rearview mirror for bad guys. Not that he particularly wanted to go back to the same old, same old, but the changes might be easier to deal with if only he understood women a little better...this woman in particular.

"I'm going to need to eat something pretty soon. Breakfast was a long time ago."

He turned to smile at her, but she still stared out the front window. At least she didn't sound quite as hostile. This he could handle. Eating was easy enough. "If you can last a bit longer, there's a good Italian place in Occidental. It's a neat little town on the way to the cabin. We're about half an hour away."

Kat glanced in his direction, frowned, then nodded and turned her face away, snuggling into the seat like a sleepy kitten. For the moment she'd retracted her claws. Seamus grinned at the image, then frowned. Damn, he didn't care if she had claws or not.

He turned off at the Highway 12 exit in Santa Rosa and headed west. Before long they were winding up the Bohemian Highway. Towering redwoods enclosed the road on either side and thick ferns filled the dark spaces between the trees.

Kathleen stretched and turned to look out the window. Her sudden motion caught Seamus's attention. "Have you seen the redwoods before?"

"Riley took me to a spot somewhere around here, right after I moved out to California. Armstrong Redwoods, I think it's called. I've never seen anything so spectacular in my life. The trees are so huge...I felt as if I'd entered a massive cathedral." She smiled, obviously caught up in the special memory.

Seamus knew the smile wasn't meant for him.

All he saw was Riley walking hand in hand with Kathleen through the familiar grove of towering trees.

The deep forest lost some of its luster.

Seamus swallowed the sudden anger that threatened to choke him. "We're almost to the restaurant," he said.

Kat didn't reply. Obviously, her thoughts were still with Riley.

Seamus grabbed the steering wheel even tighter. They left the cool shade of the redwoods and passed a few dilapidated buildings and old homes on the outskirts of a small town. A minute later they drove into a parking lot half filled with cars. Seamus glanced in the rear view mirror once more before shutting off the engine. Only a couple of tourists on bicycles rolled down the main street of the picturesque little village. He released a quiet sigh of relief, unaware until then he'd been holding his breath.

His neck and shoulders ached. His head pounded. He stretched his back and turned his head in a vain attempt to release the tension.

How the hell'd you do it, Riley? How'd you keep from cracking under the strain?

Riley'd been a successful FBI agent most of his adult life. Seamus realized he'd never considered the pressure associated with the job, the mind-numbing stress of danger.

Maybe Riley'd had a reason for his devil-may-care attitude...one Seamus had never tried to understand. Maybe it had helped him survive.

He was beginning to think there was a lot about Riley he'd never known.

He was also beginning to remember it hadn't always been like that.

Seamus shook off the sense of foreboding. They'd eat here, maybe pick up something extra for tonight, then get settled at the cabin. He'd set up his computer and make sure Kathleen had plenty to read, enough to keep her busy. He'd make a quick grocery run in the morning, once they figured out what they'd need. With any luck they'd survive the next few weeks.

With even more luck, he'd keep his own fears at bay and keep her safe.

This time.

He clenched, then unclenched his hands. Took another deep breath.

I've got to keep her safe.

It was as simple as that.

So much depended on his ability to protect the woman carrying Riley's child. A stray thought lodged itself in his brain, called him a liar, reminded him there was more at stake than the life of the baby.

Not merely for your baby's sake, Kathleen. For your sake. For mine.

Because I couldn't stand to lose you.

I promise I will protect you both.

Seamus uttered his silent oath as he helped Kat out of the car. Her scent tickled his senses and her silky hair brushed lightly over his hand. A cold shiver raced along his spine with the gut-wrenching knowledge it wasn't only the stalker that frightened him.

WHERE COULD THEY BE? He sat in the newly rented Chevy and watched the police milling about the large mansion, painfully aware he'd somehow lost his prey. The coroner's van parked in the driveway meant the housekeeper's body had been discovered. He'd hoped for at least a day or two. He glanced at his Rolex. It had only been four hours.

He hadn't planned to return so soon, but the power had driven him, forced him to come back. Thank goodness he'd listened to its strident voice! There was nothing more to be gained here, though. He had to find them. Soon, before the baby was born. He wanted—no, needed—one more chance to remind Kat Malone who was really in control.

Then she, and her baby, would die.

SEAMUS HANDLED THE JAG with a sure hand, guiding the car slowly along a narrow, packed dirt and gravel road that curved and twisted across a ridge line high above the Russian River. Occasional gaps in the thick forest allowed a view of the tree-covered hillsides below. A few miles beyond, Kat knew the Pacific pounded the rocky shore, but the only evidence they were so near the ocean was the thick fog bank pressed up against the towering treetops.

The road was obviously well maintained but there'd been no other driveways, no evidence of neighbors, for the past fifteen minutes or so. Kat rolled the window down and took a deep breath, expecting the smell of pines, but instead inhaling the pungent odor of humus, an earthy, mushroomy scent that filled the damp air.

"How much farther 'til we're there?" she asked, leaning back against the door so she could see both Seamus and the forest beyond.

Seamus chuckled.

"What'd I say?"

The man was grinning like a damned Cheshire cat. A chuckling Cheshire cat. Amazingly, the tension that had filled the car, even followed them into the comfortable old-fashioned restaurant and out again, suddenly diffused and dispersed. Kat realized she was grinning broadly for no apparent reason, other than the fact Seamus found something terribly funny.

Seamus slowed the car, grabbed a clean handkerchief out of his back pocket and wiped tears of laughter from his eyes. "I'm sorry...it's not you. It's...it's...well... Yeah, it is you."

He laughed again, caught himself, stopped the car altogether and turned to smile at Kat. "Your timing couldn't have been better. See that big tree over there? The one with the burned trunk?"

Kathleen searched the forest for the tree and spotted it, identical to all the others as far as she could see except for a black slash that started about four feet off the ground and disappeared into the thick foliage.

"My parents used to bring Riley and me up here when we were little. The rule was we couldn't ask 'how much farther' until we'd passed the burned tree. I was thinking of that when you asked me the same thing. Talk about a voice from the past!" He lowered his head and took a deep breath. Kat wished she could see the memories roiling about in his mind. She hoped they were good ones.

When he raised his head, Seamus was smiling. "We must've been about eight years old the last time we came up here with Mom and Dad. I still remember arguing and wrestling with my brother in the back seat. You know how twins can sometimes communicate without talking? Riley and me...Wow! I'd almost forgotten about this, but when we were little, we knew exactly what the other one was thinking. He'd look at me, all blue-eyed innocence and I'd know exactly what he wanted me to do or say. Of course, usually he wanted me to do or say something that would get me in trouble. Then I'd tattle and we'd both get yelled at. I'm sure we drove our parents nuts."

Kat thought of Riley, of that blue-eyed innocent look. He'd certainly used it on her more than once. She shook off the memory. "Why'd you stop coming? It's so beautiful up here."

Seamus blinked quickly, then brushed the back of his hand across his face. Kat realized the tears filling his eyes now had nothing to do with laughter.

"A few weeks after that last trip, our parents died in a plane crash on the way to Acapulco. Gran brought us up here when she could, but it was never the same. I come back occasionally when life in the city gets too hectic, but..." He paused and took a deep breath. "C'mon. We need to get there, get unpacked and settled before dark."

"I'm sorry, Seamus, I didn't mean to make you remember anything to upset you." She meant to give his knee a quick, comforting pat. It was a gesture that would have been perfectly natural with Riley.

Seamus's big hand covered hers the moment she touched his leg, held her fingers there against the taut muscle, not by force but by the mere sense of need for shared contact.

"Don't be sorry. Do you realize that's the first really good memory I've had of Riley in a long time?" He smiled sadly at her, the look so much like his brother's it made her heart ache.

"I need to remember more things like that. I need to remember Riley was the best friend I had for a long time, even when he was getting into trouble. Our parents' deaths hit me hard, but it must have been much worse for my brother. He was closest to Dad. They were practically inseparable, always going off and doing things together. I was sick a lot as a kid, so I stayed home. I hate to admit it, but guess I was kind of a mama's boy."

His face took on a faraway expression. "Ya know, it seems like a lifetime ago now. We went to live with my mother's mom, Gran, and she was a lot like Mom, which more or less filled the need for me.

Riley kind of got left out, I guess. He must have missed Dad terribly. I never realized that before."

He gave her fingers a quick squeeze then released them. Kat snatched her hand away as he put the sleek car in gear and headed up the road. Her mind tumbled with thoughts of two little boys, suddenly orphaned. The irresponsible, irrepressible Riley; quiet, introverted Seamus. How different would their lives have been if the brothers' parents had lived?

Before Kat could imagine an answer, they had rounded a final curve, crossed an ancient stone bridge over a small creek and pulled into the driveway that ran along one side of Seamus's cabin.

"Cabin" wasn't exactly the description Kat would have given the multi-level redwood structure blending so perfectly into the surrounding forest. Instead of the typical A-frame she had somehow expected, this building had a roof that sloped steeply to one side, as if a box had been sheared at an angle. The late afternoon sun glinted off the western side of the house, which appeared to be nothing but glass. A huge deck gracefully circled three sides of the structure and a broad staircase framed in lush ferns and wild rhododendron led to the front door.

"I'll get your things." Seamus held the car door open for her. Kat wondered how long he'd been waiting as she stared open-mouthed at his home.

She shook her head in disbelief. "Thank you. I have to admit, I'm still amazed that a food columnist does this well." She swung her legs around and stepped out of the car. The ground was soft and springy, littered with needles and leaves from the damp forest. The air felt clean and damp against her skin.

"My writing didn't pay for this." Seamus grabbed the sports bag filled with her clothes. Kat wondered if he realized part of the weight came from the 9mm Ruger tucked inside her neatly folded nightgown.

"My mother was an heiress, the last descendent of a prominent banking family from San Francisco. Dad married well."

"Is that meant as a put down?" Kat followed Seamus up the stairs and into the house. At least he hadn't insisted on carrying her this time.

"Not at all." Seamus held the door open and Kat walked into the large great room. She shivered and rubbed her arms for warmth. The cabin was ice cold, the air stale and musty with the distinct scent of resin from the natural pine covering the interior walls.

Seamus immediately headed for the fireplace, squatted down and began stacking kindling for a fire.

"My father adored my mother." He glanced back toward Kat, his expression somber. "I imagine he went to his grave believing she was too good for him, but it was obvious to everyone around them that she loved him very much. They had a lot of fun together. It just didn't last long enough."

Not for his parents...not for their son. Kat tried to picture Seamus and Riley as twin hellions, sliding down the curving banister that led to the upper floors, reading in front of the huge native stone fireplace stretched along the entire north wall of the lower level.

She imagined Seamus's parents snuggled together under the multi-colored afghan now folded neatly at one end of a massive dark green leather couch. She thought of the free-spirited Riley, laughing, loving her as much as he was able, slipping through life with a smile on his face and not a care to his name. Silently she agreed with Seamus. *It didn't last long enough.*

Then she turned to Seamus, the man who had promised to protect her, to keep her safe from harm, and quietly stored Riley's memory away. She hadn't been able to put him aside when her memories of the laughing Irishman had been clouded with anger. It seemed fitting that her stalker's words, words meant to give her pain, had finally given her peace.

Now it was time to find another form of peace, if she and Seamus O'Rourke were going to survive the next long weeks together without going quietly insane.

If only he didn't confuse her so much!

Maybe with Riley settled quietly away in her heart, this strange attraction to his brother would slip away as well.

In your dreams, Malone.

Had to be hormones. Nothing but hormones gone awry and a life so screwed up she'd be attracted to any man offering her sanctuary. She rubbed her hand across the slight swell of her abdomen, felt the bandage Seamus had placed so carefully over her injury, and knew she owed him more than gratitude.

It was obvious everything she said and did irritated him. He was used to women with class and style—something Kat was well aware she'd never have. Her ex-partner, Mike Ramsey, had always called her a classy broad. Of course, his idea of class was Kat in her hooker get-up during undercover assignments.

She missed Ramsey. Hell, she missed his new wife, Rose, just as much. Rose had been her first real woman friend, someone she'd bonded with like she'd never done with another woman. Now,

Rose...Rose DeAngelo Ramsey, had class. Lots of it. She also had Mike Ramsey.

Kat sighed. If it took class to keep a man, she was shit out of luck. She knew she had tenacity, a skill to survive and a stubborn sense of right that had somehow endured in spite of growing up with a drunk for a mother and a non-existent father.

Somewhere along the line, Kat had learned how to get by. Getting by often meant playing by someone else's rules, if only for the moment. She could do that now, which meant she would try and be a civil guest while under Seamus's care.

All she had to do was play a part, which was something she did often enough in her work. Then, once the baby came, once she and it were strong enough to travel, she'd leave. She'd leave and take her baby with her, someplace where neither the stalker nor Seamus could find her.

Kat drew in a deep breath, let it out, took control of her racing heart. It was always like this once she made a decision to act. Then, once the decision was made, she neatly stepped into the role. Not a hooker, this time. A lady. A lady with manners.

Think about Rose. How would she act?

Rose didn't have to act. Her class was natural.

Here goes, Malone....

"This is a really gorgeous place." Kat walked across the room, knelt in front of the fire and laid her hand gently on Seamus's arm, aware of a tightening of the muscle, a tension that raised the cords along his forearm. "I hope you know how much I appreciate you bringing me here."

Seamus turned his head and looked at her, but he didn't say a word. He frowned, then turned back to the fire he was building.

Kat ignored his obvious dismissal. "I accept the fact you don't like me very much. I'm not always a very likable person. I know your only interest in me is your brother's baby...and you know I'll fight you on that every step of the way." She took another deep breath, released it, and held her hand up to stop him from interrupting. "Still, I appreciate your help. I trust you to keep us both safe." She paused a minute, aware she still played a part.

Even more aware this situation was much too dangerous for games. "You will protect me, Seamus. Me and my baby."

He lit the dry tinder and stood up, brushing his hands across his thighs before pulling Kat to her feet then quickly releasing her hands. "How do you know you can trust me?"

His deep voice rumbled up out of his chest. She loved the sound of it. Didn't want to. Couldn't help it.

"I couldn't protect you in my own home. What makes you think I'll do any better here?"

"Because you have to." Kat folded her arms, rested them across her belly and sighed. "You have no choice. If you don't keep me alive, you'll never see your brother's child."

"Kathleen, I..."

"Seamus. Please. Let's drop it. We both know where we stand. That's enough, isn't it?" She licked her dry lips and pushed her hair back out of her eyes. Suddenly the day felt way too long. "I'm tired. Would you show me where you want me to sleep?"

He nodded, his dark green eyes studying her with an unnerving intensity. He checked the fire, added a log, then picked up her bag and silently led Kat to a room beneath the stairs. She followed behind, marveling once again how Seamus could look so much like his twin, yet be so completely his own man.

She was wondering as well how she could have ever thought herself in love with a man who was merely a pale shadow of the real thing.

No. Don't even think that. It won't work. Not in a million years. Remember what he wants, why he's so damned protective.

You can do it, Malone...it's only three more months. Three more months, and whether or not her stalker had been apprehended by then, she'd quietly slip away and make a new life for herself. For herself and her child. Why did she have to keep reminding herself there'd be a child. A baby. A tiny, vulnerable life, completely dependent on Kat. She'd find a place where no one, not Seamus, not the killer, would ever find her...or her baby.

Oh God! It wasn't just the pregnancy or "whatsit". It was going to be a living, breathing little person, a child to love and hold.

My baby. Not *the* baby. Not Riley's, certainly not Seamus's. Kat brushed her hand lightly across her stomach and a tiny foot or elbow fluttered against her palm. Fierce, hungry, overwhelming love flooded her heart. Warmth raced through her veins until she felt as if she must be glowing.

This baby is mine, Seamus O'Rourke. Mine.

She watched impatiently as Seamus set the bag on the double bed and turned to leave. "I know this isn't much," he said, gesturing toward the bed and shrugging his shoulders. "But it's the only bedroom downstairs and it's got its own bathroom. I don't want you climbing up and down the—"

"It's perfect. Thank you." Kat stepped to one side and held the door wider for him, hoping her intention was obvious. He cocked one dark eyebrow.

Kat returned his stare. She had to get him out of here, *now*. No way was she willing to share this revelation, this sense of impending wonder, this *love*. She wanted nothing more than to curl up on the bed, to wrap herself around her growing baby...to absorb the feelings warming her heart. Finally, she wanted to dream of her child, to plan.

Why had it taken so long to *feel* like a mother? She'd been wondering what was wrong with her, wondering in the dark recesses of her heart if maybe, just maybe, Seamus would be the better parent.

Thoughts of Seamus's kindness suddenly filled her mind, traitorous thoughts mingled with the knowledge of his ultimate reason for helping her. Well, he wasn't going to get her baby and he wasn't going to get her. Kat straightened her spine as Seamus glanced once more in her direction, then turned to leave the room.

He doesn't want you, you idiot.

But what if he did? Seamus brushed against her as he walked past and Kat's muscles tensed involuntarily. He shot one crystalline glance in her direction, affirming the contact had been intentional.

She didn't need all this confusion in her life! She shut the door quickly behind him, searched for a latch and felt oddly relieved when she couldn't find one. Then she pushed thoughts of Seamus out of her mind, slipped her shoes off and wrapped herself snugly in the heavy bedspread. *Three more months.* Just three months until she held her baby in her arms, packed their bags and left.

Half asleep, Kat pondered the fact she'd finally started thinking of her baby as a separate being, of someone alive and waiting to be born. Someone she couldn't wait to cuddle and love. She drifted to sleep amid conflicting dreams of holding her baby to her breast and the comforting sound of Seamus adding more wood to the fire.

IT WAS COMPLETELY DARK when Kat opened her eyes, but a pale sliver of light under the door helped her orient herself. After a quick trip to the bathroom she ran a damp washcloth over her face, finger-combed her hair and stepped out into the great room.

Seamus was there in the semi-darkness, his head and shoulders framed by the light from the dying fire. His back was to her. He slouched in an old rocker he had pulled close to the hearth. His head tilted to one side, and his left arm hung loosely over the armrest, the fingers almost reaching the floor.

Other than the soft hiss and snap of embers in the glowing fireplace, the room was quiet. A shiver ran along Kat's spine and she quickly glanced around the large room, wondering if the unease she felt meant danger or was merely a reaction to waking after a late afternoon's sleep.

She stepped around beside Seamus and quickly relaxed. He slept soundly and peacefully, his lips slightly parted, one hand across his flat stomach, his long legs stretched out as if seeking the heat from the slumbering fire.

He wore argyle socks with a hole in the left foot. His big toe stuck out through the hole. Something about that imperfection in this oh-so-perfect-male touched Kat. It was nice to know the paragon was human after all.

If this had been Riley she would have run her fingers through the thatch of dark hair, would have wakened him with a kiss and an invitation for more.

But this wasn't Riley. Seamus wasn't anything like his brother and yet he was so similar to Riley it hurt to stand here and study him. Hurt to want to touch him, yet know that touch was forbidden by her own need for self-protection.

Kat couldn't move away. She'd never felt so torn, nor had she known such a sense of loneliness. The baby kicked, a sharp emphasis to her situation. For the first time Kat thought of the struggle that awaited her, thought of raising the baby by herself.

Seamus stirred, stretched, then, as if aware of Kat silently watching him, turned his head to study her in the darkened room. He blinked, then pulled himself more upright in the chair. "How long have you been there?"

"I just woke up. Thought I'd check and see if you were awake."

"I wasn't." He grinned, arched his back and stretched again. "Didn't realize how tired I was." He glanced at his watch. "Geez, it's after eight. Are you hungry?"

She hadn't thought about it until Seamus brought it up. "Yeah, guess I am. Is there anything here to eat?

"Dumb question. Let's go see what looks good."

A loud buzz startled them both. Seamus grabbed his beeper from the small table next to the chair. "Do you recognize this number?" He held the digital screen out so Kat could read it.

"That's Sandy Wilson's home number. It must be important." She shivered, though the room was warm, and wrapped her arms around herself.

Seamus punched in the numbers on his cell phone. Kat watched the dark expressions cross his face, sensed the deep despair that filled him, but she waited until he finished the call, waited while he closed his eyes in an obvious attempt at composure.

Finally he turned and looked directly at Kat. His green eyes glistened with tears. "Hazel's dead. They found her body right after we left. Just outside the kitchen. She'd been strangled."

"Oh, my God." Kat reached for Seamus's hands, grabbed them both and held on. "What...? Who...?"

"Sandy had a team out there to look for clues right after we left. They were checking your room, the stairs... They didn't find her body for a couple of hours. She never had a chance. Her neck was broken."

He bowed his head, his hands still grasping Kat's. "I thought she'd gone to the store. Hell, I left her a note on the kitchen table and told her to take a few days off, that I'd call as soon as I could. I never imagined..."

"Seamus, I'm so sorry. It's all my fault."

He stood up and pulled Kathleen gently into his embrace. She let herself melt against his strong frame, but guilt wouldn't let her rest. "If I hadn't been there, he never would have come. She'd still be..."

"Hush. You're not to blame. If anyone's to blame it's me. For not taking the threat seriously enough, for risking both your lives. He never should've gotten on the grounds. I can afford a security force. I didn't think we needed it. No, I figured I could take care of everything. Well, I sure screwed that up, didn't I?"

Kat closed her eyes against the bitterness in his voice, the fear in her heart. The baby kicked, a tiny staccato of beats against her belly.

Kat shuddered, more aware than ever of how much she had to lose.

Chapter Six

"I'VE GOT TO MAKE some phone calls." Seamus carefully unwrapped Kat's arms from around his waist and set her away from him. It felt too good to hold her close. This was neither the time nor the place. Not now, maybe not ever.

"I'll get something together for dinner." Kat wiped her eyes with her sweatshirt sleeve and sniffed.

"Thanks. I appreciate it." Seamus reached for his cell phone. "I need to call Hazel's daughter and I should get in touch with my agent before this hits the evening news...if it hasn't already."

Kat nodded her head in answer and left the room. Seamus watched her walk away, his sense of unease like a lead weight in his chest. He wondered if Kat realized how much things had changed. An anonymous reign of terror was one thing. In the course of one afternoon, her stalker had crossed two major barriers.

He'd gone from written threats and vandalism to outright confrontation of his victim.

He'd murdered an innocent bystander.

Seamus rubbed his hand across his burning eyes. There couldn't have been a more innocent bystander than Hazel Andrews.

If Kat was right, if her stalker had killed Riley, it meant the downward spiral had begun even earlier.

Seamus doubted it would end with his housekeeper's death.

"Geez, Hazel. I'm so damned sorry." Seamus looked down at the phone in his hand, dreading the call to Linda. He'd known Hazel's eldest daughter for years, enjoyed her quick wit and the wonderful relationship she shared with her mother. Now, in the blink of an eye, it was over. Hazel was gone. Linda would live with the pain of her mother's untimely death for the rest of her life.

Just as he would live with the guilt.

The clatter of pots and pans caught his attention.

In the blink of an eye. He could easily have lost Kat as quickly. The stalker had held her life in his hands this afternoon. For whatever twisted desires drove him, he'd allowed Kathleen Malone to live, had toyed with her like a cat with a mouse.

Then he'd left her with a threat of more to come.

A shudder passed through Seamus. He clenched his fists, then just as quickly spread his fingers wide. He stared at his broad palms, unmarred by calluses and scars as Riley's had been, at the long fingers, the neatly trimmed nails.

Not the hands of a fighter, and certainly not the hands of a killer.

What if he couldn't protect her? What right did he have promising Kat he would keep her safe? Could he, with these hands?

He shook his head dismayed by the direction his thoughts kept spinning, and dialed Linda's number.

"WHEN'S HAZEL'S FUNERAL?" KAT dried the last dish and stuck it in the cupboard over her head.

Seamus finished rinsing the sink, then shut the water off and dried his hands. He turned and leaned against the counter, immeasurably fascinated by the toes of his shoes as far as Kat could tell.

"Seamus?"

"I'm sorry." He raised his head, frowning, looking even more troubled and distracted than he had earlier. "It'll be in three days...Friday morning. The family is planning a graveside service, same cemetery where Riley's buried. Linda, Hazel's daughter, didn't think she could handle a big funeral."

"Can we make it down and back in one day?" Kat hung the towel on a hook next to the sink and sat down at the kitchen table. "It's not that far, is it? I slept most of the way here, but..."

"We aren't going." Seamus pulled out the chair across from her and sat. "It's too risky. The killer's going to expect you to be there. I'm not about to hand you over to him on a silver platter and that's exactly what we'd be doing."

He rubbed his hand across his face and shoved a heavy lock of dark hair off his forehead. Deep lines bracketed his mouth. Kat thought he looked incredibly weary.

Guilt ripped through her again. None of this would have happened if she'd been stronger. She should have gotten a hotel room in the very beginning. Hazel would still be alive. Seamus's world wouldn't be in complete turmoil.

I'd probably be dead. Me and the baby.

Seamus's quiet voice interrupted her thoughts. "I explained the situation to Linda. She understands and she agrees. She knows how fond I am...was...of her mother." He closed his eyes, bowed his head, then suddenly looked up and glared at Kat, as if expecting an argument.

The baby chose that moment to plant a strong kick just under her ribcage. Kat's automatic rebuttal died in her throat.

"I understand. I guess I just feel so awful... I keep thinking..."

"I know what you're thinking." He practically growled at her. "Just stop it, Kat. It won't change anything. Hazel's gone. She shouldn't have died the way she did but it happened. You're alive. The baby's alive. Keeping you both safe is my primary concern right now."

His eyes narrowed as if he dared her to argue, but Kat sensed the helpless rage and sorrow behind his angry guise. She fought a powerful urge to go to him, to hold him in her arms, to do anything that would take the emptiness and sadness from his eyes.

Knowing full well he would probably push her away with the same cool efficiency as he had earlier in the evening kept her glued to her seat. His rejection left her confused and hurting, especially after the loving way he'd held her earlier, after the stalker had attacked her. Would she ever figure him out?

"How long do you think we'll have to stay here?" she asked. She told herself the inactivity was making her crazy.

Liar. Seamus was making her crazy. She didn't want to be confused by him, attracted to him. Hell, she didn't even want to *like* him.

Lately, it didn't seem to matter what she wanted.

"Until they catch him, I imagine. Sandy told me he's following some leads. Now at least he has an idea who to look for." Seamus slammed his palm down on the table, frustration evident in every move he made. "Damn, I wish you'd gotten a look at him so we could be certain..."

"It has to be Tim Anderson. He's scary. My friend Rose, the woman he kidnapped during the hijacking, said he was a real sicko. Her ex-fiancé ended up protecting her from Anderson. If he hadn't, Rose was convinced Anderson would have killed her...and taken great pleasure in the process."

"What about the ex-fiancé?"

"James Dearborn? I don't think so. Comes from money. Got involved in hijacking to cover gambling debts. Such an idiot! He'd been embezzling from his own mother! In the end, he was just as much a victim. The head of the operation was blackmailing him to keep him in line. Dearborn's a real dip, a complete loser, but I don't think he's dangerous."

"He never threatened you?"

"No. The only threats came from Anderson. He threatened to kill all of us. Guess I'm lucky to be first on his list." She didn't mean to sound so bitter. She'd rather Anderson come after her than her best friends...or Hazel, the chatterbox housekeeper she'd grown so fond of over the past few weeks.

"I'm so sorry about Hazel. She didn't deserve to die like that." Kat looked down at her folded hands, amazed they weren't trembling. This sense of fear, of vulnerability, was unnerving.

She'd never felt like this before.

You've never been pregnant before, idiot.

No wonder she felt helpless. The physical abilities she'd always depended upon were no longer an option.

Isolated as they were, if Anderson found them she'd have only her wits and Seamus to protect her.

Even Seamus had admitted the truth...he'd failed her once before.

Thank goodness for the gun tucked under her mattress.

Seamus reached across the table and took both Kat's hands in his. She felt his strength cross the barrier, flesh to flesh, filling her with a sense of calm she hadn't expected. "We'll be okay, Kat. He has no idea where we are. Sandy's got a team working on this, so we'll just sit tight until we hear from him."

"Sit tight, you say." She laughed and carefully slipped her hands out from under Seamus's. "I'll go nuts here with nothing to do." She stood up and walked away from the table, turned in the doorway and leaned against the frame. Seamus watched her, the steady gaze from his dark green eyes a bit unnerving. "You realize, I've spent the last few weeks going quietly insane," she said. "Now that I'm feeling better the inactivity will really drive me crazy."

"I've got a deck of cards." He mimed a dealer's quick moves.

"Cards, you say?" She winked at him. Immediately wished she could take the flirtatious move back. Wondered how she could have possibly lost control of that damned eyelid!

The smile he flashed in her direction made her heart beat double-time. Maybe a game of cards wasn't the best of ideas....

WHERE WERE THEY? DRESSED in tan coveralls with a fake name tag over the pocket and his hair slicked back against his scalp, he'd placed the flowers at the foot of the casket, and had even set out some of the late arriving arrangements, but there was no sign of either O'Rourke or the bitch. He stepped back, making himself as inconspicuous as possible at the edge of the olive grove.

The same grove he'd waited in a few short weeks earlier.

So much had changed since then. He'd felt the power grow,

experienced the soul-searing rush of heat when he'd held a life in his hands, when he'd taken that life.

His fingers twitched with the recollection of what followed, that most satisfying lesson in terror he'd given the bitch. Slashing her across the belly... He took a deep breath, replaying the moment, closing his eyes against the deep welling of pleasure.

Sounds of footsteps jerked him out of his silent world.

He watched the mourners enter the quiet grove. Their voices slipped in and out of his range of hearing, a subtle cacophony of grief. Hell, she was just an old broad, a nobody! Didn't they understand the power?

"No," the woman was saying. "He couldn't be here today. The police think the killer was after a woman he'd offered protection to. Mom never said too much about her, only that she was pregnant and almost lost the baby."

"How awful. Are they at the house? Were they there when your mother was...well, you know?"

"I don't know. They're not there now. I talked to Seamus the other day...did you know he's paid for everything? It's such a beautiful casket, and the flowers are lovely. He was always so good to Mom."

"Where do you think they've gone? Is the woman, the one who's pregnant...is she his girlfriend?"

"Oh, I don't think so."

The woman laughed. It wasn't right, laughing at her mother's funeral. Bitches. They were all alike. Out for themselves, never cared a whit about anyone else.

"Mom always maintained Seamus was gay. She never knew him to bring a woman home in all the years she worked for him. Otherwise I'm sure she would have been trying to set us up."

"Gay? Seamus O'Rourke? Gawd, what a terrible loss to womankind!"

"That's what I always said. The man is so good looking, he's obviously successful and to top it off, he's really nice."

Their voices softened, blended in with the general hum of conversation. He tried to pick out details, and finally decided he'd have to move a bit closer. Suddenly he recognized a familiar face. Sandy Wilson...the police detective working the case!

He slipped back in amongst the olive trees.

"Hello, Linda. How are you holding up? I'm really sorry about your mom. I only met her a few times, but she was an absolute delight."

"Thank you. Thank you very much. Guess I'm doing as well as

can be expected. I still expect her to come flying through the door at the end of the day, chattering a mile a minute. I never realized how much I'd hate the silence."

She wasn't laughing now. Hell, he'd done the broad a favor. That old woman could talk your leg off. She reminded him of his mother...which meant he'd really done her a favor. He edged a bit closer.

"Officer Wilson? I'd like to introduce you to my friend Mona. Officer Wilson is working on Mom's case."

Once again the conversation blended into a rumble of meaningless sounds. He moved quietly among the twisted trunks and branches, finally reaching a point close to the two women and the police detective.

"...not really sure. Someplace safe from harm, I'm sure."

"I remember Mom telling me about a place over near the Russian River, a summer home Seamus's parents used to have. I think if I were looking for a place to get lost, that's where I'd head. Good food, good wine..." *Soft laughter followed.*

He strained to hear more.

"Wherever they are, I hope it stays private."

He slipped back into the shadows. So, Officer Wilson didn't want to talk about the Russian River? It wasn't far, just up the highway in Sonoma County. This sounded promising. It was time to call for reinforcements. Time to call in some markers. He could barely contain the smile that twisted his lips. He wasn't all that familiar with California, specifically Sonoma County, but there was someone who knew it well. Someone who owed him big time.

His fingers twitched. So close. She was really very, very close. Grinning broadly, he headed back through the dark grove of olives for his car.

SEAMUS STRAIGHTENED UP IN front of the open door of the refrigerator and glanced over his shoulder at Kat. She stood framed in the kitchen doorway wearing the same pair of blue sweats she'd been wearing all week long, the pair she had to wash and dry every night if she wanted something other than her nightgown to wear during the day. "Think you could handle a trip into town?" he asked.

"I'd take a trip to the moon if you offered. The walls are closing in." She flopped down on one of the kitchen chairs and dropped her running shoes on the floor. He watched as she awkwardly slipped her feet into the shoes, working around her ever-expanding middle. "I can't believe how far away my feet seem to be getting," she grumbled.

"Need any help?" Seamus shut the refrigerator door and ambled over to the table. "I learned to tie my shoes even before kindergarten, you know. Always was a precocious child."

She glanced up at him, one blue eye twinkling through a part in the hair that had fallen over her face. "I can tie my own shoes, thank you. This week," she amended. "Clothes are another matter. If you think it's safe to go into town, I need to find some other things to wear. Look at this."

She pulled the sweatshirt up to reveal the waistband of the pants cutting into the flesh below her abdomen. Then she stretched the band out and away from her stomach.

Seamus gulped. He could see the upper edge of the gash where it ended near her hipbone. The knife wound had healed to a pale pink scar, but he didn't think there could be anything lovelier than Kat Malone entering her seventh month of pregnancy. The skin stretched smooth and sleek over her growing baby, and what had once been a tiny little indentation for her navel was now a full-fledged belly button.

"What used to be a cute little innie turned into an outie overnight. I think I need some bigger pants. Are there any clothing stores in this little town of yours?" She rolled the sweatshirt back over her belly.

Seamus knelt down to tie her shoes, pleasantly surprised when Kat stuck a foot out for him without protest. "We'll find you something. We're just about out of groceries, too, and I'd like to top off the gas tank in the Jag. I didn't take the time to fill it when I made my last run to town."

"Think we'll need to make a quick get-a-way?" Her voice held a teasing quality, but Seamus was certain he sensed an underlying fear.

"No, that's not the reason. Here, give me your other foot." He tied the laces and stood up. "I don't want to risk running out of gas if we're still here when you decide to go into labor. The last thing I want to do is deliver a baby."

"I'm at least two-and-a-half, three months off. You don't think we'll be here that long, do you?" She held her hand out and Seamus pulled her to her feet.

"Hopefully not, but until we get the all-clear from Sandy Wilson, I'm not budging. C'mon. Let's put together a list of what we need."

GUERNEVILLE WAS JUST AS Kat remembered from her brief visit months before with Riley, an eclectic gathering of shops and restaurants stretching along the highway, surrounded by towering redwood trees and bordered along one side by the lazy flow of the Russian River.

Riley'd explained to her that the community was a magnet for people who lived what he'd termed "alternative lifestyles," a Mecca for gays and lesbians, transsexuals, transvestites and everyone in between.

For a small town girl from Pennsylvania, Kat's first visit truly had been an eye-opener, but she'd thoroughly enjoyed the brief time she and Riley had spent here. She'd suffered enough intolerance in her life, merely because she'd chosen work in what was essentially a man's field, to ever be intolerant of another's lifestyle.

Seamus found a parking place on a narrow side street and helped Kat out of the low-slung car. "Let's just wander," he said, slipping her hand into the crook of his arm and taking off at a leisurely pace.

People smiled as they passed and it suddenly occurred to Kat it was her pregnancy that caught their attention. She glanced at Seamus just as he turned in her direction. His glance held hers for a heartbeat before he looked away.

He's thinking the same thing I am, that people assume we're married. They look at the two of us and see husband and wife, with baby on the way.

She didn't know whether to be angry or amused. This was the first time she'd been out in public with a man since her pregnancy had become noticeable.

Riley should have been the one at her side, not Seamus. She tensed, began to slip her hand away from his arm before another thought intruded.

Riley should have been here...but would he have? She'd never know, and would always wonder whether her easy-going, devil-may-care lover would have accepted responsibility for the baby.

Seamus had. Without any hesitation at all.

Of course, part of that acceptance was due to the fact he wanted her baby.

She tightened her hand on his arm, as she refused to think beyond today. There was no point worrying about the future.

Whenever she did, her first thought was to ask herself if she and her baby even had a future. She glanced nervously about, almost expecting Tim Anderson to jump out from behind a display rack.

Seamus pointed to a woman dressed in a brilliantly hued tie-dyed dress, then led Kat into a store with similar dresses on display.

Twenty minutes later they walked out into the bright spring sunlight. Kat giggled and hugged the plastic bag close to her chest.

"Did you have to pick the one with the big blue sun on the front? It looks like a bulls-eye on my belly. Not quite the thing for a hard-working, gun-toting agent to wear."

"I thought it was rather becoming." Seamus lifted the bag out of her hands and wrapped her fingers back in place around his forearm. There was a definite twinkle in his eyes. "It's you, Kat. The subdued shades, the intricate design..."

"Subdued? How can you call turquoise, chartreuse, hot pink, yellow and purple tie-dye subdued? As far as the intricate design, it looks like every other dress in the shop!"

"Not when it's on you." Seamus halted in mid-stride and smiled down at Kat. That alone made her pause. Very few men were tall enough to smile *down* at her. Then he frowned slightly, as if thinking through his words.

"On you it's unique. You looked like a wild-eyed gypsy when you put it on. Definitely not the look of an investigative agent."

She thought about how Seamus must see her. Even pregnant she knew her carriage and demeanor radiated a self-confidence she didn't always feel. It did, however, lend her an aura of authority she'd put to good use in her work—and her private life—over the years.

She returned Seamus's unwavering stare with her own, wondering. How did one define "the look of an investigative agent?"

As if working out the definition for himself, Seamus silently studied her, his eyes as dark as the primal forest. Kat felt herself drawn into their depths, and sensed something deeper in the moment, something indefinable taking place between them on the narrow sidewalk.

Seamus blinked and the moment ended. His eyes twinkled with mischief and he chuckled as if enjoying a private joke. "Let's amend that," he said, once again taking her hand and placing it over his arm. "You look like a very pregnant, wild-eyed, blond gypsy."

"Gee, thanks."

Arms linked, they continued on down the street.

THEY WANDERED IN AND out of almost every store on the block, picking up a few baggy knit dresses and some tee shirts for Kat, blue jeans and soft flannel shirts for Seamus. A bookstore caught Kathleen's attention and she dragged Seamus across the street, dodging the slowly moving traffic.

"We definitely need to go in here," she said. "The reading material at the cabin is a bit dated."

"What? You don't like my Hardy Boy mysteries?" Seamus followed her into the store.

"I liked them better when I was nine." Kat slipped out of his grasp and headed for the romance section.

Seamus followed her. "Somehow, I pictured you reading Stephen King or John Grisham or even Tom Clancy. Not..." He plucked the book Kat selected out of her hands and glanced at the cover. A bouquet of flowers with the title and author's name in script told him absolutely nothing. "Hmmm...never heard of her."

"It's a romance and I've read everything she's written. Except this one. Now give it back."

"So. The tough detective reads romances." He held the book out to her. "What's the draw."

Kat's expression suddenly grew very serious. "The draw? Only the bad guys get hurt. The hero and heroine may have their problems but they work them out and fall in love. Best of all, there's always a happy ending." She bowed her head a moment, hiding those brilliant blue eyes from Seamus. "There aren't enough happy endings in life, Seamus. I don't want to read something that makes me sad, especially now. Understand?"

He studied her a moment, clearly seeing the woman beneath the façade, the tough, sweet, sometimes vulnerable woman he'd grown to care about so much. He tucked another bit of Kat's personal information away in his heart.

She wanted happy endings. What was so unusual about that? He wouldn't mind one himself. "Yeah," he said, stepping back out of Kat's light. Distancing himself before the need to touch her won out over his common sense. "A happy ending would work really well for me right now. I'll be over there..." He gestured toward the far end of the store. "Stay out of trouble, okay?"

She was adding books to a growing pile and merely nodded when he left. Seamus headed straight for the women's section of the store, where he picked up a couple of books on childbirth and delivery. One had a picture of a very pregnant woman on the cover. It took a few moments before he realized he wanted the book because the audacious tilt of her chin reminded him of Kathleen.

He set the book down and grabbed another instead.

He'd moved on to the action/adventure section when a sudden movement to his right caught his attention.

"Seamus? What the hell are you doing here?"

His agent clasped him on the shoulder in greeting. *Damn!* The last thing he wanted was to run into anyone he knew.

"Of course, I guess I should've known you'd love this town." The smaller man grinned broadly. There was no ignoring the knowing twinkle in his eye.

Seamus suppressed a groan. "Hey, Frank. How ya doin? Didn't you get my message?" Seamus fought the urge to glance in Kat's direction. He hoped she wouldn't choose that moment to join him.

"No. Must've missed it. Hope it wasn't important. It's good to see you. I'm surprised you're not home working on that book. The editor won't wait forever, you know. Especially since it's out of your usual genre."

Seamus plastered a jovial grin on his face, one he definitely wasn't feeling. This meeting could really complicate matters. "Needed a break, Frank. Figured I'd take a run up here and clear my head. What're you doing here? This isn't your usual stomping grounds."

"Unlike yours, eh?" Frank laughed knowingly and winked at Seamus. "I'm at a writers' conference in Santa Rosa. Thought I'd take the afternoon off and check out the local color." He nodded in the direction of a pair of handsome young men dressed in matching leather pants and vests. Heavy chains linked them together. The shorter of the two rested his head against his partner's shoulder.

"It doesn't get much more colorful than Guerneville." Seamus had seen the two enter the shop a moment earlier, but at the mention of local color, his imagination slipped back to the vision of Kathleen in the tiny dress shop modeling the full-length tie-died dress.

Suddenly the object of his vision appeared directly in front of him. "Seamus, I think I've got more than enough. Are you about ready to go?"

"Well, well. Hello." Frank's naturally bulging eyes bulged even further as his gaze moved from Kat's face to her belly, then back to Seamus. "This is a surprise, Seamus."

In more ways than one, I bet, Seamus added.

Frank's gaze darted from Seamus to Kat to Kat's middle and back to Seamus. "Aren't you going to introduce us?"

"Uh, yeah, Frank. Meet—" He caught Kat's startled expression, smiled and said, "—my friend Kitty." He returned Kat's frown with one of his own. "Kitty, this is Frank Montero, my agent. I was just telling him we were here on a day trip."

"Nice to meet you, Frank." Obviously sensing Seamus's discomfort, Kat turned back to him and smiled sweetly. "It's a long drive home, darling. We'd really better be going. Are you going to get these or am I?" She nodded at her armful of paperbacks.

"My treat." He nodded at the befuddled looking agent, took the stack of books out of Kat's arms and added them to the basket he'd partially filled, then turned back to Frank. "I'll call you in a couple of days to let you know when I've got something more to send. Good seeing you."

Then with a hand planted firmly against Kat's back, he walked her to the cash register by the front door, paid for the books and bundled her outside before Frank could hit him with questions.

They'd barely reached the sidewalk when her laughter exploded, deep and earthy and filled with humor. "Kitty? Where in the hell did you come up with that? I don't see myself as a Kitty, Seamus. No way."

"I'd already started the K sound before I though better of giving your name. I doubt he'll remember it anyway. Frank's still trying to reformat everything he thinks he's known about me for the past ten years."

Chuckling, Seamus led Kat down the block to the street where he'd left the car. They stowed their purchases in the trunk, climbed into the car and headed for the grocery store at the far end of town.

"Well? Are you going to tell me what it is Frank's reformatting?" Kat leaned casually against the door as Seamus negotiated the narrow streets.

"Frank thinks I'm gay. It didn't bother him a bit to run into me in a bookstore in Guerneville, but it really threw him for a loop when a very pregnant, gorgeous blonde stepped into the picture and called me 'darling.'"

"I see. Blew your cover, did I?"

"Big time." He turned and smiled at her.

She didn't return his smile. "You're not, are you? Gay?"

He didn't answer for a moment, uncertain how to explain himself.

"A simple 'no' would suffice." Now Kat was the one who sounded uncertain. He couldn't blame her, the way he'd ached to hold her one moment, then pushed her away the next.

Did his sexuality matter to her? He'd only thought of how much he was attracted to her and how wrong it was. He hadn't really considered she might actually be interested in him.

"No, Kat. I'm not gay. I am very definitely heterosexual." He slowed the Jag, then turned left into the parking lot surrounding a large grocery store. He found a space near the back of the lot and parked under a tree.

"Then why? Why let your agent and even Mrs. Andrews assume you..."

"Hazel, too?" He sighed, wondering how to answer her questions without coming off like a complete idiot. He turned and studied her a moment, noting the flush to her cheeks, the questioning look in her eyes. "A lot of reasons, most of which you won't like, most of them having to do with Riley. He was outgoing and a little crazy, I was shy and withdrawn. We both reacted to our parents' deaths in our own ways. He got wilder, I became quieter. Girls flocked to him, they scared me to death. Unfortunately, if they couldn't have Riley, they wanted me. I was tired of being second best. I didn't know how to deal with my feelings, so it was just easier to let them think I wasn't interested."

Kat grinned broadly. "You've spent a lot of time thinking about this, haven't you? Lots of hours in therapy? You know, flat out on the couch with the shrink asking you to delve deeply into the workings of your tortured soul? Gettin' to know your feminine side?"

Suddenly Seamus saw himself from an entirely new perspective. She was right. He'd spent way too much time self-diagnosing his hang-ups, his longings and desires. He'd been hashing it over like the whole universe depended on his knowing why he did what he did...and all that time Riley'd been out living life to the fullest.

Once again the sassy blonde in his front seat was forcing him to reevaluate his manner of living life versus Riley's...and once again he was finding Riley's approach a lot more sensible.

His short bark of laughter sounded bitter even to Seamus. "No shrink, Kat. I managed to do it all on my own...but you're right. I did spend too much time thinking about it. Face it...what else do you do when you're sitting home alone on a Saturday night? The truth of the matter is, I wasn't ready to get involved with girls when I was young, avoided them to the point my friends tagged me as gay, but since no one seemed to care if I was gay or straight and it ended all the hassles with women, I just let the tag stick. Unfortunately, it made it difficult to find dates when I was finally ready..."

He let the sentence drag, accompanied by what he hoped was a doleful grin.

"I take it you're ready." Kat's eyes darkened to an intense shade of blue, and her voice, soft and breathy, rasped over his senses like a physical entity.

"Oh yeah..." *No! Geez, what the hell am I thinking?* He swallowed, caught his breath, smiled brightly in her direction. "Yeah, one of these days I'll meet someone willing to put up with all my hang-ups. Now that Frank suspects I'm as hetero as he is, he'll be parading every single woman he knows past my door. At least he will once he figures out where you fit in the scheme of things. C'mon. Let's stock up and get back to the cabin."

Kat threw back her head and laughed. "You really are something, Seamus O'Rourke." She opened the door and swung her legs out, then glanced back over her shoulder and grinned at him. "When you figure out what that is, let me know, okay?"

He grunted, climbed out of the Jag and slammed the door. Kat was still laughing at him when he hauled her to her feet and led her into the grocery store.

"THAT'S NOT ACCEPTABLE! I know the Russian River is a long river, you idiot! There are not that many resort areas. It should not be difficult to find a couple as distinctive as Seamus O'Rourke and Kathleen Malone. They couldn't blend into a crowd if their lives depended on it."

He chuckled, laughing at his own wit. Of course their lives depended on it. He'd see to that.

"Find them!"

He slammed the phone down and felt the rush, the power within surging through his veins, filling his muscles with an almost superhuman strength. Suddenly he looked around, realized he was standing inside a phone booth and laughed out loud.

He was invincible. He had the power. He was Superman.

Chapter Seven

KAT SHUFFLED THE DECK one more time, then dropped the cards in a pile on the kitchen table. "I can't do it, Seamus. I cannot play another game of cards, I don't want to even look at the chess board, and if you suggest we take one more leisurely stroll down the drive and back in this godawful rain, I'll bean you with your walking stick."

She glared at him, daring him to disagree.

"You could always read a book."

"I've read all my books. Every damned one. I've even read your dumb cop stories." She leaned forward, her blue eyes flashing, and jabbed the air between them with her finger.

He thought of his seventh grade math teacher, the one he'd had such a terrible crush on. She'd made her point in exactly the same way.

Seamus bit his lips to keep from grinning. He figured Kat wasn't in the mood for a nostalgic walk down memory lane any more than she was for a walk down the hill and up again.

"Those authors haven't got a clue what a real cop's life is like. There is no glamour in stakeouts, undercover work is usually scary and exhausting, and I can count on the fingers of one hand the number of times I've actually had to fire a weapon. If I shot as many perps as those storybook cops, I'd spend the rest of my life writing reports and or explaining myself to the captain, the media and half a dozen lawyers out for my throat!"

"Then why do you do it?" He reached out and grabbed her finger, momentarily holding it immobile. Kat jerked it out of his grasp.

"Do what?"

"Why did you choose to be an agent? Why not a..." He paused. "Why not a truck driver?"

"I hate driving. It's boring."

"How about a school teacher? You said you like kids."

"Low pay, long hours and it's too political." She jabbed her finger at him once more. Seamus decided she was a lot cuter than his math teacher.

"Do you know you can't even hug your students now if they really need a hug? You can get fired for 'inappropriate contact.' That would drive me nuts."

"Did any of your teachers ever hug you?" He tried to imagine Kat as a little girl, hurting enough to be needy. He thought of her now, of everything she held inside.

If only she'd recognize she needed him.

"Oh, yeah." Kat's smile was wistful. "I was forever in need of hugging. I didn't get it at home, but thank goodness I had teachers who cared enough to recognize what I craved...who cared and had the freedom to act. It would kill me to know a child needed that human touch and not be able to give it. No, I could never be a teacher, not in today's society."

Seamus stared at her a moment, then slapped his palm on the table. "I've got it. You could've been a secretary?" *Now that was pushing it!*

"Yeah, right." She mimicked a prissy voice. "Yes, sir, I'll make that appointment, sir. And you'd like coffee with that? Of course. Right away. I'll pick up your cleaning on my lunch hour. Shine your shoes? Whatever you want." She made a face. "Not in this lifetime, buddy."

"A chef then?"

"I can't cook."

"Won't argue with that." She'd proved that with her few feeble attempts at cooking dinner over the past few weeks. He paused, put a finger to his lips in thought, thoroughly enjoying this game of words that was telling him so much about Kathleen. For all the time they'd been together, he hardly knew her. He just hadn't known where to start.

"I know," he said. "A housewife. You could stay home and make babies. You've got a good start."

He expected a quip, not the look of longing that crossed her face or the subtle withdrawal, as if she'd just pulled the shutters closed on her life.

She stared down at her hands. Her fingers spread across the surface of the table for a moment, then curled into fists. When she raised her head, her expression was closed, cool. "I think I'd really like to go to town." She looked away, then pushed her chair back from the table. "I want to pick up some more books and a few personal items."

"How do you feel about seeing a doctor?"

"Go back to San Francisco? My doctor there? Do you think it's safe?"

The look of anticipation on her face made him wish it was. He knew better. Knew Sandy Wilson had reported sightings of someone resembling Tim Anderson near Seamus's home. He hadn't told Kat because he hadn't wanted to worry her.

"No," he said. "I don't think it's safe to go anywhere near the city yet until we know where your buddy Anderson is. I've got a friend who has an obstetrics practice in Santa Rosa. I was thinking I'd call Sharon, see if she would agree to see you after hours, at least make sure everything's all right with the baby."

Silence filled the space after his sentence.

Finally, Kat struggled to her feet, indignation evident in every cumbersome move she made. "Don't want to take any chances, right, Mr. O'Rourke? Here I thought we'd reached a kind of truce, you working on your writing, me staying out of your way and going nuts, but still a truce. I thought maybe you'd started thinking of me as something other than a means to an end, someone besides a way for you to get that child you're so set on." Her voice cracked and she cleared her throat. "I thought..." She closed her eyes, left the sentence dangling.

"You thought what, Kat?" Seamus fought the urge to jump to his feet, grab her up in his arms and shake the answer out of her. Instead, he gripped the edge of the table with both hands and stared intently into her sparkling, tear-filled eyes.

She blinked, brushed her face with the back of her hand and turned away.

Seamus repeated his question, keeping his voice purposely low. "Kat? What did you think?"

She spun around and glared at him. "None of your damned business. Now are you going to take me to town or do I go by myself?"

Seamus stared back at her, willing Kat to tell him what he hoped she'd almost said. Tension crackled between them, tension and anger and a sense of desperation at all the words unsaid, all the wrong ones spoken. Finally, after an interminable moment in time, Seamus sighed then rose slowly to his feet. "I'll take you to town, but we're going to Santa Rosa and you're going to the doctor. You're eight months pregnant. I know for a fact you should've been under regular medical supervision all along, so don't argue with me."

Kat spun around and stalked out of the kitchen.

Seamus called out to her, sharper than he intended. "Kathleen."

She paused in the doorway, but didn't look at him.

"It's not just the baby I'm worried about, Kat. It's you, too. I don't want anything to happen to you." He moved around the table but stopped just short of touching her. Only inches away, he was aware of her body trembling, of the rigid set of her muscles. He reached out, tentatively, and barely touched her shoulder.

She flinched. Looked away. "Don't touch me. Please. It'll only make it worse."

He jerked his hand back. If her words had been said in anger he might have forced the issue. He might have spun her around the way he wanted, wrapped her in his arms. Grabbed on to her and held her until the trembling stopped.

Her quiet plea stopped him as anger couldn't. Seamus stepped back. He had no choice. He gave her the space she seemed to need so desperately.

"I'll call Sharon. Maybe she can fit you in this afternoon. You'll like her. I've heard she's an excellent obstetrician. It doesn't hurt to be on the safe side."

"I'll be ready in fifteen minutes." Kat slipped quietly out of the kitchen and disappeared into her bedroom.

Seamus stared at the vacant doorway, much too aware of his empty arms, the painful knot in his gut. He'd done it again. It must be a particular talent of mine, he thought. To always say and do exactly the wrong thing.

Someday, maybe he'd get it right.

THE RAIN FELL IN a steady torrent, overflowing the small creeks, turning the long gravel driveway from Seamus's house to the main road into a muddy ribbon bordered by rushing currents from the heavy run-off. The forest seemed darker, the ferns more lush, the humus-rich soil almost black.

Kat stared out the window and concentrated on the fat drops sliding down the glass rather than the silent man sitting so closely beside her. How could she have misjudged him so? These last weeks, they'd settled into a comfortable co-existence. Seamus wrote for about four hours a day, locking himself away in his upstairs bedroom where he kept his computer. He sent his columns off to his editor by e-mail, handled his other business affairs and communication, worked on a book he refused to discuss, then put his work away by noon.

Kat had used those quiet hours to teach herself to crochet, finding an unexpected pleasure in the repetitious work. Amazingly, the tangle of pale yellow yarn she'd started with was fast becoming a warm little blanket.

With each loop and knot, her confidence grew.

With each passing day, her love for her baby deepened.

She and Seamus spent the afternoons taking quiet walks when weather permitted, or like today, playing cards or board games. Seamus knew as much about the flora and fauna of the coastal redwoods as any science teacher. He'd taught her the names of the flowers and trees and the birds that filled the forest around his home.

She'd learned little about Seamus. He talked easily about politics and plants, his love of cooking and even his columns, but never discussed his personal life even when Kat had tried to tease him into it. He rarely mentioned his childhood and absolutely refused to say a word about the book he was writing.

More telling, neither one of them ever mentioned the baby. *It's like the proverbial elephant in the parlor in more ways than one.*

Kat blinked back tears. It was her own damned fault. She'd let herself dream, creating a fantasy world with each loop of her crochet hook.

Stupid idea, Malone. Seamus O'Rourke had no more interest in a street-smart field agent than she did in an uptight writer. Who was she kidding with her daydreams of the two of them settling down together and making a real home for the baby?

Seamus had been an absolute gentleman—polite, entertaining, and as aloof as he could possibly be. It was obvious he wanted their relationship to stay as impersonal as it could with the two of them living under the same roof.

Makes it easier to try and take you away from me. At least Seamus meant her baby no harm. Kat ran her hand over her taut stomach, more aware than ever of the life growing inside. She felt a connection so intense it frightened her, a vulnerability from a love stronger than she'd ever imagined possible.

She hadn't truly understood the power of her stalker's threat. Not at first. Now fear hung over her every movement. She knew Seamus hoped to take her child and raise it as his own, but there was someone else out there, someone who wanted to kill for the sheer pleasure of killing.

An involuntary shudder wracked her body. She wrapped her arms around herself.

"Are you okay?"

She snapped her head around and looked directly into Seamus's eyes.

She'd been so lost in her fears, she'd almost forgotten him! Kat coughed, cleared her throat, then merely nodded.

"If you're cold, I can turn up the heat, or there's a blanket in the back seat."

"I'm fine." Kat watched as he turned his attention back to the rain-swept road. "The storm seems to be letting up a bit," she said. Rain was no longer falling in sheets, but the steady drizzle appeared to have settled in for the long haul.

"It's supposed to blow over this afternoon, but there's another front due in later tonight." Seamus glanced in her direction, then back at the road. He stopped the car at the end of the drive, looked both ways, then slowly pulled out onto the highway. "We'll get groceries and stock up on batteries in case the power goes out or the river floods. If this storm is as big as they're saying, we could have some flooding and not be able to get out for a few days."

"I guess I'd better stock up on plenty to read."

Seamus returned her brief smile, then turned his attention back to his driving.

IT WAS JUST AS well he hadn't found them. Let them become complacent and soon enough they would come to him, bringing the baby with them. The longer he waited, the more time she'd have to bond with the child. The more power he would draw from the killing.

He rubbed his thumbs across the tips of his fingers, relishing the death. He imagined her face, her terror when she realized he'd won, and the image sent the power surging through him.

He'd never realized how addictive the power would become. Addictive enough to take him on a most enjoyable journey home.

Memories...such wonderful, wonderful memories...thanks for the memories...he swayed with the silent tune, hearing the applause of the ages.

The screams. He'd actually been sorry when the screaming stopped....

He glanced down at the telephone. Should he call off the hunt? No. This one owed him. Let him waste his time.

While the one who owed him hunted, he could wait. He'd learned patience over the years...patience and endurance...and subterfuge. He smiled, brushing his fingers lightly over the phone.

It rang when he touched it. Still smiling, he took the call.

THE DOOR CLOSED SOFTLY as Sharon Rucker let herself out of the examining room. As much as she hated to admit it, Kat was glad Seamus had insisted on a visit to the doctor. It was a relief to know that everything was going well, the baby sounded perfectly healthy and Kat was in excellent shape.

Maybe all those long walks Seamus insisted on had been a good idea after all.

Kat shrugged out of the cotton hospital gown and gathered her clothes. The doctor hadn't been anything like Kat had expected. Oh, she'd been highly professional and obviously well qualified, but she'd known Seamus and Riley since they'd been children growing up together in the same San Francisco neighborhood. She'd laughed with Kat and told stories about the two boys, of the predicaments Riley'd gotten into, of Seamus's often futile attempts to bail his brother out. Kat realized it was the first time she'd ever spoken with anyone who knew the O'Rourke boys before they'd grown so far apart.

Sharon recalled long evenings on the front porch and the almost eerie silent communication between Riley and Seamus. Best of all, as far as Kat was concerned, she remembered a time when Riley and Seamus were each other's staunchest defenders, best friends...most powerful allies.

In spite of the doctor's long history of friendship with the two men, she'd definitely sided with Kat after hearing the convoluted story of her pregnancy by Riley and her odd relationship with Seamus.

Kat wasn't sure why she'd felt comfortable enough with the other woman to talk about such things. She decided it must have something to do with the lack of female companionship.

She hadn't mentioned the stalker, though. Sometimes he didn't seem real. The less Kat discussed him, even with Seamus, the easier it was to pretend he didn't exist.

Of course, she'd long been a master of denial, just like her old partner, Ramsey.

Denial is not a river in Egypt. How often had they thrown that stupid quip at each other?

Missing Ramsey and his silly teasing, missing Rose, his wife and her closest friend and wishing she could just sit down and spend time talking girl talk with a woman who actually knew her, brought a sting of tears to Kat's eyes.

Lord but she missed boring and normal and, as much as she knew her pregnancy and her stalker made it impossible, she missed her job and her friends.

Thank goodness for Seamus.

For now anyway.

If only... No! Kat Malone goes it alone.

Except, for the first time in her life, Kat Malone had to admit going it alone was, well...*lonely.*

She wiped her sleeve across her eyes, slipped her feet into

sandals, quickly ran a brush through her hair and stepped out of the examining room. She heard Seamus and Sharon laughing about something. Their voices carried from the waiting room. She caught Riley's name and the sound of more laughter.

Kat stood there a moment, listening. Seamus sounded relaxed as she'd not heard him in weeks, reminiscing with his old friend, laughing. It was hard to imagine him doing anything to hurt her, but when she'd told Dr. Rucker of Seamus's plans to try and get custody of her child, the doctor seemed to understand.

Her quiet words remained seared into Kat's mind.

"Seamus has always been a man who needs family, yet he's lost all of the family he ever had. First his parents, then his grandmother, now Riley. There was a lot of anger between them, but the love they shared was absolutely fierce and more powerful than the hate. He needs to fall in love and start his own family, but he's afraid of the risk, afraid of falling in love and losing that person, too. He probably sees Riley's baby as his chance for a child without risking his heart with a woman...and a way to hold on to the best of his brother."

Then she'd looked at Kat and smiled, as if waiting for confirmation of something brewing between her and Seamus.

"No," she'd said. "He looks at me and sees that I was Riley's. I'm not good enough for him."

Damn! How pathetic I sounded.

How true.

The doctor hadn't even argued with her. She'd patted Kat on the shoulder and left her alone to dress.

Dress and realize just how much was lacking in her dismal life.

Never realized just how good you were at feeling sorry for yourself, did you, Malone? You're pathetic...absolutely pathetic.

"Has to be the hormones," she'd muttered, fully aware she had been perfectly capable of screwing up her life even without the added stew of pregnancy-induced chemicals simmering in her bloodstream.

She'd taken one last glance in the mirror and fluffed her hair with her fingers, even blown herself a kiss. "It's good to have a skill," she'd said, laughing at her atypical bout of self-pity.

Now, here she stood, eavesdropping.

Pathetic.

"But at least you're consistent, Malone." She was still grinning broadly when she walked into the waiting room.

Seamus looked up and returned her smile.

The man obviously didn't have a clue what she found so funny.

"How come you didn't ask Sharon to tell you the baby's sex?" He spread his palms wide in question. "She won't tell me...said you didn't want to know."

"That's right. There needs to be some mystery in everyone's life."

Seamus's dry answer surprised her. "I think we've got more than our share of mystery, don't you?"

The doctor nodded in silent agreement. Obviously, he'd explained at least some of their troubles.

"I've told Sharon about our stalker." He held his hand out to Kat.

Startled by the unexpected intimacy, she took his outstretched hand and sat next to him. "I wasn't sure if you wanted me to say anything or not," she said.

Seamus gently squeezed her fingers. "The creep knows you're pregnant. The fact I own property up here isn't a secret. The guy's always found you before and I was afraid he might think of checking with obstetricians in the area. I wanted Sharon to be aware. Forewarned is..."

"You're right." She turned to Sharon. "I hope we haven't put you in any danger. I didn't even think..."

"Don't worry about a thing. I'm not putting this visit on the books and I'll keep your medical history in my office, under a number and not a name. I sent my staff home early today, so as far as they're concerned, this visit and any future ones, just won't exist."

THEY PICKED UP GROCERIES at a huge market in Santa Rosa, then stopped by a shopping mall to check out the bookstores. While Seamus headed straight for the action and adventure books, Kat browsed through the romance section. She picked up first one, then another, and realized the romantic suspense she usually enjoyed wasn't nearly as appealing any more.

Not while her own life was filled with more than enough suspense and tension.

She found a couple of new books by an author known for her quirky sense of humor, then realized she'd wandered into an area displaying books on infancy and child care.

"Guess it's time to do my homework, eh, little guy?" She glanced at her growing middle, sighed and picked up the closest book. What she didn't know about babies could fill an entire mall.

She checked the index, aware of an odd sense of unease, a tightening in her chest.

The feeling someone was watching?

She glanced around and saw nothing but shelves and browsing customers. Seamus glanced up from the far side of the store, smiled, waved, and went back to his shopping.

Must be the thought of actually having *this baby that's giving me the shivers.* The visit to the doctor had triggered the realization they were talking weeks now, not months.

The brief discussion they'd had about labor, about whether or not Seamus wanted to be in the delivery room.

Dr. Rucker's surprise at Kat's resounding "No way!" which of course led to the discussion of the actual parentage of the baby, of Seamus's odd relationship to Kat and his brother's child.

The feeling increased. The familiar sense of impending *something* Kat often felt in the midst of danger. Still holding the book open, she surreptitiously glanced about her, spying nothing out of order.

Couples shopped together, children giggled over in one corner and a harried mother tried to quiet them. A large number of teenaged boys hung out in an area designated for video games.

A typical, busy day in the bookstore. So why did the hair on the back of her neck tickle her nape, why did her palms and underarms suddenly feel damp, her spine as if something crawled and skittered across the nerves?

She glanced back toward Seamus but his back was to her. Growing more frantic by the second, Kat no longer made a pretense of looking at the open book in her hands.

Who watched? Someone...someone very close, someone threatening. Someone frighteningly familiar.

She took a deep breath, swallowed. Her eyes darted from side to side then suddenly her gaze was drawn upward, to a corner of the bookstore just over the doorway...to her own reflection in the large, round security mirror that took a wide-angle view of the entire store.

To the feral eyes of Tim Anderson. Watching. Catching her gaze. Holding her immobile for one timeless second.

Smiling at her, a smile of pure, unadulterated evil.

She gasped, spun around to search the room, spotted Seamus looking back at her with a questioning expression on his face. She turned again, saw her own wide-eyed face staring back at her from the mirror.

Where Tim Anderson had stood there was a young mother holding a book out to her fussing child.

Kat dropped her armload of books to the floor and moved as quickly as her gravid body would allow.

"Kat? Kathleen?" Kat and Seamus reached the doorway at the same time. He grabbed her by the shoulder, both halting and supporting her. "What the hell...?"

"He was here." She took a deep breath, trying to still the tremors that wracked her body. "Tim Anderson. I had a feeling I was being watched, just the weirdest sense of danger and when I looked into the security mirror he was staring at me. The bastard actually *smiled* at me. *Shit!* I can't believe he got away!"

"You're sure it was him?"

"Of co..." She thought about it a moment, wondering. It had been almost a year since she'd last seen him, during a court appearance. There was nothing remarkable about him, nothing to make his face stand out.

"He looks like a little weasel." She stepped out into the mall and looked both ways. Crowds surged by in all directions. He could be anywhere. "He was wearing a white shirt and a dark brown leather coat," she added. "His hair is fairly short...it's brown, and he's got a dumb little mustache and goatee."

"Like that man over there?" Seamus pointed to the far side of the store, to the action and adventure section where he'd been shopping.

Kat watched as a dark-haired man wearing a white shirt and brown leather jacket studied the shelves. He had the typical facial hair popular with some men. The young mother, child in tow, stepped up to him and handed him both the child's hand and a book. Laughing, the three of them headed toward the checkout stand.

Maybe? She tried to recall the image. The mirror was curved, the images distorted. This man looked enough like... *Oh damn...it had to have been him.*

"I am so embarrassed." She shook her head. Relief poured through her. "I was so certain it was Anderson. Guess I'm just jumpy. Must have been that guy."

Seamus took her arm and led her back to where she'd dropped her pile of books. "He doesn't look too threatening, but I'm glad you're not getting complacent, either." He knelt down to retrieve her books.

"Thank you, Seamus."

"For what?"

"For not laughing at me. I feel like such a dope."

The look he gave her made Kathleen feel anything but dopey. In fact, it curled her toes.

He stood up, reached out, stroked her hair, paused as if to speak, then shook his head.

"C'mon," he said. "Let's pay for these and head home."

MUCH TOO CLOSE, BUT worth the risk. Though if she'd actually caught the idiot it could have ruined everything! At least now he knew his suspicions were correct. It would be easy enough to find O'Rourke's so-called hidden cabin, a matter of public records.

So, the bitch looked ready to deliver at any time? He stared at his hands, wondering how he would control the power over the next few weeks. There was no help for him at home...not any more. Of course, there would always be the memories.

He nodded his head for a moment, keeping time with remembered screams. Good, but not enough. Not any more.

If only...that was it! He grinned, rubbed his hands together, practically laughed aloud.

A tiny little reign of terror...that would satisfy the power, satisfy his growing needs...for now.

It would prepare him. Prepare all of them.

The heat rushed through his veins, filled him with pleasure. He stroked himself through the light fabric of his pants, stopped just before the moment of completion.

He reveled in his discomfort. Celebrated the power. It was almost time.

SEAMUS STIRRED THE FIRE and added another log. He glanced back over his shoulder at Kathleen. She'd been unusually quiet on the way home. *Tired?* Possibly, but he thought it must be more.

She'd been terrified this afternoon, so certain she'd seen her stalker. Her fear had transferred itself to Seamus. It was a potent reminder he'd let his guard down, again, after so many trouble-free weeks.

Sandy hadn't offered much help when Seamus called to check the status of the investigation. Anderson had disappeared again. He could be anywhere.

In a bookstore in Santa Rosa?

A white shirt and brown leather coat wasn't an unusual outfit under any circumstances.

What if Kat really had spotted Anderson?

If that was the case, her stalker would find them. The location of Seamus's cabin was certainly no secret. The fact his writing had made him a minor celebrity, even this far from San Francisco, meant any number of people could give directions to the private drive leading to his property.

Seamus stood up, brushed the dust from his hands and walked across the room to the large sliding glass door. It wouldn't hurt to check the locks throughout the cabin, but he didn't want to frighten Kat.

She had enough on her mind.

The door was locked, dead bolts in place, the alarm active. Seamus originally kept it armed day and night, resetting it whenever they went in or out of the cabin. It would warn them if any doors or windows were opened or if someone walked across the deck.

He'd grown lax in recent days. This was not a time for carelessness.

Rain lashed the heavy tempered glass, sparkling like golden crystal shards in the reflection from the outdoor security light. Seamus drew the curtains closed against the storm.

Usually the curtains remained open. There were no neighbors, no nearby public roads. Both he and Kathleen enjoyed the view of the forest, the beauty of the spring storms.

These were not usual circumstances. The forest was dark and dense, home to everything from deer and wild pigs to the occasional mountain lion.

It could easily hide a man—especially one who wanted to remain hidden.

It wouldn't hurt to check the rest of the doors and windows while he was up. Seamus glanced at the book Kat balanced on her rounded mid-section as he passed by her chair. Whatever the title, it was open to a beautiful black and white photo of a woman in the advanced stages of pregnancy, her belly swollen, her breasts enlarged with dark nipples and the shadow of veins visible under the skin.

The model's hands encircled her stomach, the fingers supporting the weight of the growing baby. Seamus had noticed Kat in a similar pose in recent days.

Kat's breasts were much bigger as well. He knew she wore a bra now to support their weight, but they must be every bit as large as the woman's in the photo. His mouth went dry at the image in the book, at the thought of the flesh and blood woman in front of him. Kathleen could be the model now. Full with child, her body literally ripening day by day.

He imagined her naked, her breasts unbound, the nipples stretched darkly smooth and his body reacted as it never had before.

She is so lovely.

He'd thought she was beautiful from the beginning. Now, in the abundance of her final weeks of pregnancy, she took his breath.

Kat looked up, caught his gaze, blushed and turned away.

Seamus had never seen her blush, had never noticed the least sign of self-consciousness over her changing body.

But then she'd probably never caught him gazing at her with such unbridled lust before, either.

Not that it hasn't happened.

He'd been careful to keep his feelings hidden. Still, she had to know how he felt, didn't she?

How can she, when you're not sure what you want yourself. Idiot!

He reached out and touched her chin, turned her face to his. He had to clear his throat before he could make a sound, and when he spoke it could have been a complete stranger voicing his words. "I assume you're even more beautiful than the woman in the photo, Kat." He smiled, hoping to mask the sudden intensity of his feelings. "Of course, you realize I'm relying entirely on imagination."

She returned his gaze for a long moment, as if trying to decipher the reason for such a personal observation. They had tip-toed around each other for so many weeks now keeping their relationship impersonal and as light as the situation allowed.

Even Seamus wasn't certain why he'd said the words he'd been thinking for so long. Would she realize it was an invitation, a desperate request from a man who was almost, but not quite certain, what he wanted?

Kat licked her lips, then shook her head, dislodging the light touch of his fingertips, unobtrusively backing away from Seamus. Her soft hair, longer now, brushed his fingers. He moved his hand away, but not before he felt the contact all the way to his heart.

She smiled brightly, diffusing the tension with her light laughter.

"Your imagination must be pretty good if you get an image like that while looking at me in this." She swept her hand out to draw attention to the loosely flowing tie-dyed dress she practically lived in now her clothes had grown so tight.

"Do you want the truth, Seamus? I feel like a beached whale in tie-dye. A walrus in heat is more graceful than I am right now and I can't wait to get my old body back. I hate to think how hard it's going to be to lose almost forty pounds!"

She pushed her hair back out of her eyes and laughed again, but she didn't make eye contact and her laughter was unconvincing. Obviously his comment had made her uncomfortable.

"I have indigestion after every meal, I have to pee at least twenty times a day and if this baby isn't a boy born with soccer cleats on, I'll be absolutely shocked. Pregnancy is not my idea of fun. If you think this body's beautiful, you are one sick puppy."

So much for speaking his mind.

She patted his hand with almost maternal affection. "But thanks anyway for the compliment. I'm sure you meant well."

She flashed him a brief smile then went back to her book. The first thing she did was turn the page, hiding the photo and effectively dismissing Seamus.

She couldn't have made her point more clearly. Keep it light. Keep it simple. But most of all, keep it impersonal.

Sighing, Seamus turned away to finish checking the locks.

Chapter Eight

"WE ALL KNOW WE'RE supposed to have April showers, but hasn't anyone told Mother Nature it's May?" Tense and edgy after weeks of almost continual rain, Kat felt like crying as she glared out the window.

Her back hurt, her feet were swollen and she'd progressed from looking like she'd swallowed a basketball to having a belly that would make her competitive in a giant pumpkin contest.

She'd never felt uglier or more ungainly in her entire life. Or more prone to mildew. She stretched the soft yellow baby blanket she'd finally finished and pulled it a little tighter around her shoulders, more for comfort than for warmth.

She was *not* pleased with her life right now, nor was she dealing well with the infernal, eternally falling rain.

"This is nothing. I recall one Memorial Day weekend we had over five inches." Seamus looked up from his laptop as he spoke. "The river flooded and they had to rescue a number of stranded people by helicopter." He smiled brightly then went back to work on whatever he was writing.

"Thank you so very much for that bit of good cheer." Kat turned her attention back to the forest beyond, staring blankly at moss covered trees shrouded in heavy rain.

"You're welcome."

She ignored his snide comment.

All they'd done was snipe and insult and goad one another for what seemed like forever. Actually, it hadn't quite been forever...it hadn't gotten really bad until Seamus had said... *Damn!*

Seamus's comment repeated itself over and over in her mind. "*I assume you're even more beautiful than the woman in the photo, Kat.*"

Why had he said it? She didn't think he'd been making fun of her...his sense of humor was never cruel. Could he possibly care for her as something more than a means to an end? He couldn't possibly be attracted to her, not the way she looked now...could he? He'd stopped mentioning the fact he wanted the baby, but she knew it was only a matter of time.

If only he hadn't said anything, hadn't hinted there might be...no. He'd merely been trying to make her feel better about herself. He couldn't possibly have meant anything else when he'd said she was beautiful.

Sometimes, though, she was almost certain she caught him watching her.

Probably afraid the kid's gonna fall out on the floor.

She had a sinking suspicion childbirth wouldn't be quite that simple.

Seamus had been studying the baby books as if his life depended on it. Kat hated to admit that, if worse came to worst and the storms continued, both her life and her baby's actually could depend on whatever knowledge he gained.

She shuddered, wrapped the blanket even tighter about her, then turned her back on the rain.

AS UNOBTRUSIVELY AS HE could, Seamus watched Kat turn away from the window and wander across the room to the old rocker by the fire. She'd taken that chair as her own and he'd grown fond of observing her there, imagining her with their child in her arms.

It *was* their child, in no uncertain terms. He'd come to the realization he could never separate mother and baby, any more than he could allow Kathleen to step out of his life, but he felt a connection to Riley's unborn child as if Seamus's own seed had given it life.

He had no idea how to convince Kathleen to stay. He'd thought of asking her to marry him but feared she'd see it as a ploy to gain custody. He knew she could never love him. She still saw Riley when she looked at Seamus.

How can I blame her? Every time I look in the mirror, I see Riley's image.

"Did you hear something?"

Seamus shifted around in his chair so that he could see Kat better. "What?" he asked. "I didn't hear anything."

"Sounded like something hit the side of the house." She pointed toward the back of the room where a door led to a small garden beyond the deck.

"Stay put and I'll take a look. Probably just a branch." Seamus glanced through the stained glass window on the door before turning off the alarm and opening the door. Nothing but rain and mud and more rain. One of the potted plants Kathleen had set out on the deck lay on its side. Seamus ran out and righted it. He managed to get thoroughly soaked in the process.

"Must have been a raccoon." He turned to race back into the

house when he spotted it. A muddy footprint on the redwood deck, a long streak melting away in the rain, as if someone had lost their footing on the slick surface.

Not his footprint, obviously not Kat's. Seamus glanced quickly about, but nothing caught his attention in the dusky late afternoon light. He turned and reached for the door. His breath caught.

A muddy handprint, fingers splayed across the roughhewn wall, met him at eye level. Positioned perfectly for someone trying to catch himself from falling.

He quickly slipped into the house and carefully locked the door behind him. He reset the alarm. "Someone's been here." He kept his voice low, but Kat obviously understood. She stood awkwardly and waddled across the room to pull the drawstring on the drapes. Seamus quickly checked all the doors and locks on the ground floor.

"Stay put," he said. "I'm going to double check the windows upstairs and the door to the deck from the master bedroom."

Kat slipped into her bedroom as quickly as she could and grabbed the Ruger out from under the mattress. At just over two pounds, the familiar weight of the automatic pistol gave her an instant sense of confidence. No way in hell would the shoulder holster fit over her belly, but she felt safer with the heavy gun in her hand.

Seamus tapped lightly on her bedroom door, then slipped into the room, shutting the door behind him. He glanced briefly at the weapon and nodded. "I was hoping you'd thought to bring that damned thing," he said.

"What did you see?" Kat felt the familiar shiver of excitement, the sense of finally knowing the stalker was close by. Now, maybe, after so many months, the waiting would come to an end.

"Footprint on the deck, not mine. The sound you heard was someone slipping, catching himself against the wall. There's a muddy handprint beside the door." He smiled at Kat and shook his head. "You know, it's almost a relief to finally know where the guy is."

"We don't really know." Kat nodded in the direction of the window, now tightly covered with both shades and blinds. She reached behind Seamus and flicked off the light. "He could be anywhere out there, but he knows exactly where we are in here. C'mon. Let's shut all the lights off and find ourselves a spot where we can wait him out."

Seamus didn't question her and for that alone Kat was thankful. So often her male counterparts on the job had tried to second-guess her decisions. Seamus easily accepted the fact she knew what she was about. He moved ahead of her into the front room and hit the main switch on the wall near the front door.

The room was plunged into almost total darkness, other than the pale glimmer from a single skylight over the sloped kitchen ceiling. The approaching darkness outside meant even that light would quickly fade. Seamus took Kat's arm and guided her to the couch near the fireplace. She sat down with the gun still firmly clasped in her right hand, resting on her abdomen.

The juxtaposition of a deadly automatic pistol atop her growing baby disturbed her. She unobtrusively slid her hand to her side and tucked the pistol against her leg.

"I already turned off the lights upstairs and called Sandy Wilson. He's going to contact the local sheriff's department. We should have someone up here before too long." Seamus sat next to Kat and pushed her hair back from her eyes. It was the first time he'd really touched her, truly looked at her, for weeks now.

The contact sent a shiver coursing down her spine, a sense she equated as much with fear as excitement. She turned her head and his hand dropped away. "I feel as if we should be hiding somewhere, just in case..."

"I know. So do I, but the doors are sturdy and there's double-paned glass on all the windows. If he breaks in, we'll hear him. I'm just wondering why we didn't hear the alarm when he stepped on the deck. I changed the settings after the raccoons tripped it the other night...maybe they're set too high." He rubbed Kathleen's fingers in both his hands. "It shouldn't be too much longer before the sheriff gets up here." Seamus nodded in the direction of the hidden pistol. "I trust you know how to shoot that thing?"

Kat heard the humor in his voice. "Damn straight. Do you?"

"You're gonna laugh, but I've never even touched a gun. Wouldn't know what to do with it."

"It's not something worth laughing about." Kat lifted the heavy weapon and placed it in Seamus's open palm. He grunted, acknowledging its weight. "Don't worry, the safety's on."

She glanced up and caught the look of distaste on his face as he stared at the gun in his hand. *What's going through his mind?* So much of what Seamus thought remained shuttered behind those dark lashes of his. Did her ease with a firearm make her even more unacceptable as a mother to Riley's child?

After a moment's hesitation, Seamus turned the dull blue pistol over in his hands, exploring it. "How many bullets does it hold?"

Kat took the weapon back from him, flipped the magazine catch and slipped the full clip out of the gun. "It holds ten cartridges. I've never had to empty a clip, if that's what you're wondering." She slipped the clip back into the Ruger. "If you need to use it, you flip this lever here and that takes the safety off. Then it's just point and shoot." She demonstrated releasing the safety then holding the gun out in front of her with both hands. "It's heavy, over two pounds, so even a big tough guy like you would do better to hold it with two hands."

Grinning, she reset the safety and handed the weapon to Seamus. He quickly handed it back. "I'll bow to your expertise," he said. "Damned thing makes me nervous but, like I said, I'm really glad you brought it." He frowned. "Where was it anyway? I don't recall you carrying it in."

"That's because *you* carried it in. I wrapped it in my nightgown and stuffed it in my carryall."

"I'll never see that nightgown in quite the same light again."

They both chuckled, then held their breath. The low rumble of a car coming up the drive crept into the silence.

FEAR HAD A LIFE of its own—much the same as the power. Keeping them afraid would be easy now. They knew he had discovered their hiding place, knew their secret was no longer safe.

Would they run again? No. Her time was too close. He felt it much in the manner of the power. She would be his.

Just a little longer. The bitch was so close to delivery, big and fat and ugly, so ungainly she'd never be able to get away.

He laughed, imagining completion. Then the laughter stilled.

When she was gone, when the child lay dead beside her...what then?

Long seconds passed while he contemplated the finish. What would keep the power alive then?

A car passed by, slowly, the rumble of the quiet engine reminding him the bitch wasn't the only one out there.

Others waited. Others who might feed the power every bit as well.

Later. He'd worry about that later. Right now there was one more minor success to savor.

THE POUNDING ON THE front door did more than rattle the windows. It rattled Kat's nerves as well.

"Mr. O'Rourke? Sheriff's department." Seamus had the alarm off and the door open within seconds. A large uniformed deputy wiped his feet on the mat and stepped quickly into the foyer. He nodded a silent greeting to Kat and spoke quietly. "Before you switch on the lights, ma'am, can you open the back door and let my partner inside?"

Kat stuck the Ruger between the cushions on the couch and quickly moved to obey the whispered command as the deputy turned to Seamus and introduced himself in a louder voice. She slipped the deadbolt on the door and opened it. The roaring downpour and lashing wind outside muffled the sound of the men's voices. An attractive female sheriff's deputy, as tall as Kat and as dark as Kat was light, stepped quickly into the kitchen. She tugged a short leash, drawing a large German Shepherd through the door behind her.

Water poured off the woman's cap and puddled on the tile floor. The dog started to shake itself but his master's quick hand to the back of his neck halted the animal's instinctive reaction. He sat obediently while Kat quickly flipped on the kitchen light and grabbed a stack of towels. She handed them to the dripping deputy.

"Let me guess," she said, laughing in spite of the situation and nodding in the direction of the deputy sheriff talking to Seamus. "He's the senior partner so you got to hike up the hill in the rain."

"You got it. 'Tis the lot of women everywhere." The woman laughed as she grabbed one of the offered towels, scrubbed her face dry then knelt to towel off the patient dog. "I'm Toni Juárez," she said, holding her hand out to Kat. "Of course he neglected to tell me there'd be two streams to cross from the point where he dropped me off. That was *after* instructing me not to use the flashlight."

"Typical male. My partner would've pulled a similar stunt, I'm sure."

"The big guy in there? He's law enforcement?"

Kat turned to look at Seamus, still deep in discussion with the deputy sheriff. "His brother was FBI but Seamus is...well, not." Let's just leave it at that, she thought. How could anyone categorize Seamus O'Rourke? "I'm Kat Malone. I was referring to my DOT partner. I work...ah...worked investigations out of the San Francisco office."

"Yeah, Lieutenant Wilson filled us in on your situation. You've really got a nut case after you, haven't you?" Juárez continued drying the huge dog. He grunted and rolled over on his back, his tongue lolling out of his mouth. She laughed and stood up. "Sorry, Buddy, you're enjoying it too much."

"So what's the plan?" Kat motioned the deputy ahead of her and the two of them sat at either end of the couch. Buddy padded along behind and settled quietly on the floor at Toni Juárez's feet.

"John's gonna make a cursory check around the place and then make a production out of leaving. Only he's parking about a quarter mile down the road and waiting to hear from me. Hopefully no one saw me and the beast—" She leaned over to scratch the dog between the ears. "—so we'll just quietly settle in for a bit while you and your man go on about your business."

"He's not my man." Kat wondered why she felt it so important to correct that misconception.

Toni glanced at Kat's obvious pregnancy. "Oh." A thousand questions filled the single word. "I'm sorry. I just..." She glanced toward Seamus again, taking a longer look.

A very appreciative look as far as Kat could tell. Appreciative, speculative and somewhat predatory. Kat stiffened in her seat, well aware of her ungainly body compared to the sleek deputy sitting beside her. It shouldn't matter that another woman would obviously find Seamus attractive. He was an attractive man, one any woman might be interested in.

Unfortunately, she quickly realized it did matter and she didn't like it.

Kat must have broadcast her feelings in some unknown manner, because Toni immediately turned back to the matter at hand. "If your stalker makes a move, Buddy'll know about it before any of us. Won'tcha, big boy?" She scratched his ears again and Buddy moaned in pleasure.

"Honey, I'm going out with Deputy Rodgers, show him where the footprint was. You stay put and keep the doors locked."

Honey? Now where the hell did that come from? "Be careful." Kat wasn't sure what was going on, but she made a point of sounding like the dutiful little lady.

The door clicked solidly behind the men, filling the room with silence punctuated with the sound of Buddy licking at his damp coat. "Can I get some water for your dog?"

"That would be nice. Thank you. Just a bowl on the kitchen floor would be great."

Kat moved awkwardly into the kitchen. Lately, everything she did was done awkwardly. She was more aware than ever of Toni Juárez's lean strength and sleek, attractive form. A form very much like Kat's former self.

She bent uncomfortably to look through a bottom cupboard, wondering if she'd ever see that former self again. After a quick search she grabbed a stainless steel bowl and struggled into an upright position. Lately it seemed as if everything hurt, but her lower back was especially painful today. *Just one more thing to bitch about.*

"When's your due date?"

Toni stood in the doorway, Buddy waited silently beside her.

"A couple of weeks...too damned long, as far as I'm concerned."

"I hear ya. When I had my last one, I went two weeks over. Thought I'd never make it. Never thought I'd look forward to labor, but I couldn't wait to get it over with."

Kat blinked in surprise. "You've got kids?" The woman looked more like an exotic fashion model than a sheriff's deputy; nothing at all like a wife and mother.

"Yeah, three. Two boys and a girl." She dug into her back pocket and pulled out her wallet. Further digging brought out a crisp new photo, the kind department store photographers do. Two dark-haired little boys held a baby girl and smiled at the camera. "That's Juan. He's six years old and a bundle of energy. Carlos is almost four. He's my quiet one. The baby's barely six months old in this picture. Her name's Christina but the boys call her Teetee." She laughed and shook her head. "Her dad and I sure hope that doesn't stick! High school's hard enough without a nickname like that."

"I can't believe you've got three kids." Kat took another close look at the lean, athletic deputy standing there, then studied the photo a moment longer, imagining her child in such a picture. "At least you give me hope. I was beginning to wonder if it was possible to ever get my shape back again." She handed the photo back to Toni.

"It's not easy, but it's cheaper than buying new clothes." Toni stuck the picture back in her wallet. "This your first? You probably feel like a beached whale about now, but you'll be so busy once the baby comes, you'll be surprised how fast the weight comes off. At least it did for me."

Kat began to relax for the first time all afternoon. "Have a seat," she said. "Would you like a cup of hot tea?" She flicked on the gas burner on the stove.

"You're kidding, right? You have to ask?" Toni hung her damp jacket over the back of the kitchen chair, checked to make certain her firearm was in place and shifted her nightstick out of the way to sit in the straight-backed chair. Buddy curled up on the floor beside her.

Kat watched the woman's automatic adjustments to her equipment as she sat down, recalling a time not so long ago when she would have done many of the same things.

Another lifetime ago. She thought of it with a sense of nostalgia, but surprisingly without a sense of loss.

When the water was hot Kat flipped the burner off, carried the tea to the table and sat across from the deputy. Within moments she felt as if she'd known Toni Juárez all of her life.

They talked comfortably about pregnancy and childbirth and Toni's husband, Raul. Kat briefly explained her relationship to Seamus without dwelling on Riley and was relieved when Toni didn't ask for more details. Kat realized, as she had with the obstetrician, the conversation filled a void she hadn't known existed—a need to communicate with another woman what she felt, what she feared.

She could almost forget the reason Toni was here, sitting at the kitchen table drinking a cup of tea, chatting about diaper rash and teething problems.

Almost, but not quite.

There was a tap at the back door. Toni grabbed her teacup and quickly slipped out of the room with Buddy close behind her. The latch turned and Seamus and the big deputy stepped into the kitchen. They stood in the open doorway, talking about the chance their visitor had been Kat's stalker and, if so, whether or not he was still around.

"I think he's long gone," the deputy said. "I can't imagine him hanging around in this storm. You've got my number if you hear or see anything unusual. G'night, ma'am." He turned and doffed his cap in Kat's direction, then shook hands with Seamus. He totally ignored his hidden partner. "Nice meeting you. Take care now."

Seamus closed the door behind him, set the alarm, double checked the dead-bolt and walked across the kitchen. He sat down at the table next to Kat.

A tall Hispanic woman in uniform entered the kitchen, trailed by a huge German Shepherd. Seamus immediately rose to his feet.

"Hello," he said. "I'm Seamus O'Rourke." He shook hands with the attractive deputy. Her grip was as strong as any man's and her attitude matched Kathleen's. Seamus immediately felt at ease with her, as if he'd known her for years. It was a pleasant experience, unusual for him. Meeting new women generally left him feeling awkward and self-conscious. He smiled broadly. "Kat and I really appreciate you staying here."

"No problem. I'm glad we can help. I'm Toni Juárez. This is Buddy."

As she sat down, the huge German Shepherd walked around the table and sniffed Seamus's hand. He stared at Seamus a moment, then back at his master before returning to his spot at the deputy's feet.

"You're lucky. Buddy likes you." Toni laughed. Seamus noticed that, while Kat smiled, she was definitely studying the dynamics between him and the attractive deputy. He thought of his own reaction when Toni's male counterpart had commented on Kat's appearance. Sandy Wilson must have informed him Kat and Seamus weren't married.

"She certainly carries her pregnancy with style," he'd said. "Bet she's really something when she's not expecting."

Seamus figured Kat Malone was something any way you looked at her. The hot flash of jealousy he'd felt when the big deputy made his casual observation though, now that had surprised him. Surprised him so much he'd actually called her honey! *The lonely man's version of staking a claim?*

The look she had on her face right now reminded Seamus of the way he'd reacted. He glanced quickly at Toni and the big dog, then back at Kat.

She couldn't be jealous, could she?

This time when he looked at Toni, he smiled engagingly.

"I hate to imagine the consequences of Buddy not liking me." He winked, consciously risking Kat's ire.

Hoping for it.

"Oh, you don't want to think about it." Toni glanced from Seamus to Kat and back to Seamus. Suddenly her face lit up with a broad smile. She winked back.

Kat abruptly stood up. "Well, if you two are *on guard*, I think I'll go lie down and take a nap. I'm tired and my back hurts." She glared at Seamus, ignored Toni and waddled into her room.

"Mind telling me what all that was about?" Toni grinned and nodded in Kat's direction.

"It was a test actually. Just checking to see how she'd react." He couldn't help the smug grin that split his face.

"Let me give you a word of advice. It's not smart to test a pregnant woman." She laughed, a pleasant throaty sound that brought an answering chuckle from Seamus.

"I guess I'll have to remember that."

"Another thing," Toni added. "She told me you're not her man." She reached down and patted Buddy on the head. The dog grunted. "I find that hard to believe, watching you two interact. I couldn't help but notice she had her eye on you the whole time you were talking to my partner. My opinion, unsolicited, of course, is that she doesn't know what she's talking about."

Seamus gazed at the earnest young woman and wished he could

explain a situation that seemed to grow more confusing as each day passed. "Whether she knows what she's talking about is beside the point, at least until we get this other problem settled. Let's just say, Ms. Juárez, that as usual my timing sucks."

He pushed his chair away from the table and stood up. "I'm going to fix something for dinner. Have you eaten?"

"Not yet."

"Can't hunt bad guys on an empty stomach."

Seamus reached for the door to the refrigerator. He might not know diddly-squat about women, but at least he knew his way around the kitchen.

NO WAY ON GOD'S green earth was she going to actually fall asleep, not with that...that *hussy* out there flirting so outrageously with Seamus. Kat clenched her teeth until her jaw ached. Damn, she was actually beginning to like the woman. Typical...she wasn't any better at judging a woman's character than she was a man's. If Toni Juárez was so happily married why was she trading winks and barbs with Seamus O'Rourke?

Why was Seamus encouraging her?

Hell and Damnation!

Kat punched the pillow and tried to roll over, but like the cumbersome sea lions she and Seamus had watched at the beach one afternoon, she merely flopped in place. Here she lay, big as a house while Seamus sat out in the kitchen with that trim, slim little brunette—*flirting*, for crying out loud!

She wanted to scream in frustration, she wanted to kick something, she wanted... She wanted her old body back, her old life without all the complications of Seamus O'Rourke and his hang-ups, without some nut wanting to kill her, without this pain in her heart that didn't have anything at all to do with Riley.

When had she fallen in love with that jerk Seamus? At what point had the little bit of common sense she still retained disappeared altogether?

At first, when she'd looked at Seamus, she'd seen Riley. When Seamus spoke, she'd compared his words to what she imagined Riley might have said. She hadn't done that for so long now.

When had she stopped seeing and hearing Riley?

When had Seamus become the only man in her life?

"When did I start losing my mind?" Kat pushed herself to a sitting position and leaned against the headboard. Even when she and Riley had been together, she'd still managed to keep her own life intact. Now it felt as if everything lay in shattered pieces around her and she had no idea how to put it back together.

A quiet knock on the door interrupted her thoughts.

"Go away, Seamus." He was the last person she wanted to see.

Toni Juárez opened the door and stepped into the dark room. "Dinner's on, Kat. I think it's gonna be wonderful. You didn't tell me he could cook."

The scent of something delicious wafted into the room. Kat's stomach growled. "I'm not hungry." The last thing she needed was to sit and watch Seamus and Toni make eyes at each other.

Silence stretched between the two women, eventually broken by Toni's deep sigh. "I love my husband to pieces, Kat, but I'll always be a flirt. It doesn't mean a thing. It's just the way I manage in a male-oriented profession. Seamus was merely teasing you."

"Whatever are you talking about? Seamus can flirt with whomever he pleases. He means nothing to me."

Toni quietly closed the door, plunging the room back into total darkness. "I don't believe that for a minute. If I did, I guess I'd have to feel really sorry for Seamus because I think the guy is way in love with you."

"Yeah, right. You've been here what, all of two hours? And in just that amount of time you've figured everything out? I don't think so."

"Honey, I figured it out in the first two seconds. All I had to do was look at the way he watches you...and the way you watch him. Subtlety isn't your strong point or his. Now, c'mon. He's got a wonderful dinner fixed, and like he said, you can't hunt the bad guys on an empty stomach."

Toni laughed and flicked on the light. Kat blinked at the sudden brightness in the room, then focused on the woman standing next to the bed. "You really think he might be in love with me?"

"No think about it. I may be dumb, but I'm not stupid. Just don't let on I gave away his secret. You see, I'm not quite sure he's completely convinced he feels what he thinks he feels, and he sure as hell doesn't think you care a whit about him." She chuckled, a throaty laugh that had Kat laughing along with her.

"It's a guy thing, I guess. They have an answer for everything except what's goin' on in their hearts. Now wash your face and come eat dinner."

Kat slid her legs around and stood up. "You're talking to me like

I'm one of your kids."

"You're acting like one of my kids. Now move it, lady, or no dessert."

Chapter Nine

"GOOD LORD, SEAMUS. THIS is wonderful. If I ate like this every night, I'd look like the Goodyear blimp." Toni sopped up the last of the rich gravy on her plate with a slice of warm sourdough bread.

Kat tapped her fork on the side of her plate. "Uh, Deputy Juárez? Haven't you noticed? I've been eating like this every night and I *do* look like the Goodyear blimp."

"Yeah, but you can't blame it all on my cooking." Seamus held the salad bowl out to Kat. After a moment's hesitation, she grimaced and took the bowl out of his hand. "I don't need this." She proceeded to refill her empty salad plate.

"It's not fattening." Tony passed the container of creamy Ranch dressing. Kat rolled her eyes and laughed.

"Yeah, but this stuff is." She dumped a large spoonful of the dressing on top of her salad. "I think he's doing it to me on purpose."

"I'm innocent. All I did was cook." Seamus held up his white napkin like a flag of truce.

Both women stopped eating and glared at him until they were all laughing.

Dinner had been surprisingly entertaining. Seamus wasn't certain what Toni had said to Kathleen earlier, but the two women had quickly slipped back into their easy banter with Seamus their willing target. Buddy remained on guard, quietly prowling about the ground floor of the cabin and the three of them had relaxed and enjoyed their meal as if this were a mere gathering of friends, not a stakeout for a killer.

In fact, Seamus couldn't recall ever enjoying a meal or an evening as much, in spite of the circumstances or the storm howling with growing anger outside.

He figured that must say something awfully pathetic about him...that he could find pleasure in a situation such as this. A meal shared with a deputy sheriff and her attack dog and the woman he loved...who just happened to be pregnant with his brother's child.

Definitely a soap opera in action.

Seamus was still thinking along those lines when Buddy suddenly paused by the kitchen door and growled. Conversation halted.

Toni immediately moved to the dog's side. "Whatcha got, big

guy?" She patted the dog with one hand and reached for her radio with the other. Buddy stared intently at the back door. The hackles along his back stood straight up. The growl never ceased. The steady rumble reverberated throughout the cabin, vying with the muted roar of the storm.

Toni flipped on her radio and contacted her partner. "I think we've got something, John. North side of the house, possibly the driveway. I'll wait for your signal."

She unholstered her service revolver, then turned and motioned Seamus and Kat to move into the front room, away from the door. Seamus quickly turned off the alarm, then helped Kathleen to her feet and the two of them stepped into the next room, out of the potential line of fire.

"Should I turn off the light?" Seamus reached for the switch but Kat touched his hand, halting the motion.

"Don't do anything to let on we know someone's out there." She turned and sat down on the couch, then reached between the cushions. After a few seconds she pulled her firearm out of its hiding place. "We don't want to compromise anyone's safety."

She set the Ruger on the couch, close to her thigh.

Seamus glanced at the pistol, suddenly aware he no longer found the weapon as distasteful. Whoever stalked Kat, and now him, was most likely heavily armed.

Toni's quiet voice and the crackle of the radio alerted them. Her partner had to be close by. Buddy's growl rose to a higher level and his toenails skittered on the tile floor. It couldn't be easy for Tony to hold the big dog back when he obviously wanted to go after the intruder.

A blast of cold air whooshed through the room as the back door flew open. Buddy snarled and yelped. A single sharp crack of gunfire split the air. Toni shouted a command to Seamus and Kat. "Stay inside!" That was followed by her partner's booming voice, Buddy's frantic barking, and the panic-stricken scream and pleas for help from an unfamiliar voice.

Kat reached for Seamus's hand. He grasped her cold fingers in his own. His muscles quivered with the sudden rush of adrenaline. He had to go out there, had to find out what was happening.

He had to know. Was it their stalker? Was Kathleen finally safe?

The dog's steady barking punctuated the blasts from the storm. Toni's voice rang out, then John's deeper command. More voices, more barking, a series of ferocious growls. Seamus tightened his grip on Kat's hand. Her fingers squeezed his tightly.

Sudden silence, a lull in the wind and a series of sharp yips from the dog brought both Seamus and Kat to their feet. They reached the kitchen in time to see the two sheriff's deputies dragging a third man, his hands tightly cuffed behind him, up the steps, across the deck and into the room.

Buddy heeled close to his master's side, tongue lolling, tail wagging, but the captive's torn pants and blood-stained thigh told a story all their own.

"Recognize this guy?" Deputy John Camden yanked the prisoner's hair at the same time Toni reached out and closed the kitchen door. The man's head jerked back, exposing his face.

Kat shivered. "He's Tim Anderson. One of the hijackers I helped capture last year. The one Sandy Wilson thinks might be stalking me."

"If that's the case, he's the one suspected in the murder of Hazel Andrews. We caught him in the process of rigging what looks like a pipe bomb under the Jag. I'll call for back-up. We'll get the bomb squad up here to dispose of the explosives. I think you two can wait until tomorrow to come in and make a statement."

Anderson glared at Kat, his malevolence an almost physical entity in the crowded room.

Kat hardly recognized the man. His hair hung in wet, greasy tangles about his face, his clothes were filthy and he stank of unwashed flesh and stale cigarettes. Where Anderson had once looked the part of the well-dressed, well-educated but sadistic criminal, he now appeared as disheveled and spaced-out as any druggie on the street.

"I don't want him in here any longer than necessary." Seamus slipped his arm around her waist and Kat leaned into the comforting warmth. "Kathleen's been through more than enough."

"I agree." John Camden jerked Anderson by the arm, propelling him toward the kitchen door. "I just wanted you to ID him, Ms. Malone. I'll go stick him in the back of the squad car until the others arrive." He paused at the door. "Toni, why don't you see if these folks would mind making up a pot of coffee. I think it's gonna be a long night."

IT WAS ALMOST TWO a.m. before the last of the coffee had disappeared, the law enforcement officers had departed, and Seamus could take a moment to check on Kat. Pleading exhaustion, she'd gone to her room around midnight.

Seamus felt oddly unsettled, but it had been an unsettling night. The storm still raged wildly. One of the men from the bomb squad had informed Seamus the Russian River had reached flood stage and the highway through Guerneville was closed. The Bohemian Highway was still open to local traffic, but a couple of trees blocked portions of the road and travel was difficult.

Deputy Camden told him not to worry about coming in right away to make a statement. Since Anderson was already wanted for escape, there was no risk of him being freed on bail. With Kat and Seamus's statement and future testimony as well as the evidence gathered after Hazel Andrew's murder, Tim Anderson would most likely never be free again.

That would be welcome news for Kathleen. In an odd sort of way, though, not so welcome to Seamus. He paused a moment outside her door, thinking over all they had been through over the past months. With her stalker behind bars, what reason did Kathleen have to stay?

Seamus didn't knock. He merely sighed in defeat, opened the bedroom door a crack and looked into the darkened room.

"I'm awake."

Her soft voice startled him. "I thought you'd be sound asleep. I just wanted to make sure you were okay. I was worried about you. It's been a pretty traumatic night." He stepped further into the room, stood awkwardly by the bed for a moment, then sat on the edge.

Kat's fingers found his hand in the dark. "Thanks. I couldn't sleep. I keep thinking how anti-climatic it feels. All these months of fear...it's like I don't know how not to be afraid. Like I can't accept the fact the threat is gone. It feels really weird."

"I know." His fingers tightened around hers. "Part of it's probably exhaustion. When you've had a good night's sleep you'll be able to put everything into perspective."

"I wish I could sleep. I guess I just don't want to be alone. Not tonight." Her sigh ended with a catch. "I bet you're relieved it's over." Her voice had taken on a winsome, questioning quality. "Ever since I barged into your life, I've brought you one problem after another."

"That's not true." He smiled into the silent darkness, listening to the sound of Kat's breathing, the thudding of his own heartbeat. "Scoot over, okay?"

He heard the blankets rustle as Kathleen made room for him on the small bed. Still holding tightly to her hand, he lay down next to her. "Before I forget...I stuck the Ruger in the kitchen drawer with the cooking utensils. Figured it was one thing I didn't want to explain."

"I completely forgot. Guess I left it on the couch. That shows you how well my brain is functioning."

"Like I said, you're tired. I'll stay here with you until you fall asleep. Maybe having someone close by will help."

"Thank you, Seamus. I appreciate it. Are you warm enough? There's an afghan at the foot of the bed. I'm just so tired..." Her voice drifted off. Within moments the even tone of her breathing told him she was asleep.

He lay there, wide awake, soaking up the feel of her, the soft curve of her body next to his. She turned her face against his shoulder and a wisp of soft hair tickled his cheek. He reached down and grabbed the afghan to pull it up. Kat stirred and he covered her as well. She rolled over on her side, molding her buttocks against his belly, snuggling back under his chin to fit perfectly into the contours of his body. Though his clothes and the bedding separated them, Seamus had never imagined such perfection, had never suffered such a surge of arousal.

He wanted her, not merely to bed, but beside him like this until they grew old and crotchety together. He imagined trading barbs and kisses, gibes and hugs, insults and lovemaking with this woman until he was too old to hear and too feeble to care.

No, that time would never come. He would always care, even if she chose to walk out of his life tomorrow. What was there to hold her now? Tim Anderson was under lock and key, so the threat of her stalker no longer existed. She could go off and live her life as she had intended all along.

Seamus knew if she did that he would die. Not physically. He was too damned healthy to die of a broken heart, much too Catholic to take the easy way out. His soul, though, was another matter. His soul would not survive if she left him. He didn't want to imagine life without Kathleen Malone.

His arm slipped around her waist, resting on the rounded curve of her belly, encircling his brother's child. How would he ever convince Kathleen he loved her because he'd fallen for the woman, not because he wanted the baby she carried?

For the first time in his life, Seamus found himself thankful for Riley's indiscretions. Not merely because this growing life was the result, but because Seamus would never have met Kat if not for his brother.

Could Seamus make Kat love him, though, and not his twin? Would she ever look at Seamus and see the man before her, not the man she'd once loved?

Suddenly the mound beneath his arm heaved and bumped as the

baby repositioned itself within Kat's womb. Tears filled Seamus's eyes. He felt a connection to this baby as if it were his own child, a connection every bit as strong as he felt for its mother.

If only he had the confidence Riley had had with women! If only he could somehow, in some way, convince Kathleen to stay. Seamus could accept the fact she might never love him, but could he make her accept him as a father to her baby? As a man to protect her and her child?

Why should she? She's perfectly capable of protecting herself, especially now that Anderson has been captured.

His mind roiling with turmoil and questions, Seamus lay quietly with Kathleen in his arms. The storm battered the cabin, rain beat against the windows. Lulled by the angry wind, Seamus fought to stay awake, unwilling to miss even a moment holding Kathleen.

I can't even do that right, he thought. Exhaustion engulfed him, weighted his arms and legs, dulled his thoughts. He drifted, surrounded in Kathleen's warmth, vaguely aware of the wind, the rain and the woman sleeping in his arms.

"SEAMUS? ARE YOU AWAKE?"

Seamus blinked, then squinted against the glare from the overhead lamp. Rain still battered the windows, wind roared and whistled around the cabin, but the pale glow of a dreary dawn made the light almost unnecessary. He sat up and leaned against the headboard.

"I am now." He focused on Kat, the unusual pallor of her skin, the dark circles under her eyes. She held his old terry bathrobe wrapped tightly about her. "What's wrong?"

"I think my water broke. I was just getting out of the shower when..."

Galvanized, he leapt out of bed. "Are you sure? Are you having any contractions, any pain?" His mind whirled...the main road to Santa Rosa was closed, the other had been partially blocked by trees. After the night-long storm Seamus was certain it would be impassable.

"Just a backache that won't go away. I don't know if it's labor or not. Seamus, I'm really scared."

He pulled Kat into his arms, felt her trembling. "We'll call the doctor and..."

"I already tried. The phone's out. I tried the cell phone, but it's not working either."

"Okay. Everything'll be okay. Let's figure out what to do."

"Can't we just drive into town? The hospital is less than an hour from here."

"No, it's not. After you went to bed last night the deputy told me the river's up and they've closed the highway. We might be able to get out on the same road we came in on, but it was already partially blocked by downed trees. The storm hasn't let up all night, so I imagine it's in even worse shape this morning. The only way I know of would be to head west, toward the coast, then loop south and back to Santa Rosa that way. It's a lot longer, though, so we better get you dressed and get..."

"Aaaaahhhhh!"

Kat suddenly tightened and doubled over. Seamus swept her up in his arms and carried her to the bed. She drew her knees up in obvious distress, her breath whooshing in and out like a bellows.

"How long have you had that backache?" Seamus demanded. He leaned over Kat, breathing every bit as deeply as she. He wondered if he looked as wild-eyed as he felt.

"Late yesterday afternoon, I think. Just before all the trouble started." Her words puffed out between labored pants.

"Why in God's name didn't you say anything?"

Kat opened her mouth but no sound came out.

Seamus backed away and ran his fingers frantically through his hair. "I'm sorry. I didn't mean to shout at you. It's just that...honey, haven't you read any of those books I got? You've probably been in labor since yesterday. Good lord, woman!" He spun around and paced back across the room, then turned to look at Kat. She had suddenly focused inward, her concentration on what was obviously a contraction of monumental proportions.

Seamus fought panic. Her last contraction had been just moments ago. He'd read about women who passed the early stages of labor relatively free of pain.

She could be close to delivery right now and he didn't have a single thing prepared! "Don't push! Not yet...you're not pushing, are you?"

"Son of a bitch! No, damn it, I'm not pushing. I thought I was supposed to get some warning here! Not...supposed...to...surprise... *melikethis!*" She took deep draughts of air, breathing in and out much too quickly.

Seamus spotted a small paper bag on the dresser. He grabbed it, dumped the contents out on the floor, then had to step around the jelly beans that rolled in every direction. Just as Kat took another deep breath, Seamus placed the bag over her mouth.

She struggled to push it away.

"Breathe into this or you're going to hyperventilate. I don't want you passing out on me!"

Kat ripped the bag out of his hand. "If I pass out, it'll quit hurting, damn it! Leave me alone!"

"Do you really want me to leave you alone?" Seamus held the bag to one side.

Kat looked at him with stricken eyes. "You wouldn't do that, would you?"

"You know better. But please, at least I read the books."

"You find the place in your damned books where it says you shove a paper bag over the woman's face. *Then* maybe I'll put up with it."

Suddenly she blanched as another contraction hit. Seamus dumped the bag on the floor with the jelly beans and held tightly to both of Kat's hands. "Breathe with me, then. C'mon, honey. Take it slow...that's a girl. In, out. You're doing great."

Kat merely glared at him. She didn't have to curse for Seamus to know what she was thinking.

Time seemed to stand still, at least for Seamus. He figured Kathleen might not see it the same way. Between contractions he managed to get a bowl of warm water, some clean towels, string and sharp scissors. When Kat worried about ruining the mattress, he ripped the plastic curtain off the shower and managed to slide it under her, then covered it with soft towels. Nothing was sterile. Nothing was as the books described it.

Neither was Kat's labor. It seemed to progress much too rapidly, to intensify with each contraction. The birth had to be close. Right now she lay back, exhausted, her face pale, her blond hair hanging in tangles around her shoulders. She'd grunted with pain, cursed, he knew, at her own inability to control what was happening to her body even though she aimed most of the curses at Seamus—all the while breathing like a draft horse on a long pull with each contraction.

She hadn't screamed. He was thankful for that. Seamus died inside with each painful grunt. He didn't think he could handle it if she screamed.

"Kat, honey, I really should take a look and see if the baby's head is showing." *Crowning, the word is crowning*...why couldn't he remember anything? Kat's life depended on him, Kat's baby....

"Hurry, Seamus. I feel another one, like I've got to... Oh, God, it hurts, Seamus. I feel like I've got to shove this...aaaaahhhhh." She tucked her legs up and grabbed hold of her shins. Her scream drowned out the cry of the storm.

Frantically Seamus pushed Kat's drenched robe out of the way and knelt at the foot of the bed...barely in time to catch the squirming infant that slipped from her body into his waiting hands.

Shock, a moment etched forever in his memory as the perfect, tiny little boy opened his eyes and stared directly at Seamus. No sound, no life-giving gasp for air, just the steady gaze of Riley O'Rourke's only son, a look Seamus took deep into his heart.

"Oh, my God, Kat. It's a little boy. He's, he's... Oh, shit, he's not breathing, he's..." Seamus quickly cleared the baby's mouth with his finger and turned him face down to clear his airways.

Instead of the feeble cry he'd prayed for, the baby let loose with a loud, indignant wail. Tears streamed down Seamus's face as he sheltered the baby in his hands and placed him on Kat's stomach. Her slender fingers encircled her newborn son. Seamus cut the cord and tied it off with a clean piece of string.

There were no words. None Seamus could think to say that would make this moment more perfect. He could only care for Kathleen with what little knowledge he had. Care for her and keep her and their baby safe.

KAT HEARD THE BABY cry. She awoke, climbing out of a half-formed dream to see Seamus leaning over her, placing the tiny little being at her breast. She'd tried to nurse earlier in the evening without much luck, though the baby had eventually fallen asleep. Now he took her nipple between perfectly formed lips and drew it into his perfect little mouth.

Everything about him was perfect. How could she have ever wondered if she could mother this child? She felt the sharp pain in her breast and instinctively knew it was a good feeling, sensed the first milk flowing even before the baby sputtered, choked, then reattached himself with a contented sigh.

His tiny fists kneaded her breast, his face scrunched up with supreme concentration. A cap of dark hair covered his head, soft as silk and black as night. Kat felt the tears flow, knew the deep bond of motherhood at its very core. When she raised her eyes to stare directly into Seamus's dark gaze, she knew he shared the same emotion, the same bonding.

Everything was going to be perfect. She drifted off to sleep, the man she loved at her side, her son nursing at her breast.

Sometime later, Seamus's voice penetrated her drowsy mind. He was whispering to the baby, his words so filled with love and emotion they brought tears to Kat's eyes.

"You are the son I never expected, little one. A gift more precious than any other. I promise to always be there for you. I promise to love you and care for you no matter what happens. I want you to know your mother and I love you more than anything or anyone in the world."

Kat drifted with the sound of Seamus's promises, one question uppermost in her mind. *Do you love his mother? Will you care for her no matter what happens?*

Kat awoke hours later. The baby was gone! Startled, she sat up, fought the brief dizziness, then realized Seamus had moved the rocker into the bedroom. He sat in the corner holding the baby.

No...it wasn't Seamus. Something was different, the slant of the head, the turn of the shoulder. The man raised his head and Kat realized she looked into Riley's blue eyes.

"He's so beautiful, Kat. So goddamned perfectly beautiful. Thank you. You've given me more than I could've ever wished for."

"Riley?" She pushed herself upright, struggling to come fully awake, to prove to herself this wasn't a dream.

"Sleep, sweetheart." Riley stood up and carried the baby to her. Just as Seamus had done earlier, he placed his son at her breast. His fingers brushed the hair back from her forehead. Though the hair moved, she could not feel his touch.

"I loved you. I loved you more than I ever loved anyone, but to be honest, Seamus loves you more. He was always more than me, Kat. He just never quite figured it out. Tell him I love him, please. Tell Seamus and our son I love them both. You know I will always love you."

He leaned over as if to kiss her cheek, but the caress was without substance. When she opened her eyes, Riley was gone. Their son suckled at her breast. The rocking chair sat unmoving in the corner.

She dozed then, and when she awoke Seamus sat in the rocker, watching her. His hands drooped listlessly between his knees, his eyes were dark pools, filled with despair.

"What's wrong, Seamus?" Kat carefully dislodged the sleeping baby and tucked him close beside her. "Are you okay?"

"Have you thought of what you're going to name him?"

"What?" She shook the sleep from her mind and brushed her hair back out of her eyes. Immediately, Kat thought of Riley, of the touch that wasn't a touch. "What are you talking about?"

"The baby. What do you plan to call him?" Seamus raised his

head. His eyes held a haunted look, a look of need and loss and something more. Something Kat didn't understand.

He dreamed of Riley, too, she thought. He's haunted by the loss of his brother, more than he'll ever acknowledge.

"I'd like to name him after his father," she said. She'd call him Seamus, after the man who was more a father to him than Riley had ever been, ever could be. Even his spirit, if that's what had visited her last night, agreed.

Seamus bowed his head. "I agree. We'll call him Riley."

"No, I..."

"I need to see if I can get to town." Abruptly he stood up. His quick movement sent the chair rocking. "I think I can still get to the store. It's on high ground. I'll see when the roads are supposed to open. You really should be seen by the doctor. The baby needs to be checked."

"Seamus. That's not what I meant." How could he think she would mean anyone but him? This was Seamus O'Rourke's son. Her baby had no other father.

"We'll talk about it later. I need to buy groceries and pick up some diapers." He grinned, the first smile she'd seen on him since he'd handed her son to her. "Tea towels and duct tape definitely aren't my first choice."

At that comment, Kat looked down at her son. His tiny bottom was firmly wrapped in one of Seamus's hand embroidered tea towels. Shiny strips of duct tape held the linen in place.

"I don't know. It's definitely a fashion statement." She smiled at Seamus, but he looked away. She wanted to scream at him! How could he cut her off like this? How could he, after sharing the most intimate moments in her life? He'd delivered her child. He'd placed the tiny burden on her stomach, helped her deliver the afterbirth, cleaned up the horrible mess, and bathed her as if she'd been a baby.

He'd packed her to stop the bleeding, brushed her hair back from her eyes, brought her nourishing soups and meals, cared for her as tenderly as she'd ever been cared for in her life.

How could he turn away from her now? Didn't the past months, the past hours, mean anything to him?

They mean he's finally free of you. You've done what he wanted...delivered a healthy baby. Now he just wants his son, but he wants you gone.

Kat looked down at her son. She didn't want to call him Riley. She wanted to call him Seamus. Barring that, she'd name him Michael, after the partner who had stood by her for so many years.

Michael Seamus Riley O'Rourke was quite a mouthful for a little guy like this. "Did you weigh him?" She touched one tiny finger.

"Yeah, on the vegetable scale. Just a bit over five pounds. He's eighteen inches long, but for almost a month early that's not bad."

"Will you bring me some ice cream?" She smiled at Seamus, but his somber expression left no room for teasing.

"Yeah, if you want. I'll be back in about an hour or so." Without a further glance, he left the room.

Kat felt a shiver run along her spine. She didn't want him to leave. She wanted Seamus here, protecting her and their son.

Michael was *their* son. Somehow, she just had to convince Seamus they all belonged together.

Chapter Ten

THE LONG DRIVEWAY WAS in worse shape than he'd imagined, especially for a car as low-slung as the Jaguar. It took him at least twenty minutes to negotiate the gravel road. Luckily none of the larger trees had gone down, but Seamus had to stop and clear a number of fallen branches out of the way.

The highway wasn't much better. When he finally reached Guerneville, the Russian River stretched from bank to bank, boiling under the bridge like thick chocolate milk. Seamus passed a sign partially blocking the road he'd come in on: ROAD CLOSED. That option for escape was out for at least a few days.

He felt uncomfortable being this far from Kathleen and the baby, but after last night, he had to get away.

He'd dreamed of his brother before, but last night had been...something. Seamus broke out in a sweat again recalling his brother's presence. Riley, standing beside the recliner where Seamus had fallen asleep. His words the words of old, the silent communication they'd shared as boys, loud and clear in his mind.

"You love her," Riley had said. Not an accusation, merely a statement of fact. Seamus had nodded in agreement, still convinced this was a dream.

"You love Kat and you love our son. You'll be a good father, Seamus. A better father than I ever could have been. Probably a better husband, too." He'd smiled at Seamus, a sad smile of love and longing. "Take care of them. Watch over them. Love them both for me. I'm sorry for all I put you through, big brother. Remember I love you best of all."

Had it really happened? Or had Seamus imagined both the words and the image of Riley to ease his own conscience?

Would he always be haunted by his twin?

God, Riley, I want to believe it was you.

He had to believe. He had to believe Riley gave his blessing, or Seamus knew he could never offer his love to Kathleen.

He pulled into the parking lot at the grocery store and waded through six inches of water to reach the building. Local residents scurried about, grabbing the last few items available, readying themselves for what looked to be a long siege.

It had always been that way here. Just another inconvenience for people who lived along the river. Stock up on supplies, batten down the hatches and watch the river rise.

It always went down, sooner or later.

Seamus grabbed a basket and headed down the first aisle in the store.

THERE IS A SEASON and this is mine. They are such fools to think capture can stop the power. It grows. I feel it growing. One is but an instrument, a tool to be used and cast away. The other holds the true Power, the one true light that guides the hand.

The child will die. Ah, but the mother will die screaming. The Power? The Power will never die. It will grow and feed, and feed again.

Now? Now it hungers.

Not for long.

No, it hungers not for long.

IT SEEMED AS IF Seamus had been gone forever. Kat checked her watch for the hundredth time and knew it had only been two hours. Michael slept. He'd emptied her breasts completely at his last feeding. She had a feeling Michael was not going to be a child who would ever do anything half way.

It was so easy to call him Michael. She knew her old partner would be thrilled with the name. His first son, to his immense delight, had turned out to be twin daughters.

Kat shivered. It didn't make sense, this strange unease. The feeling that all was not as it should be. Her life had never been more perfect. Whatever problems existed between Seamus and her could be solved. She was certain of that.

She was not so certain what caused this strange sense of foreboding.

The storm had stalled, the winds died down a bit. The rain still fell as a steady torrent, running in rivulets across the drive, filling the creeks and streams. What if Seamus had car trouble? What if the road washed out?

"Don't make trouble where none exists, damn it! Oops, sorry." She covered her mouth and laughed at herself. *Apologizing to thin air. You're losing it, Malone!*

The moment she'd first held little Michael in her arms, Kat had promised to clean up her language.

It wasn't going to be easy, but unless she wanted a toddler with a mouth like a longshoreman, she figured she'd better start now.

Kat sensed the Jag before she actually heard it, the low growl of the powerful engine vibrating deep in her bones. She pulled the curtain aside and looked out the window just in time to see Seamus pull into the drive, park, run around to the back of the car and grab a couple of large bags out of the trunk. He ducked his head against the pouring rain and headed up the stairs.

She met him at the back door.

"I was worried about you. I was afraid the roads might have washed out or you might..." She caught herself and turned away.

"Might what, Kat?" Seamus closed the door, filling the kitchen with more than just a physical presence. He placed the bags on the kitchen table, draped his soaking wet coat over the back of a chair. "Might not come back?" He reached out and touched her chin, tilting her head back so she was forced to look him in the eye.

"I'll always come back. You should know that."

Of course he would. She had what Seamus wanted. She had Michael.

She said as much.

He frowned. "I thought you wanted to call him Riley. Why Michael?"

She backed away, out of his reach. "Michael was my partner for almost ten years. I probably know him better than any man alive."

"You said you wanted to name him after his father. I don't understand."

Kat threw her hands in the air in frustration. "You never do, Seamus. You don't listen. Sometimes I think you misunderstand me on purpose. When I said I wanted to name him after his father, I meant you, not Riley. You've been here all along, taking care of me, taking care of the baby. You've promised to be there in the future for him. I heard you. That's the role a father plays. No matter what kind of man you think Riley was, no matter that his seed created this baby, he's dead. You, Seamus, as hard-headed and irritating as you are, are still very much alive. Whether I like it or not, for all intents and purposes, you are this baby's father. I won't try and keep you apart. I promise you that."

"You can't keep us apart. I would never let that happen. That baby is as much my son..."

"You're doing it again! Listen to yourself, Seamus! I'm telling you I *agree* with you. I *want* you to be a part of this child's life. I *want* you to be his father. Hell, even *Riley* wants you to be his father. You're so busy hating your brother and everything associated with him, you can't even listen to your own heart."

The silence was deadening. Seamus stared at Kat as if he'd seen a ghost. She realized, belatedly, that maybe he had.

"What did Riley say to you? When...?"

Exhausted, Kat slumped heavily into one of the kitchen chairs. "Last night. At first I thought it was a dream, but it was just too real. He was sitting in the rocker, holding Michael. He said he loved the baby, he loved me, and he loved you. You saw him, too, Seamus. Don't deny it."

Seamus sat just as heavily in the chair directly across from Kat. He rested his elbows on the table, pressed his temples between his hands. "I thought it was a dream. I thought it was all that damned guilt looking for a way to have what Riley can't—a son, a family, love. But if you... Kat, I don't know if I can accept this. I really don't know."

"Well, you're just going to have to, Seamus O'Rourke. Accept the fact your brother is dead but he doesn't seem to hold it against you. Accept the fact he loves you enough to give you his blessing."

A thin cry sounded from the back room. Kat sighed. *The stubbornness of men.* To think she'd just brought another one into the world. "We'll talk about this later. Your son is calling."

MY SON. KAT'S WORDS ricocheted around inside his skull, reverberating over and over until he almost believed she meant what she said.

It was more than he'd dreamed, more than he'd ever hoped. Only one more thing would make the dream perfect.

If Kat could accept him as the baby's father, could she also accept him as her husband?

He thought of Riley's words last night with a sense bordering on disbelief. He could have sworn Riley had been there in the room, essentially absolving Seamus of everything that had come between the brothers over the years.

The pain of missing Riley clutched at his chest. So many years wasted, so much love forgotten.

No, not forgotten. Buried under anger and frustration. Buried but not lost.

No matter how much he wanted to, Seamus couldn't blame Riley for anything. Riley had just spent his life being, well, Riley. No, Riley had never done a thing, intentionally, to hurt Seamus. He'd merely lived his life the way he wanted, regardless of the consequences.

Now Riley was dead and Seamus still very much alive. What he chose to do with that life was up to him. Riley might have been a constant thorn in his side, but Seamus realized his memories of his brother had suddenly been tempered with love.

Love and an overwhelming sense of appreciation. Seamus knew he'd been given a second chance. Not only that, he'd been given a son. Two miracles, two unexpected dreams come true. Maybe this time he'd finally get it right.

Seamus wasn't certain if he'd ever convince Kat how he felt, but unless he gave it his best shot, he was wasting Riley's life as well as his own.

He glanced over his shoulder, uncertain whether or not he actually sensed his brother's spirit. "Thanks, kid," he whispered, hoping. "I'll do my best."

Seamus realized he was standing just outside Kat's bedroom, uncertain as to how he'd gotten there. The rain still fell, the wind had once again picked up, but the soft sound of Kathleen murmuring to her son drew him like a magnet.

Seamus quietly slipped through the partially open door.

"Is he asleep?"

"Yeah." She shifted slightly in the rocker, easily adjusting the tiny bundle in her arms. "I could sit here and just hold him for hours. Come see?"

Seamus walked across the room, mesmerized by the sight of the tiny little boy. Equally mesmerized by the full swell of Kat's breast, the puckered nipple next to the tiny rosebud lips. By all rights, Michael was a miracle, a baby neither he nor Riley could ever have hoped for.

Kat Malone was a miracle as well. Seamus still felt hopeless where she was concerned. Hopeless and so much in love he ached.

"Why did you tell me Riley was sterile?" She looked up at Seamus, obviously unconcerned with her lack of covering. "This little squirt looks so much like you guys there's no way either of you could deny parentage."

Seamus studied the black hair, the eyebrows already visible in their dark fuzz version, the arch to one a copy of both his and Riley's. He felt as if his heart would burst, so full of emotion with the fact of this child's very existence.

He pulled up an ottoman and sat close beside the rocker. "Our parents traveled when we were babies and we missed a lot of the regular check-ups most kids get. I don't know if we ever got vaccinated for mumps, but if we did, it didn't work. Riley and I both got sick when we were about five. The infection tends to settle in glands, and in our case the glands it settled in supposedly left both of us sterile. We were two miserable little boys!"

He reached out and trailed a finger across the baby's satiny cheek. "Thank God the doctors who tested both of us were wrong about Riley, though as far as I know, this is the only child he ever fathered."

"So you can't have babies?" Kat frowned when she looked at him.

Seamus wondered what she thought, if he was less than a man for being unable to father children. One more reason to back away.

Kat smiled, but her eyes glistened with tears. "Then that makes Michael even more special, doesn't it?" She pulled her shirt closed to cover her breasts and tucked the baby more snugly in the yellow blanket she'd made for him. "Why don't you hold your son for awhile? Little boys should spend lots of time with their fathers."

FATHER. THAT WASN'T A term he'd ever expected to apply to himself. Baby Michael yawned and stretched one tiny fist free of the blanket. His body fit perfectly into the curve of Seamus's arm, warm and solid and very much an O'Rourke. Seamus stared at the tiny bundle and felt as if his heart would explode. There was too much happening in that overworked organ right now, too many new emotions, too many fears, too much confusion.

With little Michael Seamus Riley, he felt nothing but unwavering love and a terrifying sense of vulnerability. So much responsibility, so much risk, so many decisions ahead, all of it tempered by dreams of playing catch in the backyard, of flying kites along the marina, of loving his son.

When he looked across the softly illuminated room at Kathleen sleeping so soundly in her bed, he practically trembled with frustration. He loved her, he needed her, he wanted her more than he could imagine wanting anything other than the tiny baby in his arms.

She'd offered him her baby then she'd backed away. She'd made it plain to Seamus he would always be a part of Michael's life, but hadn't offered to share her own.

She was independent, intelligent and more self-sufficient than any woman he'd ever known. Barely two days after giving birth, she was up and moving around as if the pregnancy hadn't even happened. She still wore the flowing tie-dyed dresses, but they clung to her shape and hinted at the slim, supple body she would soon regain.

She didn't need him anymore. Tim Anderson was in jail, the baby was healthy, and Kat could return to her old life and her job without a single backward glance. She'd let him know, in no uncertain terms, that she really missed her work, her friends, the challenges of the job.

Seamus could have exactly what he wanted.

Riley's baby. Not completely, not all the time, but she'd promised Seamus never to come between the two of them. It was so easy to picture Kat slipping back into her active roll as an investigator with the Department of Transportation, going undercover for long periods of time and leaving the baby with Seamus.

Well, wasn't that exactly what he wanted?

No. Not any more.

It would never be enough. He wanted the whole package...mom, dad, baby. Kathleen, Seamus, Michael...the house in town, weekends in the country, the three of them sitting down around the table at night and talking about their day.

Putting their son to bed, maybe sharing a late-night glass of port, then slipping off to the master bedroom and making love until their limbs were weak and their hearts racing.

He floated with the fantasy, dozing in the chair with Michael's warm little body held securely against his chest, thoughts of Kat's warm body pressed intimately with his own.

Suddenly Seamus jerked awake, blinking against the darkness in the room. When had Kat turned off the light?

As his thoughts cleared, he realized there was no light coming from the rest of the house, either, which meant the power had gone off again...which meant a wet trip out to the shed to fire up the generator. Michael stirred in his arms, snuffled against the soft blanket and sighed. Seamus carefully stood up and carried the tiny infant across the room.

He lightly touched Kat's warm shoulder. "Kat. Wake up, honey. Power's out. I need to go start the generator. Do you want the baby or should I put him in his bed."

They'd fashioned a dresser drawer as a makeshift crib, but Seamus knew Kat preferred to keep her son close by her side.

"I'll take him. My breasts hurt. Must be time for dinner." Kat struggled out of sleep and squinted against the darkness. She reached out and found Seamus, then Michael with the light brush of her fingers. Seamus expertly transferred the baby to her in the darkness. "Is it another wire down?"

"Could be. The wind's really picked up."

His voice always comforted her, the rich sound of it so smooth and powerful. "Be careful, Seamus. I'd hate for you to get whacked on the head by a branch."

He patted her hand. "Thanks. It's so nice to know you care."

She heard him chuckle as he turned away, then a soft *thunk* and a curse.

"Are you okay?"

"Yeah," he muttered. "I'd be better if I could remember to either leave the door open or closed...then maybe I wouldn't walk into it all the time."

Kat smiled as she heard him digging through the cupboard in the dark kitchen, obviously hunting for the flashlight. The narrow beam sliced along the hallway then disappeared as Seamus headed out through the back door. It slammed loudly behind him, caught in a heavy gust of wind.

Michael jerked and cried out at the sudden noise, then rooted hungrily at her breast. Kat sighed and settled into what was quickly becoming her favorite position, propped up with fluffy pillows, her son tugging hungrily at her nipple.

She ran one finger along the downy black silk that covered his head. She'd never seen newborn babies with so much hair, never held a baby as perfect as her son. His tiny fists kneaded the taut skin of her breast, his forehead puckered with a deep frown of concentration as he went about the most important business of filling his tummy. Kat couldn't help but think of Seamus and Riley as newborns, their mother probably overwhelmed by the responsibility of two tiny lives totally dependent upon her for everything.

A shiver crawled along her spine, the same shiver Kat felt whenever she allowed herself to think of the enormity of what she'd done by bringing a new life into the world. She hadn't merely needed Seamus for protection when Tim Anderson was still at large. She realized now she needed him for all the years to come, for the toddler years, the teen years, the years when Michael would finally be grown enough to leave and go out into the world on his own.

It wasn't merely the vulnerability that came with the task of raising a child, of keeping him safe. It was the sense that without Seamus, Kat was less than whole. Without Michael she was incomplete as well.

Kat Malone goes it alone.

She'd been so proud of her independence, of her ability to fight the world on her own terms.

Not any more. Not if she was going to give Michael the best of all possible lives. Not if she was ever going to find happiness for herself.

Now all she had to do was convince Seamus.

Kat patted a burp out of the baby, then switched him to her other breast and settled back against the pillows. Convincing Seamus wasn't going to be easy, but at least she had something he wanted.

Kat smiled, aware she could think of Seamus wanting the baby without anger or fear. She trusted him. If she'd learned nothing else about Seamus O'Rourke over the long weeks of living with him, she'd learned her earlier impression of him had been right—he was a man of honor. He would never forcefully try to take her child. That sort of thing would definitely go against his personal code of honor.

Too much honor, as far as Kat was concerned. There'd been times during her pregnancy, even when her belly swelled out in front of her and she'd moved about the house like the *Queen Mary*, when she'd fantasized crawling into his bed and doing her damnedest to seduce him.

She shifted her position in the bed, easing the pressure on her sore crotch. Seducing Seamus right now was the last thing on her mind.

That didn't mean she couldn't think about it as a *future* endeavor. Smiling, Kat snuggled down into the pillows, dozing lightly while Michael nursed.

The familiar crack of gunfire split the night just outside her window.

Kat shook her head in mute denial. She couldn't possibly have heard a gunshot here at the top of the mountain, miles from another residence.

Seamus hadn't come inside. The power was still out. A thought flitted through her mind. Maybe he'd fired her gun to frighten off a wild animal. Reason took hold. That wasn't the sound of her Ruger. It sounded more like the heavy concussion from a larger caliber weapon.

Cold sweat beaded Kat's forehead as she carefully slipped the sleeping baby from her breast. She carried Michael to the dresser drawer lying on the floor, its interior padded with a folded towel, and laid the baby carefully inside. Almost by instinct, she slid the drawer holding the sleeping baby across the soft carpet. With her hands she found the edge of the closet opening, shoved the door aside and pushed the drawer holding Michael into the tiny space.

She closed the door and prayed he would continue to sleep.

Her robe was thrown across the end of the bed and Kat carefully wrapped the navy blue garment around her nightgown. It would offer more cover in darkness than the light colored gown she wore.

She halted at the open bedroom door and listened. The wind continued its ungodly howl, branches lashed at the windows and walls. She wanted to call out to Seamus, but hesitated giving away her position.

Who fired the gun? Where is Seamus? Lord, please keep him safe.

He'd said the Ruger was in the kitchen drawer. Only a darkened hallway and a few steps across the tiled kitchen and at least she'd be armed with a familiar weapon.

She took a deep breath, well aware of her shaking hands and trembling legs. Childbirth had taken its toll. The body she'd always trusted in any situation was no longer the same, the strength she'd relied on only a faint memory.

She thought of Michael sleeping peacefully unaware in the wooden drawer, tucked away in the dark closet. No harm would come to him. No harm unless her own life were forfeit.

Which meant whatever action she took, whatever choices she made, required she survive to protect her son.

Kat stayed close against the wall and slipped quietly into the kitchen. The wind outside shifted and rain beat against the window over the sink. Lightning illuminated the clean tile counters, glinted off the faucet, pointed the way to the silverware drawer where Seamus had stashed the Ruger.

Thunder rumbled directly overhead.

Seamus, where are you? A sob caught in her throat, a sound borne of fear and love. A gun had been fired. Seamus hadn't come running in to check on her and Michael. Ergo, Seamus was hurt. He was hurt, or he was dead.

I can't think of that. I have to protect Michael.

Lightning flashed again and her fingers found the handle to the drawer. The Ruger was just inside. Seamus said he'd left it here. Silently, so slowly, Kat eased the drawer open.

Thunder growled and lightning flashed again, glinting duly against the dark blue surface of the automatic pistol. She reached into the drawer.

Strong fingers clasped about her wrist, jerked it behind her back, high, between her shoulder blades. A thick forearm snaked across her chest.

The scent. The feel. The essence of the man who had followed her for months. The same man who had held her captive in San Francisco.

Now. Here in the protected kitchen of Seamus O'Rourke.

It hadn't been Tim Anderson after all. No, this man was the one.

Whoever he was, this was the man who had stalked her, attacked her, had threatened to murder her child.

The pressure eased across Kat's chest. Before she could react the cold blade of a knife pressed into her throat, held her immobile.

She gasped, drew in a quick breath of air.

His chest heaved against her back.

Oh God, he's laughing.

His foul breath gagged her. She held perfectly still. Ignoring the pain in her shoulder, she prayed that Seamus lived, that Michael wouldn't wake.

Prayed for the strength to survive.

Thunder rumbled through the room. Once more the lightning flashed. Rain tattooed against the window.

Where was Seamus?

Kat gasped for air. The blade of the knife pressed even closer. Hot blood seeped into her gown.

Her captor didn't speak. Kat's harsh breathing echoed in her own ears. The wind eased, rain no longer pounded the cabin.

Michael's thin cry pierced the silent darkness.

Chapter Eleven

THUNDER...SO CLOSE AND the flash of lightning right on top of it. One Mississippi, two Mississippi... What did Riley say? Something about counting the seconds between the crack of thunder and the flash of lightning...but what if they happen at the same time? Riley? Hey, bro...how's that go again?

Hurry, Seamus, there's not much time. I hate to tell ya, but you're the only chance they've got. C'mon, big brother...get up! Kat needs you. Our son needs you!

"Quit bugging me, Riley. My head hurts."

Seamus rolled over onto his hands and knees in the soggy patch of bracken. Two beams from his flashlight spiraled into the darkness. By concentrating on the light he managed to focus his vision on a single beam. It took all the energy he had to reach out and grab the cold metal handle.

Lord, but his head hurt. Seamus sat back on his heels and reached up to touch his right temple. His fingers came away sticky with a mixture of blood and rainwater. He stared at his reddened fingers as memories flooded his mind.

Walking out into the storm to start the generator, a sense of movement in the shadows, the sweep of the beam from my flashlight catching the image of a man, the glint of something metallic in his hand...the crack of thunder, the flash of lightning...

"Good Lord, that son-of-a-bitch shot me!" Stumbling to his feet, Seamus quickly switched off the flashlight. He swayed a moment, gained his bearings and stared at the dark silhouette of the house.

Kat was in there. Kat and the baby.

And a killer.

A sliver of moonlight peeking between dark clouds barely lighted the walkway leading to the back door. Swaying, fighting nausea, Seamus worked his unsteady way into the deep shadows surrounding the deck. He pressed against the damp redwood, disoriented by strange lights flashing behind his eyes, the blood pounding painfully in his ears.

How long had he been unconscious? His clothes were wet, but not soaked through. He reached up to touch the side of his head. The blood seeping from the wound on his temple had not yet coagulated.

The house stood silent. He had no doubt the killer was inside.

If only his head would clear! He closed his eyes tightly, once again reliving the moments by the shed.

Seamus had caught only the briefest glimpse of his assailant when he'd swept the beam of his flashlight through the darkness and pouring rain. There was a man, but no one familiar. Long stringy hair, unkempt appearance, a fanatical gleam in his eyes.

One thing Seamus knew for certain.

It was *not* Tim Anderson.

Then who the hell is it?

What did it matter? Whoever it was, he was after Kathleen.

Kathleen and Michael!

Adrenaline surged through Seamus, driving the fog from his thoughts and clearing his vision. He quietly climbed up over the edge of the deck, forgoing the easier route up the stairs in case anyone watched.

The back door stood ajar. Trusting his instincts, Seamus slipped through the opening into the dark kitchen.

The room was empty. The kitchen drawer stood open. In the faint gleam of pale moonlight, Seamus caught the dull glint of the Ruger. Quickly he snatched it up, realized the safety was on and tried to release it.

How in the hell did she do that? For the life of him, for Kat and Michael's lives, he couldn't recall Kat's simple instructions.

The weapon mocked him.

Michael's thin cry echoed through the darkness.

"No, damn you." It was Kat's voice, angry and frightened. The baby cried louder. Impotent frustration galvanized him. Seamus stuck the useless weapon in his coat pocket and grabbed the cast iron skillet off the stove.

He raced across the hallway between the kitchen and Kat's room. A loud grunt, Kat's furious scream, and a harsh cry filled with rage and anger drew him in.

Seamus reached the doorway just as Kat twisted free of her captor and shoved him away. A shadow stumbled in the darkness, directly toward Seamus.

Before the man could catch his balance, Seamus smacked him soundly with the frying pan.

The intruder crumbled in a heap on the bedroom floor.

Seamus reached for Kathleen but she turned from him in a fluid motion that took her directly to the closet and the wailing cries of her baby. She shoved the door aside and snatched Michael out of the wooden drawer. Soothing the infant with nonsensical words and kisses, she held him close to her breast.

Seamus stood over the unconscious man, drawing in great draughts of air. His fingers remained clenched tightly about the handle of the heavy frying pan.

"Are you okay?" He barely saw Kat in the dim light from the moon, but he could tell by the sound of her movements when she carried the baby to the rocker and sat down.

"Yeah. I'm okay." He heard the catch of fear in her throat and his gut tightened. Thank God, for once he'd made it in time.

"Get him out of here, Seamus. Please? Do you have anything to tie him with?"

Kat's voice was barely above a whisper. Frowning, Seamus stared through the darkness but saw only her shadow. "There's some twine in the laundry room." He reached down to grab the man by his ankles and the room spun. Seamus held the position a moment, got his bearings, and dragged the man's inert body out of the bedroom, across the hall and into the kitchen.

He grabbed the roll of twine off the laundry room shelf and carefully tied the unconscious man's hands behind his back, then bound his ankles tightly together. He looped another piece of rope between ankles and wrists and tested the taut rope.

The man grunted, but didn't struggle. Seamus didn't think he'd fully regained consciousness yet, but he checked the knots once again to make certain they were secure.

Seamus glanced toward the window and noticed a dark wall of clouds moving to cover the moon. He grabbed an extra flashlight and headed back to Kat's room.

That's when he noticed the blood seeping through her gown and robe, covering her chest with a rapidly spreading crimson stain.

"My God. Kathleen!"

He raced to her side. Her head had fallen to one side, the long blond hair covering a gash that twisted from just under her ear and down, across her collarbone, ending just above her heart. She still held Michael tightly in her arms, a mother's instinct more powerful than her wounds.

"Kat! Sweetheart..." Seamus pressed his fingers against the uninjured side of her neck and felt the pulse there.

Kat turned her head towards him and licked her lips. "I don't know how badly he cut me, Seamus. It hurts..."

Seamus raced into the bathroom and grabbed a towel. He pressed the soft fabric against the gaping wound, noting that the blood flow seemed to have slowed. No major arteries had been cut, thank God, but she'd still lost a lot of blood.

"We're going to the hospital. Now. Let me have Michael. Do you think you can make it to the car?" Seamus carefully took the child from her grasp, snuggled him securely in the crook of his left arm and leaned over to help Kat to her feet.

She leaned forward and he put his arm about her waist and helped her stand. She swayed against him, then seemed to draw strength from some unknown well. "I can make it."

"You hold the flashlight, I'll hold you."

She turned and smiled. He felt her spine stiffen, but she fell into a slow step beside him. Michael snuffled and rooted against Seamus's chest. "Sorry, little guy. I'm not mama," he whispered.

They crossed the hallway. Seamus hated to have to pass so closely beside her assailant's body in the kitchen, but he'd left the bound man blocking the closest path to the car.

The beam from the flashlight wavered in Kat's grasp, then stopped.

Where Seamus had left his captive, only a pile of tangled twine remained.

"Oh, shit." He glanced at Kathleen, at the look of horror on her face.

"Hurry. Let's get the hell out of here."

Kathleen flicked off the flashlight. "We don't need to give him a target."

Her voice sounded stronger. Seamus took it as a sign to move faster. He opened the back door and helped Kat down the steps and into the back seat of the Jag. "Buckle yourself in and I'll hand Michael to you." He glanced over his shoulder at a rustle in the shrubbery.

"Okay. I'm in."

Seamus slipped Michael into Kat's outstretched arms, slammed the door shut and raced around to the driver's side. He grabbed the keys from under the mat, turned on the engine and immediately hit the automatic door locks.

The moon disappeared behind a heavy curtain of dark cloud as Seamus threw the car into reverse and backed out of the driveway. He made a quick turn at the bottom of the drive and glanced over his shoulder.

Kathleen's frightened gaze met his. "Hurry, please?"

Her quiet plea galvanized him. Seamus swung the wheel around and hit the accelerator. The Jag bounced over the small bridge at the end of the drive and spun into the first turn on the gravel road.

A man jumped out as if to grab for the door handle. Seamus caught an impression of blond hair flying, wild eyes flickering in the glare from the headlights and then they were past him, racing through the darkness for the highway beyond.

"Who the hell is he?" Seamus gritted his teeth in impotent frustration. "It's not Anderson, Kat. Who is he and why does he want to kill you?"

"I think...but it can't be. He was so meticulous, so uptight and clipped and trimmed..." Her voice wavered with confusion.

"Take a guess, Kat. Give me something to call in to Sandy Wilson. Who do you think it is?"

"You don't need to shout, Seamus!"

Michael started to cry.

The car spun, almost out of control. Seamus let up on the accelerator. "I'm sorry. It's just... God, Kat. I'm so damned sorry. I promised I'd keep you safe. I told you I'd keep Michael safe. I screwed up again... I don't mean to yell at you..."

He stared straight ahead, following the twists and turns along the gravel ribbon.

"James Dearborn. I think he's James Dearborn, Tim Anderson's partner. But..."

"The mama's boy? The one you said was engaged to your friend?"

"I'm not sure. He looks so different. James was almost pretty. His hair was perfect, nails trimmed, suit neatly pressed even during a kidnapping. The guy was a freak."

"So's the guy who's been after you."

Kat couldn't answer. She glanced up into the rearview mirror. Seamus stared back at her. Eye contact lasted only a moment, but she felt the depth of his feelings, his remorse, his anger...at her?

Why not?

If not for her, there'd be no murderer in his life. His wonderful, quirky, little housekeeper would still be alive. If not for Kat, Seamus would still be living the comfortable, wonderful life he'd led before.

If not for her, even Riley might still be alive.

She held Michael close and tried to keep pressure on the towel covering the knife slash across her throat. She knew she'd lost a lot of blood, but she'd been hurt before.

She'd been hurt before, but never when she had a child to protect. Never when she'd loved a man who could never love her back.

She wasn't a crier. She never cried.

She was a survivor.

Kat Malone goes it alone.

But Kat Malone wasn't alone. Not now. Not anymore.

She held Michael tightly against her. She gave her trust over to Seamus and her tears dampened the soft yellow blanket covering their son.

THEY THINK THEY'VE won. Fools. I've been beaten before but my tormentors always pay. They think they won because they know me, but they don't, really. They never do. It's better now...they know who to fear. They expect to die. I don't intend to disappoint them.

They'll die afraid. Not me...I will find the ultimate satisfaction. I will win. I always win, don't I? I showed you I always win, didn't I, Mother?

Mother? Is that you, Mother? I'll see you in hell before the night is over. I'm coming, Mother. I'm coming.

SEAMUS DIDN'T EVEN LET up on the accelerator when they hit the highway at the end of the gravel road. He swung the wheel to the right, and the back tires slipped and skidded before he brought the Jag under control then headed toward Guerneville.

Fat raindrops splashed against the windshield. The wipers emphasized the danger. When Seamus had gone to the store, he'd learned the road south was closed due to falling trees and a landslide. The road east was closed as well with flooding in the low-lying areas. Their only route to a hospital was to head west, toward the ocean, make the loop south along the coast highway and cut back toward Santa Rosa. There was a small hospital in Sebastopol, but the roads to that little town were questionable as well.

The Jag sped along the dark, rain-swept road, eating up the miles. Kathleen murmured softly in the back seat, talking to Michael. Her voice soothed Seamus as well, reminded him of the importance of this mad dash through the night. His vision still hadn't cleared completely. The yellow line in front of him often split and meandered with the beat of his pulse.

He'd never had a concussion, but the symptoms were all there. Damn, he had to hang on. Long enough to get Kat and Michael to the hospital. That was all. He could do this.

He glanced in the rearview mirror. A brilliant set of headlights bore down on them.

"Kathleen. I think he's on us."

Kat spun around in her seat, then turned back to Seamus. "Can you outrun him?"

"We'll find out."

He pressed the accelerator to the floor. The powerful car leapt forward. The bridge across the Russian River suddenly loomed in the headlights. Seamus hit the narrow span at almost sixty miles per hour. The streetlight was red, but he ran it without a qualm. The tires on the low-slung Jag squealed. The car spun left, then straightened out.

A deep puddle threw them into another spin. They slid through the intersection at an oblique angle. Seamus prayed for a highway patrolman.

None appeared. Silently cursing his frustration Seamus regained control of the Jag and headed west. Highway 1 and the small town of Jenner were just a few miles down river.

Headlights filled the rearview mirror. Their stalker pursued them in a manic race along the narrow highway.

Suddenly the clouds unleashed their burden. Rain drummed against the windshield, bounced back off the dark asphalt surface, poured in thick cascades of mud and rock from the high cliffs to their right.

Saturated from weeks of heavy storms, the hillsides slipped. Slumped. Edged ever closer to the road. The river boiled on their left. Huge waves, laden with fallen trees and other debris, reached almost to the edge of the slick asphalt.

"Hang on to Michael!" Seamus spun the wheel. He barely missed a huge boulder tumbling across the road. It crossed between the Jag and the car racing close behind, then disappeared into the flood-swollen river.

Kathleen gasped. Michael's voice rose in a piercing wail. "He's okay," Kat shouted. "Hurry, Seamus. Dearborn's right behind us!"

Seamus couldn't look back. He wished he could reassure Kathleen. Looking away from the road wasn't an option, not if they expected to survive.

Hell, who was he kidding? They couldn't possibly survive, not this, not the storm and a manic killer hot on their trail. Seamus O'Rourke had no skills. He wasn't a hero. He'd never had the right stuff to be other than what he was. It was a little too late to change now.

He was a writer, for crying out loud. A foodie, a geek who thought the newest kitchen gadget was worth an entire column in the Sunday paper. He wasn't Riley. He didn't even know how to take the damned safety off a gun! If he'd been able to figure that out, the man now threatening their lives could well be dead.

With your luck, Seamus, you would've shot Kathleen. The frying pan was more your style.

Almost...he thought he heard his brother laughing. *Oh God, I'm really losing it here....*

Seamus braked to avoid a fallen tree. The car behind him didn't. The force of the impact set Michael crying louder and Kat to cursing. Seamus accelerated once again, sliding around the tree, leaving their pursuer behind.

Lightning flashed. Directly in front of Seamus the side of the hill fell away. Trees. Boulders. Tons of mud crossed the road and crashed into the raging river.

Seamus hit the brakes. The Jaguar slid sideways, a howl of tires on wet pavement before impact.

There was an eerie silence, a loud *crunch* as the Jag hit the churning wall of mud. Trapped amid the debris, they slid toward the river.

Seamus heard Kathleen's scream and Michael's whimper.

His heart lodged somewhere in the vicinity of his throat.

Then, as if it had always been a part of the mountain, the car settled amid the rocks and mud and plunged into the dark water.

KAT FELT AN ALMOST preternatural calm, a sense of peace that frightened her more than panic. The car was underwater, upright at least, but there was only darkness outside the windows. Darkness and the deep roar of the river.

But no sound from the baby.

Michael wasn't crying.

Oh Lord, please....

Kat pressed her face against the baby's silken cheek. He immediately turned his head at the contact, rooting against her face as if in search of dinner.

Kat's tears flowed and she held him tighter. *Thank you, thank you, thank you....*

The car lurched. Seamus's voice penetrated the odd silence. "Kat? Sweetheart...are you okay?"

"Seamus...yes. We're fine. How...?"

"I'm okay. We don't have much time. There's water coming in around my feet..."

"How are we going to get out?"

"Move up to the front seat. I'll kick out the windshield. You hang on to Michael and I'll pull you to the surface."

Suddenly the car lurched forward, raising the back end so that Kat was above Seamus. Something scraped heavily along one side of the Jag, then shuddered to a stop. The roar of the river increased.

"Hurry, Kat. Now!"

Lethargy weighted her bones and muscles. She fumbled with the seatbelt. Nothing happened. The clasp held.

Michael whimpered as the car jolted with the impact of some unseen debris. There wasn't time. Seamus couldn't possibly save them both.

"I'm ready," she lied. "Go. Now!"

She heard Seamus grunt with the effort, felt the pressure change as the windshield popped free and water rushed into the car. The slash across her chest burned as the icy water swirled around her. She screamed at Seamus, felt his arms on hers and thrust the baby into his hands.

"My seatbelt's jammed. Take Michael. Go, Seamus. For the love of God, save him!"

"Kat! No!"

Water cascaded around him. She wished she could see him, just this once. Wished she could tell him how much she loved him.

But she couldn't. Seamus and Michael were gone.

THE AIR POCKET KEPT the water at a level just beneath her chin. It wouldn't last for long, not the way the car jerked and wobbled in the rushing torrent. At some point the Jag would break free of whatever held it in place. She'd seen cars in floods, watched them roll and tumble like so much garbage.

Kat fumbled again with the seat belt, her fingers growing more unresponsive from the cold, from fear, from loss of blood. What did it matter? She'd never make it to the surface. Maybe, if she'd been stronger. Not now, not so soon after giving birth, not bleeding from a gash across her throat... Seamus hadn't said he was coming back. Not a word. He'd taken Michael and disappeared into the flood.

Kat Malone goes it alone.

"No, damn it. Not any more!" Kat sobbed against the restraint. Icy water sloshed around her.

This was what he'd wanted all along, wasn't it? Seamus finally had his baby. Had his baby free and clear without the added burden of a streetwise female investigator.

No, Seamus was an honorable man, wasn't he? He'd come back for her. He wouldn't leave Michael's mother to drown.

How long had he been gone? It seemed like hours. How long could she last? How long would it take for her to finally believe he wasn't coming back? She'd always been so damned gullible. Kat almost laughed, thinking of all the times she'd believed.

Hell, she'd even thought Riley loved her.

I do, Kat. I'll always love you. But never as much as Seamus loves you. He'll be back. Hold on, please. He'll come for you. Trust me, Kat. He loves you.

"Riley? Where are you?" There was nothing to be seen...not even her hand in front of her face.

I'm here, Kat. I'll always be here. Hold on, sweetheart. He's coming. Seamus is coming for you. He was shot, you know. Dearborn shot him. He's hurting. He's coming as fast as he can....

Riley smiled at her from the front seat. His rumpled suit was dry. *How could that be?* The front seat was completely underwater. A faint glow outlined his features, but it was Riley. She knew it and felt him in her heart. Took peace from his presence, accepted his words.

Maybe this was what it meant to die.

The car jerked, slipped and tilted. A great whoosh of bubbles escaped through the open window, leaving Kat with a tiny bubble of air caught against the back window.

She struggled against the restraint of the seat belt, reached for that tiny bit of life sustaining air. She felt Riley beside her, felt the essence of the man as he had been.

The latch holding the jammed belt released.

Gasping, Kat curled against the back window, drew what air she could from the tiny pocket that was left.

Riley was gone. All that existed was this little bit of life, one frantic breath after another...one frantic breath and the strong, bruising grasp of fingers grabbing at her ankle.

Pulling her away from the air, pulling her into the raging river, her lungs burning, eyes shut tight against the flood. Suddenly Seamus had his arms around her and she felt the powerful thrust as he kicked them to the surface. It took forever, the passage from death to life. Forever and a heartbeat, then suddenly the rain was pelting down and a huge wave of water cascaded over their heads.

Arms and hands reached for them and pulled them ashore. Both she and Seamus bent over, coughing and gasping for air. Someone helped both of them away from the river's edge and wrapped them in blankets. Kat heard cheering, the sound of applause.

"Michael? Where's my baby?"

"I've got him. He's fine."

A heavyset man dressed in a yellow slicker opened the front of his coat to show Kat the warm bundle tucked against his chest. Kat took a deep breath, thanked God and Riley, then turned around to Seamus and threw her arms around him.

"You came back for me." She was sobbing, crying all over him, but it didn't matter. "Riley said you would. I didn't believe him. I thought you'd take Michael...leave me. I thought...I thought you'd leave, not ever come back."

Seamus stiffened in her embrace. He reached down, took hold of her arms, put her away from him.

She looked up at him, her eyes full of tears, her soft mouth begging to be kissed.

She thought I'd leave her. She thought I'd let her drown? She honestly thought I'd take her baby and let her die?

This pain was worse than anything he'd known before. More than when his parents died, more than when he lost Gran. Even Riley's death couldn't compare.

This was a death of all his dreams, all those fantasies he'd conjured up while watching Kat as she carried the baby, even more when she finally gave birth and held the infant to her breast. He'd seen them as a family, a loving family raising their son. Seamus, Kathleen and Michael.

She thought I wouldn't come back? Why shouldn't she?

He'd managed to fail every time he'd promised to help her. Why shouldn't she expect him to fail at saving her life?

And when she thought she was dying, whose image had she turned to?

You win, Riley. Dead or alive, you always win.

Seamus took a deep breath, curled his fingers into fists when they would reach for Kathleen. "Riley's dead, but I guess he'll never be gone. At least, not for you...or, it appears, for me either." He took a deep breath, wiped the blood and river muck out of his eyes. "I promise you, Kat. I won't try to take your son, but my lawyer will be in touch regarding support. Don't worry. This time I won't come back. You have nothing to fear from me."

The wail of an approaching ambulance echoed off the canyon walls.

Seamus watched as the paramedics raced toward Kathleen. Then he turned and walked away.

"WHERE IS HE, SANDY? It's been three days." Kat pushed herself to a sitting position and peeked at Michael, sleeping soundly in the bassinet next to her hospital bed.

"I don't know, Kat." Sandy sat down on the edge of the bed and awkwardly patted her leg through the blankets. "The emergency room technician said he wasn't admitted, just treated and released. I called his house but didn't get an answer and he's got his cell phone turned off. You might be able to reach him through his agent."

Kat absentmindedly scratched at the stitches running along the side of her neck. The wound wasn't deep, but she'd lost a lot of blood. The plastic surgeon who'd sewn her back together had been inordinately proud of his work.

"Sandy, it's not like Seamus to just bail out. He's much too responsible for that." Kat blinked the tears back and sniffed. Sandy passed her a box of tissues. "I mean, it's obvious he doesn't want to see me, but it's just not like him to..." She bit back a sob. "Damn him."

"I thought you weren't going to cuss anymore." Sandy grinned at her.

"You're right." She took a deep breath. "Guess I'm doing the denial thing, eh? He's not coming back, is he? It's all my fault."

"I think he'll come back." Sandy squeezed her leg. "Right now, he's hurting. When I saw him in the emergency room, he was still pretty rattled. You have to admit, you've brought a bit more excitement into the man's life than he's accustomed to. Seamus doesn't usually get shot, chased by a killer, run off the road or have to pull a woman and baby out of a flooded river."

"If you're trying to make me feel better, it's not working." Michael squirmed in his sleep and Kat patted his back. He immediately settled down. She turned back to Sandy. "Did he say anything about me?"

Sandy's averted eyes told Kat more than she wanted to know...and not nearly enough. "C'mon, Sandy. What did he say?"

"It didn't make any sense, Kat." Sandy stood up and wandered around the small, private hospital room, obviously ill at ease.

"Sandy? Let me try and figure it out. What'd he say?"

"He kept talking about how you'd never be able to trust him

because he couldn't keep his promises, that even when he did, you didn't believe him...and how Riley'd won again. Riley's been dead for a long time, Kat. What'd he mean?"

Kat took a deep breath and closed her eyes. It really shouldn't hurt this much, but hadn't she hurt Seamus just as badly? What must he have thought when she'd blurted out she didn't think he'd come back for her? That he only wanted her baby?

A man as sensitive and caring as Seamus. A man more vulnerable than he'd ever admit. A man who'd sworn to protect her and her child and who had done exactly that.

"It means I'm really a jerk, Sandy. But thanks for telling me."

"Sorry, Kat. I do have one bit of good news. Well, good and not so good." He pulled a metal chair up close to the bed and sat on it. "We pulled Dearborn's car out of the river yesterday. His body was still inside, along with a gun, two knives and a lot of duct tape. It was obvious he had plans for you."

Kat shivered and glanced at Michael, sleeping so peacefully beside her. She leaned over, reached into the bassinet and picked him up. Right now she felt a very strong desire to hold her baby close to her heart. "I'm just glad he's dead. I've been lying here trying to figure out how to get lost so he'd never find us again. It was either that or kill him myself. I still don't understand why he targeted me. I was a minor player in the case."

"Tim Anderson gave us some background. He'd coerced Dearborn into a lot of illegal activity over the years, including siphoning off a huge amount of Alicia Dearborn's estate. The day the smugglers were apprehended, you were pretty high profile, staying with Rose DeAngelo throughout the interrogation by the FBI. Dearborn must've blamed you and the arresting agents for all his legal problems. He'd been too close to Rose to want to put the blame on her. You guys were more convenient.

"His mother bailed him out, but once she found out how much money her baby boy had stolen from her, she pressed charges against him herself. She figured she'd teach him a lesson, let him spend a few nights in jail."

Sandy shoved himself away from the bed and paced the small hospital room. "He got more of a lesson than she'd planned. Turns out he was tossed into a cell with a bunch of guys who beat the crap out of him then gang raped him. According to Anderson, Dearborn snapped. Anderson always felt like he'd had the upper hand with his buddy, but Dearborn came out of that jail cell a changed man...convinced everything bad that had happened to him was your fault...yours and Agent O'Rourke's.

"By that time, both he and Anderson were hooked on drugs. Dearborn still managed to have enough money to feed his and Anderson's addiction, so the power shifted. Anderson was working for Dearborn when you caught him trying to plant the bomb on the Jag."

"My God, Sandy." Kat shook her head in disbelief. "If you could've seen James Dearborn when he was arrested, you'd know why I never suspected him. He was such a mild-mannered sort, a real wimp. Blond hair, blue eyes, a real pretty boy. His mother was the original bitch on wheels, but she had to have known what she was setting him up for, sending him to jail. Rose told me that was his greatest fear— ending up in prison—a guy with his looks." Kat stroked Michael's cheek and he turned to her hand in his sleep, his mouth instantly puckering.

How could any mother do something so awful to her only son?

Sandy cleared his throat. "That's the other part of my news. Turns out when the Pittsburgh cops went to notify Dearborn's mother of his death, they found her decomposing body in the basement, all bound up with duct tape. The autopsy hasn't been completed, but it looks like she'd been tortured and stabbed to death within the last few weeks. Dearborn's the obvious suspect, though we won't know for sure until all the results are in. The neighbors all thought she'd taken off on a European trip she'd been talking about, so no one checked up on her. Gardeners kept gardening, maid kept cleaning and her accountant kept making payroll."

"How awful...and sad." *To be so isolated that no one even misses you? To die at the hand of your own son...* Kat shuddered, remembering the fear, the sheer terror she had lived through for almost a year. She had never known such dread, but then she'd never had so much to lose.

Sandy said something, but Kat missed it. "What did you say?"

"The doctor said they're gonna release you tomorrow morning. Jane and I insist you come home with us for awhile, 'til you get stronger."

Damned...er...darned tears... "Sandy, that's so nice, but—"

"No buts, Kat. Jane'd never forgive me if I didn't give her a shot at holding that little baby. She's a frustrated gramma." He stood up, grinning. "The closest she's got to grandchildren is our son's hyperactive border collie."

Kat laughed. "Well, guess we can't disappoint her."

"It's settled then." Sandy headed out of the room. "I'll pick you up at ten."

Kat held her smile until Sandy left the room. Then she cried softly for a long time, holding her sleeping son.

"JANE, I'VE SPONGED OFF you and Sandy long enough. I really have to move on." Kat threw the last of her few items of clothing into the sports bag she'd picked up at the drug store that morning, then stared at the huge pile of belongings Michael had accumulated over the past month.

His baggage outstripped hers by more than half.

"But where will you go?" Jane Wilson had taken Kat into her home and her heart without question when Sandy brought the new mother home from the hospital. She'd helped with Michael and mothered Kat, something Kathleen hadn't realized how much she'd needed.

"I talked to my ex-partner and his wife last night. Rose and Mike Ramsey own a bed and breakfast in the Sierra foothills. They've been bugging me for ages to come and help run the place. She and Mike have twins who just started walking." Kat couldn't help smiling, thinking of Mike Ramsey with twin daughters.

She grinned at Jane and deadpanned, "I truly believe their offer is entirely sincere."

"What about Seamus?" Jane was well aware of Kat's feelings.

"What about him?"

"Don't you think you should let him know you're leaving?"

"He'll find out. Eventually. If he really cared, don't you think I'd have heard from him by now?"

"So, you're really gonna leave us, eh, Kat?"

Sandy Wilson walked into the spare room and handed Kathleen a fat envelope. "This just came for you. I signed for it."

Kat took the thick vellum envelope Sandy held out to her. "You had to sign for it? What is it?"

"Why don't you open it and see?" Sandy hovered over her shoulder, obviously curious.

"Why don't we let Kat open it in private, dear?" Jane grabbed her husband's sleeve and dragged him from the room, laughing.

Kat watched them go with a sense of sadness that she would never share that kind of closeness with a man again.

With Seamus O'Rourke.

"Oh, Seamus, you're such a dolt." Why couldn't he see what was right there in front of his face? He loved Michael. Kat was certain of that. She was almost certain he loved her as well.

Almost.

Kat knew she loved Seamus. How else could she explain the horrible sense of loss she'd felt when she finally accepted the fact he wasn't coming back for her?

She stared at the thick envelope, noticing for the first time that it had been sent from an attorney's office. *Probably another subpoena.* It was one of the drawbacks of working in law enforcement that convinced her she'd made the right decision to request a long leave of absence.

Kat slipped her thumb under the flap and removed the contents.

The first thing she saw was a bank statement in her name with a balance larger than any sum she'd ever earned in any given year. There was a checkbook enclosed with her name on it, and a bank signature card for her to fill out and return.

The note was brief and to the point. Seamus O'Rourke, through his attorney, was naming himself financially responsible for Michael Seamus Riley Malone until said child reached the age of twenty-one years, at which point, if further funds were needed, Seamus should be contacted through his attorney.

Other than that, and unless the child should wish to know his uncle, there would be no further contact between Seamus and Michael, except at Kathleen Malone's discretion.

This time Kat didn't cry. She merely dug through her papers for Michael's birth certificate, stuck it in the stamped return envelope provided by Seamus's attorney, grabbed her bags and Michael's and stalked out the door.

She left the bank statement and checkbook on the dresser.

ALMOST EXACTLY ONE MONTH later, Seamus O'Rourke pounded on Sandy and Jane Wilson's front door demanding to see Kathleen Malone. Sandy wasn't home, but Jane calmly handed Seamus a slip of paper with an address on it and shut the door in his face.

Seamus didn't recognize the street name, but he knew exactly where the town of Jackson was. If he could find the Honeysuckle Inn, he knew he'd find Kat Malone.

Chapter Twelve

"ARE YOU CERTAIN YOU'LL be okay here by yourself? I just hate leaving you and the baby all alone out here like this."

"Rose, relax." Kat turned her friend by the shoulders and pointed her toward the door. "Ramsey's waiting in the car, and if you don't hurry, he'll leave without you. Trust me...I know how the man thinks."

Rose laughed, spun around and gave Kat a quick hug. "When you guys worked together, you didn't have twin toddlers. Believe me, he is not going anywhere without The Mama. My status has been greatly elevated since the birth of the girls. The man really needs me now."

"He's always needed you, kiddo. Even before he met you, he needed you. Now go. Give your Aunt Rosa a hug for me, enjoy Hawaii and come home with a tan. Michael and I can handle the inn just fine."

"There aren't any guests scheduled for the entire month and you've got Rosa's number if you need to reach us for—"

"Go. That's an order." Kat finally managed to push Rose through the front door and shut the screen behind her. Just then Michael started to cry. "The lord and master is calling. Send me a postcard." Kat pulled the screen open to wave at Mike Ramsey. "Have fun, guys. I'll keep the home fires burning."

The mini-van pulled out of the driveway and disappeared in a cloud of dust. Kat watched them leave, grinning at the thought of her macho Department of Transportation partner, the best shot on the force, the guy who always got his man, driving away in a mini-van with two adorable raven-haired daughters firmly strapped in their carriers in the back seat and his beautiful wife beside him.

None of them had ever dreamed of such a life. Now Mike and Rose Ramsey had it.

Michael raised the volume, demanding to be fed.

Kat grinned even wider. Well, she didn't have the husband beside her, but she definitely had her own man...and this little guy was demanding enough, thank you very much!

At least I know how to keep him happy.

After a quick diaper change Kat settled into the old rocker Rose had given her. Michael rooted and snuffled, impatient to latch on to her nipple and have his lunch. Nursing continually amazed Kathleen, that she could feed this growing child from her own body, nurture him completely and keep him healthy and happy.

Too bad I couldn't do the same with Seamus. Immediately, the fantasy image of Seamus's lips at her breast sent a shaft of heat through Kat. Michael snorted and wriggled, suggesting in his own way it was time to switch to the other breast.

Kat held Michael up against her shoulder and patted a deep belch out of him, then bared her right breast. The baby latched on immediately, already an expert at finding his next meal.

Kat rested her head against the back of the rocker and let her mind drift. Once again Seamus was the center of her thoughts...along with a conviction, deep in her heart, that if Seamus would only let her, she could make him happy.

"C'MON, SWEETIE. TIME FOR your bath." Kat set the small plastic tub in the sink and added just enough warm water to bathe Michael. He'd grown so much it was difficult to recall how frightened she'd been the first time she'd bathed him.

"You were the equivalent of bathing a slippery seal, beast."

Michael grinned up at her—something he'd been doing for the past couple of days. Just heading into his third month, Michael was the most entertaining, wonderful thing Kat could possibly imagine.

If only Seamus were here to share his growing, changing, amazing ways.

Kat blinked rapidly, as usual brought to tears by thoughts of Seamus. She'd never understand how he could have dropped out of their lives so completely.

She'd played the only card she had. Seamus hadn't shown his hand. If Michael's birth certificate couldn't bring him to her, Kat was forced to admit he wasn't ever going to come.

She wrapped Michael in a soft towel and carried him into the bedroom. Once he was diapered and dressed she settled into the comfortable old rocker to nurse him—hopefully—to sleep.

"You are such a sweetheart." She stroked his satiny cheek, smoothed her fingertip along the dark wing of his eyebrow. So much like Seamus...and Riley. Odd, how she hadn't thought of Riley at all since she'd come running to the Honeysuckle Inn in search of healing. The peace of the old house had seeped into her soul, had gradually left her with nothing but quiet memories of her time with the FBI agent.

Had the conversations she'd had with his vision actually happened? Even those amazing moments had mellowed in her thoughts.

Unlike her moments with Seamus. Good Lord, she'd never even kissed the man. They'd shared nothing more intimate than an occasional comforting hug.

Hugs, a pregnancy, Michael's birth, a killer's attack, near death by drowning...Seamus's strong arms pulling her to the surface...saving her life.

No, they hadn't shared anything intimate at all.

Kat's eyes brimmed with tears. They came more easily these days since the birth of her son. She nuzzled her cheek against Michael's satiny hair and let the tears flow.

HE SHOULD HAVE KNOCKED. He never should have just walked through the unlocked screen door, then unerringly followed his senses to Kathleen. If he'd knocked, though, he never would have seen her like this.

She appeared to sleep, she was so still in the shaft of sunlight falling on the old oak rocker. Her hair, longer than before, covered the side of her face. Seamus studied the tip of her nose, the curve of her chin, the swell of her breast. She held Michael to nurse, but the baby slept as well. His tiny rosebud mouth still pursed, but the nipple he'd recently fed from had escaped his lips. One tiny hand fisted, held tightly against Kat's soft skin.

The urge to touch her, to run his hands through her hair, caress the soft curve of her cheek, to hold her in his arms and make love until both of them were too exhausted to move... *Ah, Kathleen. Will you ever forgive me? Will you ever let me into your heart?*

Seamus swallowed, forced himself to breathe. She was lovelier than he recalled, more beautiful than he'd even imagined.

He lifted his hand and caressed the folded envelope in his shirt pocket. She was Kathleen Margaret Malone, the mother of his son.

SHE MIGHT HAVE DOZED for hours. More likely it had only been minutes, but when Kat opened her eyes she sensed Seamus in the room. She wasn't certain how she knew he stood close by, but somehow the air had taken on a new quality, her heart beat with a new cadence. Warm waves of pleasure coursed through her veins. She took a deep breath before raising her head to look toward the open bedroom doorway.

He stood there, dressed much as Riley might have on his days off, in worn blue jeans and a soft flannel shirt. The sleeves were rolled back and Seamus's strong forearms looked tan and muscled. He leaned against the doorframe, feigning a relaxed pose she immediately guessed was a sham.

Somehow Kat found the strength to raise her eyes and gaze into his. Seamus studied her with a look of absolute longing that was almost her undoing. He'd lost weight. The familiar grooves and planes of his face were more pronounced, the line of his brow sharper. There was a hunger about him she'd never noticed before, a sense of need that physically reached out to enfold her.

Kat cleared her throat, but it was Seamus who broke the charged silence.

"I hear you've got rooms to rent."

So. That was going to be his approach. Kat held her smile inside. "Not really," she answered. "The inn's closed for the month. I'm just watching the place until the owners return."

Seamus pushed himself away from the wall, but he didn't move from the open doorway. "Think you could make an exception? I'm willing to work. I..." He fumbled for his words, shrugged his shoulders and took a single step into the room.

Kat repositioned the sleeping baby to her shoulder, covered her bare breasts with her blouse, and stood up. Seamus faced her from a mere two paces across the room. Two paces and a thousand miles of misunderstanding and hurt.

Kat's thoughts had never been clearer, her purpose more focused. She centered her gaze on Seamus's dark green eyes and saw her future in their depths. "I love you, Seamus. I love you so much. Michael and I need you."

She'd hardly gotten the words out before Seamus had crossed the thousand miles in two quick steps. He held her close, carefully wrapping his arms around Kat and the baby. She couldn't understand any of the words he said, not with the sobs welling up from her chest and the tears blinding her to everything but the absolute goodness of his embrace.

Michael squirmed between them and Seamus laughed. "Lord, Kat. He's huge! I can't believe how he's grown. C'mere, little guy."

Kat handed Michael over to Seamus. The look of wonder on Seamus's face told her more than words ever could.

He cradled the baby in his arms and carefully sat down in the rocker. Michael stared up at Seamus, his gaze so intense it was as if child and man, father and son, communicated on a level Kat would never understand.

Much as Riley and Seamus had once communed?

After a long moment, Seamus looked up at Kathleen. Tears streamed from his eyes and a look of wonder suffused his face. "I can never thank you enough. You know that, don't you?"

Before Kat could answer, Seamus reached into his pocket and withdrew a familiar envelope. "My attorney just gave this to me yesterday. I've been out of touch for weeks. I... Why? When I treated you so terribly, Kat. Why?"

Kathleen reached for the envelope, opened it and removed Michael's birth certificate. She read aloud, "Michael Seamus Riley O'Rourke, born to Kathleen Margaret Malone, mother. Seamus Patrick O'Rourke, father." Kat carefully placed the certificate back in the envelope. "I told you why, Seamus. I told you when Michael was born, you were more a father to him than Riley ever could've been. We both know Riley wasn't father material. Even Riley told me you'd be the better father."

"You really saw him, too, didn't you?"

Kathleen nodded, fluttered her hands in a helpless gesture then let them fall to her sides. "Yeah. I didn't believe it at first. I thought he was just in my head, but he was there. In the room, in the car..."

Seamus nodded without looking in her direction, as if understanding her confusion, her sense of denial.

"When was the last time he came to you?" Seamus glanced up from his careful study of the baby and turned all of his attention on Kathleen. She bit her lips. She knew the truth would hurt Seamus all over again.

"The last time I saw you. I was in the car. It was filling with water so fast I didn't think you'd be able to get to me in time."

Seamus nodded. "It took me longer than I expected. People had stopped to help. They tried to keep me from going back for you. They took Michael, then one guy grabbed my arm, told me it was too dangerous. I was afraid I wouldn't be able to break free in time. I barely did."

Kat nodded, finally understanding how frightening it must have been for Seamus. He was a man who took his responsibilities very seriously. She'd been under his care...she was his responsibility.

Was that *all* she was?

Seamus hadn't said he loved her, even after she'd laid her own heart on the line.

She thought he'd come back for her. Maybe he'd only come back because of Michael. Maybe her gesture had backfired. With his name on the birth certificate she'd have no way to fight for custody now.

Riley said Seamus loved her. Could she really trust a ghost?

Kat figured she'd have to. "You were gone a long time. Long enough for me to wonder if you were really coming back for me. I started thinking how easy it would be for you to let me drown. No one could fault you. No one could dispute your claim on Michael. You and Riley were twins. I assume that means your DNA would be close enough to prove you could be Michael's father.

"You said all along you wanted the baby. You told me that from the beginning. I couldn't help but think now, when I had so much to live for, I was going to die. Suddenly Riley appeared, rumpled as usual, telling me to hang on, that you were coming to save me. Then he was gone and you were there."

She said it so matter-of-factly, as if conversations with a ghost were an everyday occurrence. Kat shrugged her shoulders and reached for the baby. "Why don't you let me have him? It's past time for his nap."

Seamus regretfully gave up the tiny burden. He studied Kat as she put Michael down for his nap. She'd never been more precious to him, leaning over the small crib and adjusting the light blanket over her son.

Our son. It was going to take him awhile to get used to that, to absorb the immense scope of Kat's generosity.

She said she loved him. She said she and Michael needed him. Had she really meant those words? Almost afraid to hope, Seamus quietly followed Kat out of the room and into the large, square kitchen. She poured two tall glasses of lemonade, handed one to him and led Seamus out onto the huge front porch.

The sweet perfume from the old honeysuckle vine covering the porch filled the air. Bees and hummingbirds maintained a constant level of buzzing and humming as they moved from bloom to bloom. Seamus stood for a moment, inhaling the scents and sounds, feeling a sense of peace that had been missing in his life for far too long. He glanced at the comfortable looking chairs, then sat down instead on one end of the old porch swing. After a moment's hesitation, Kathleen sat at the other end.

She played with the condensation on her glass for a moment, then gestured toward a small speaker on the table next to her. "That's a monitor to Michael's room. We'll be able to hear him when he wakes up. He should be down for a few hours, though. I bathed him just before you arrived so he's all clean and relaxed. That always makes—"

"Kat."

She jumped when he said her name. Then she turned and leveled that crystalline blue gaze on him and waited.

Suddenly, all the words he'd practiced, all the long explanations and rationalizations that had made so much sense on the long drive over from San Francisco sounded trite and meaningless.

The only words he could say sounded equally sad and wanting. "I'm sorry, Kat. I'm so sorry."

"For what?"

How could she sit there with that innocent expression on that gorgeous face and ask such a stupid question?

"For what? What do you mean, for what?" Seamus stood up so fast he set the swing to rocking. Kat grabbed at the armrest and planted her feet.

"It's your apology, Seamus." Kat steadied the glass of lemonade before the swing could bump into the table. "I'm just an innocent recipient of a yet-unmade apology. What are you apologizing for?"

"Good Lord, woman. Where do I start?" He shoved his long fingers through the thick black hair tumbling over his forehead. Kat saw the healing scar slanting across his forehead, noticed for the first time how long his hair had grown. Now it swept across his ears and curled over his collar, giving him a rakish, sensual look.

She decided it was a look she definitely liked. She flashed him a cheeky grin, feeling, for the first time in a long time, back in control. "You could start at the beginning, maybe?"

"I promised to protect you, but I failed. I promised your stalker wouldn't find you again. I failed there, too. I lied to you and said I only wanted your baby. That's not true."

Seamus stopped his pacing and stood so close to Kathleen their knees touched. She felt the hope growing inside, the knowledge building that what she'd dreamed might actually come true.

"What is true, Seamus? Will you tell me that?"

He knelt down on one knee in front of her and took both of Kat's hands in his own. She knew her fingers trembled, knew her heart sped far too fast.

"The truth, Kathleen Margaret Malone? The truth is that I've wanted you since the first time I saw you. There, at the cemetery, burying the brother I couldn't mourn. Then, when I walked into the kitchen the next morning and you were sitting at my table wearing nothing more than one of my good white shirts with a jam stain down the front, no less... I knew I could never let you go." Suddenly he stood up and turned away.

"The problem is, there was always Riley. I figured every time you looked at me, you saw my brother. I may have been the oldest, but I always felt less than Riley. Do you understand that?"

"Seamus, Riley loved you. He looked up to you. You were everything he wanted to be."

Kat stood up and placed her hands on his broad shoulders.

"You have to get past that, Seamus. You can't spend your life jealous of a dead man."

Seamus merely shrugged. "I finished my book."

"What?"

"That's where I've been, Kat." Seamus grinned down at her as if that should answer all her questions.

"Where have you been? Make some sense here, okay?"

"Okay. I was really upset that night...not at you. I was angry with myself. For all we knew, Dearborn was still out there. I'd failed you once again. Then you started talking about Riley and I just lost it. I'm sorry. After I left the hospital, I went straight to my attorney and set up the fund for Michael, then back to the cabin. That's where it all started coming together."

Kat sat down and patted a spot beside her on the swing. Seamus dutifully sat where she indicated. "Now," she said. "Explain, please?"

"Riley was there. At the cabin. Oh, I'd seen him before, but each time I was able to explain him away. This time, he wouldn't leave me alone." Seamus looked up and squeezed his eyes shut. Only a couple of tears managed to escape.

"He'd pop up at the weirdest times. He forced me to see what I've missed all my life, that just because we looked alike, we didn't have to be alike. Nor did we have to be polar opposites. We just had to be ourselves. He made me realize I've lived my entire life on the defensive, always reacting to Riley when I should have ignored his behavior and gone on with my life."

"You got all this from a ghost?"

Seamus took her hand in both of his and grinned at her. "C'mon. Don't deny it. You saw him, too. You talked to him."

"Not recently...not since that last night." Kat realized she hadn't even thought of Riley in that time, either.

"Have you missed him?"

"No, you dummy. I missed you. Though I must admit, right now I'm wondering why."

"I missed you too, Kat. But, in a lot of ways, you were with me." Seamus reached out and touched her hair. "You haven't asked me what kind of book I was writing."

"I guess I figured it was a foodie thing, sort of like your columns."

"It's a romance."

Kat knew she should shut her mouth. Somehow, though, she couldn't make the darned thing close.

"A romance? You?"

"I know. It sounds absurd, but when I started it, months before I ever met you, I was so damned lonely. I needed the fantasy. There was no one in my life—no one who mattered. I started writing and figured I'd have my imaginary characters to keep me company. Pathetic, isn't it? Then you popped into my life and totally screwed up all my preconceived notions of what romance could be. I was almost finished with it, but after you, I had to rewrite the whole darned thing."

"Well. I'm just too sorry for words." *Just what in the hell is he getting at?*

"I figured you'd say something like that." He grinned like the village idiot. "I've missed you so much, Kat."

He leaned close and kissed her. She'd imagined the taste of him, the feel of his lips on hers.

She hadn't even come close.

He drew away from her long before she was ready to let him go.

"I didn't have a clue what real love was until you came into my life. Kat, you've brought me so much. Given me so much. I didn't know what fun was. Hell, I didn't know what life was until you."

Once more, Kat saw the hunger in his eyes and felt herself drawn to it. Once again he stroked her hair. "It's like silk, so soft and sleek. Almost impossible to imagine what a prickly, hard-headed woman it hides."

"Thanks loads." Kat sat up straight, fighting the urge to lean into Seamus's touch. If he thought he understood romance, he was wrong. Dead wrong.

You don't tell a woman she's prickly and hard-headed, you dolt!

Suddenly Seamus was back down on one knee, his big hands cradling Kat's thighs. He wasn't smiling, but the twinkle in his deep green eyes belied the serious expression on his face.

"I love you, Kathleen Margaret Malone. I've loved you from the beginning, even when you drove me nuts. You still drive me nuts. I love your wit and your laughter, your fierce nature and your gentle soul. I love your courage and your sweetness. I cannot imagine not having you in my life. Will you marry me? Will you be my wife? Will you grow old and crotchety and wrinkled with me?"

She couldn't speak, could no more get the words past the lump in her throat than fly. Instead, she nodded her head, biting her lips to stop the rush of tears.

It didn't help a bit. Seamus stood and swept her into his arms, cradling her like an infant, kissing her face, her tears, finally settling firmly on her mouth.

"Now, about that room," he said, carrying her through the front door and into the dark foyer.

"Grab the monitor and I'll show you."

"You mean the baby comes with us?"

She looked into his forest green eyes and laughed. "Yeah, Seamus. The baby comes with us. We're a family and we stick together. No more goin' it alone. What do you say?"

"I say, grab the monitor."

Epilogue

"G'MORNIN', SLEEPYHEAD. I THOUGHT you'd never wake up."

Kat stretched, arched her back and smiled at Seamus. He leaned against the doorjamb, arms folded across his chest, the sleeves of his worn flannel shirt rolled back above his wrists.

"Mmmm, what time is it?" She pushed herself up to a sitting position so she could get a better look at him. After almost four years of marriage, Kat knew she'd never grow tired of her green-eyed Irishman. She smiled, remembering how she'd once thought him threatening and reserved. There wasn't an uptight bone in this man's body. She and Mikey had seen to that.

"It's almost ten. If we're going to get any work done before it's time to pick Mikey up from preschool by noon, you're going to have to get moving."

"Thanks for taking him this morning. I'm usually not this lazy." She yawned and stretched again. "I don't know what got into me."

Seamus pushed away from the door and sauntered across the room. "As I recall, I got into you."

Kat blushed, remembering the past night of loving. "More than once," she said, scooting to the middle of the bed to make room. "Wanna try it again?"

Seamus leaned over her, one arm on either side, trapping her in a familiar embrace. "You know I would, but we have work to do. There's a manuscript in the office just waiting for a conclusion." He kissed her, quick, playful little kisses that left her giggling and breathless.

Kat reached up to touch his jaw with her fingers, holding him still for a long, satisfying kiss. As far as she was concerned, the book could wait. She and Seamus had averaged three books a year for the past three years. Out of those nine stories of romance and suspense, five had been best sellers and a sixth was quickly climbing the list. A few more minutes wouldn't hurt.

"Think of it as research, Seamus." She deepened the kiss and at the same time wriggled her fingers between the buttons on the front of his shirt to stroke the warm flesh beneath.

Seamus groaned against her lips and surrendered. "This is not the way deadlines are met," he said, fumbling with the zipper on his worn jeans. "Besides—" He stripped his shirt off his shoulders. "—we got in plenty of research last night. Unless you have something new to show me."

He slipped his jeans and shorts down his legs and stepped out of them, then struck a pose.

"That's certainly not new, Seamus," she deadpanned.

He pinned her to the bed, toes to fingertips. The thick comforter between them couldn't hide the fact he was certainly ready for more research.

Kat wriggled beneath him. "Actually...I do have something new."

Seamus leered at her before pulling the comforter out from between them, then settled himself along the length of her. "Okay, I'm ready." He kissed the tip of her nose.

"You certainly are." She thrust her hips against him.

Seamus pulled away, teasing her. "So. What's new? Are we talking whips and chains here? Maybe a little whipping cream in odd places? How about..."

Kat wrapped her arms around his waist, arched her hips and he entered her. She pushed his shoulders and rolled him to his back so she could sit astride. "How about the first time you've ever knowingly made love to a pregnant woman?"

The look of utter disbelief on Seamus's face made her giggle.

"You? Mine? But how..."

"Well, I hope you're not making love to any other pregnant women and it's certainly not the mailman's." She spun her hips, loving the feel of him inside her. "I imagine doing what we're doing right now had something to do with it."

"A baby? We're really going to have a baby?"

"That's essentially what we're talking about, big guy." She might be talking tough, but Kat felt as if she would burst with the love she felt for this man. "I do hope you're ready to be a daddy again. At least this time, I think we can expect a fairly uncomplicated pregnancy. You know, one without a stalker?"

Seamus wrapped his arms tightly around her waist and held her close. Kat felt his tears mingling with hers, his lips moving against the line of her jaw with words so tender they made her ache.

"You have given me more than any man could ever wish. Our son is a miracle. You, my love, are a miracle. I never, not in my wildest imaginings, dreamed we might be blessed enough to have another child. I love you, Kathleen Margaret O'Rourke. To answer your question, yes. I am more than ready to be a daddy again."

It was almost time to pick Mikey up from preschool before he turned her loose.

~ * ~

Kate Douglas

Kate Douglas is a sucker for happy endings, but this romance author never makes it easy for her characters to find their own personal paradise. Kate's found hers in the wine country of northern California where she and her husband of almost thirty years live in an old farmhouse in the midst of a hillside vineyard.

When she's not writing, Kate does sports photography for many northern California cycling teams.

Printed in the United States
82585LV00001B/41

9 780759 938069